c.1

Quest, Erica
  Cold coffin.   N.Y., Doubleday, [c1990].
  181p. $ 14.95

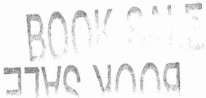

I.Title.

ISBN: 0-385-41187-1

Cold Coffin

By Erica Quest

ERICA QUEST

Cold Coffin

A CRIME CLUB BOOK
DOUBLEDAY
New York   London   Toronto   Sydney   Auckland

A CRIME CLUB BOOK
PUBLISHED BY DOUBLEDAY
a division of Bantam Doubleday Dell Publishing Group, Inc.
666 Fifth Avenue, New York, New York 10103

DOUBLEDAY and the portrayal of a man
with a gun are trademarks of Doubleday,
a division of Bantam Doubleday Dell Publishing Group, Inc.

Library of Congress Cataloging-in-Publication Data

Quest, Erica.
Cold coffin / Erica Quest.—1st ed.
p.   cm.
"A Crime Club book."
I. Title.
PR6067.U347C6   1990
823'.914—dc20   89-28153
CIP

ISBN 0-385-41187-1
Copyright © 1990 by Erica Quest
All Rights Reserved
Printed in the United States of America
June 1990
First Edition

Cold Coffin

One

Mid-July, hot and sunny for once. Saturday afternoon. Thudding hooves and the thwack of polo sticks on wooden ball, the laid-back voice of the commentator echoing over the public address system. The polo ground at Dodford was magnificently situated, its wide expanse of flat turf ringed by oak and beech, an artful gap in the trees affording a view of the Elizabethan manor house set on a rounded knoll.

Detective Chief Inspector Kate Maddox, comfortably relaxed in one of the two folding chairs her Aunt Felix had brought with them in the car, reflected that this was as pleasant a way as any to spend a few off-duty hours. The standard of play was high, even if Dodford wasn't in quite the same classy league as Windsor, Cowdray Park or Cirencester. Neither Prince Charles nor his papa before him had ever felt enticed to pay a visit here, not even as a spectator.

The chair beside Kate was temporarily vacant. Her aunt was on the prowl with her telephoto-lensed Canon, hoping to catch some good action shots. Casting her gaze around, Kate spotted Richard Gower standing over by the scoreboard, and waved to him. At once he started moving through the throng lining the ropes to join her. As he drew near she noted that the habitual limp which marred his ruggedly athletic appearance was more marked than usual. Reaching Kate, he sank into the chair beside her with a grunt of satisfaction and rubbed his left knee.

"Leg playing up today?" she asked sympathetically.

"A bit. Just to remind me that it's there."

Kate knew that he still suffered a lot of pain from the injury he'd received four years or so previously when he'd copped a stray sniper's bullet while working as a war correspondent in the Middle East. Months of hospitalization later, Richard had faced the fact that his roving career was at an end. Rejecting the soft option of a newsroom desk job, he'd taken on a new sort of challenge.

The only thing impressive about *The Marlingford Gazette, Chipping Bassett Courier and South Cotswold Post and Times* was its title. Small and ailing, on the point of folding altogether, the local weekly newspaper had been going cheap. Even so, it had taken the limit of Richard's credit potential to raise enough to purchase the premises, the ancient plant and machinery; and, as he put it, the bad will. Ten years hence, with a lot of work and a lot of luck, he might actually be turning a profit.

His first encounter with Kate had been inauspicious. Richard Gower was the prime suspect in a hit-and-run murder case . . . Kate's baptism of fire after coming to the Cotswold Division as a newly promoted Detective Chief Inspector. In nailing the real culprit she had established Richard's innocence, and their initial relief had firmed into friendship.

"Got a good lead story for next week?" she asked him.

"I'm praying for a major disaster."

"Gower," she said, "you're a ghoul."

"I'm a newspaperman."

"Richard Gower," a voice rasped from behind them, "you're barging in on my territory."

He stood up to greet Kate's aunt as fast as his injured leg would allow. "Sorry, Felix, I didn't realize you were back. I was only borrowing your perch for the odd minute."

"Oh, stay put, man, you're welcome to the chair. It's that thing you've got hanging round your neck I object to. I'm the official photographer around here, and don't you forget it."

Richard patted the camera suspended on a leather strap. "Not to worry, Felix, this is for snapping spectators, not players. You know the sort of thing. Seen at the polo final on Saturday . . . a few local nobs. Every mugshot I can cram in sells three or four extra copies."

"Just so long as you don't tread on my toes. Talking of nobs, where the dickens have the Kimberleys got to? They're supposed to be presenting the gold cup again this year, and the third chukka has already started." Looking around the picturesque scene, she spotted a metallic blue Audi that was just turning in through the entry gate. "Ah, good, it looks as if they're arriving now. I must go and have a word with them about the presentation photographs. And you keep out of it, Richard. If you want a picture of the award-giving for the *Gazette*, I expect you to buy it from me."

Felicity Moore went striding away, a large ungainly woman with a surprisingly light step. Careless about her appearance (a tentlike cotton dress in a drab tone of beige today), her hair bundled anyhow on top of her head and barely restrained by a mass of pins, she was nevertheless an impressive and formidable figure.

Richard lounged back in the canvas chair. "Any news about that cottage you've got your eye on, Kate?"

"I've been bloody gazumped again. Honestly, the property owners around here are an unscrupulous lot." She rumpled her short black hair impatiently. "Some of them belong behind bars."

"So why don't you put 'em there, the bastards?"

"I intend to, the moment greed is declared illegal."

"So that means you're stuck with living at Felix's awhile longer?"

"She makes me very welcome, bless her. I could all too easily give up the fight and stay at Stonebank Cottage permanently. But that wouldn't do at all. I need my independence, Richard, and so does Felix. I've disrupted her quiet lifestyle for quite long enough. Oh . . . well played!" Kate joined in the ripple of applause for a brilliant goal.

Her aunt was back again. "Kate, come and have a word with Vanessa Kimberley, will you? She's dreadfully worried about Sir Noah. He seems to have disappeared."

"What the heck does she expect me to do about it?" asked Kate, not budging. "Her husband's probably in the marquee knocking back a large Scotch."

"No, I mean really disappeared. Vanessa was singing at a gala in London last night, in aid of the Children in Need Fund, and she stayed over at a friend's house. She arrived back this morning in time for lunch and Noah was missing. Apparently he went out last night after dinner, and didn't return. The housekeeper went to bed early and it wasn't until this morning that she realized he hadn't come home. Vanessa is desperately worried, naturally, so I said I'd ask you to come and tell her what she ought to do."

Kate shook her head. "It's not a police matter, so I can't get involved. Sir Noah Kimberley is a grown man and he's entitled to absent himself for a few hours without starting a hue and cry. If he'd had an accident last night the police would have informed Lady Kimberley by now."

"Well yes, of course, and I've already suggested to her that no news is good news. But you know how devoted those two are. They're both meticulous about letting the other one know if they're going to be delayed. She said Noah would never let her worry about him unnecessarily."

"Maybe," put in Richard, "as Lady Kimberley was away from home last night he didn't think it mattered. Or maybe he tried to phone and the housekeeper wasn't around."

"Even so, he'd have phoned again by now, surely? It's really very strange. You must admit, girl, that Vanessa has cause to be worried."

"Sure I do. It's tough on her. But husbands go temporarily missing all the time. He probably met some woman last night who was so entrancing that he's completely lost track of the passing hours. Pound to a penny he'll be back very soon, full of apologies and with some complicated story that his fond wife will finally swallow because she doesn't want to have to face the truth."

"Oh, Kate, you are a cynic!"

"Not a cynic, just a cop. All my rosy illusions about people were shattered years ago."

"Well, you'll just have to sound sympathetic and concerned when you come over and talk to Vanessa."

"But I've just told you, there's no justification for police action. There's nothing I can do."

"I suppose not, but you can make the right sort of noises, can't you? I *promised* Vanessa."

"Dammit, Felix, you had no right to drag me into it." But remembering the stack of favours she owed her aunt from over the years, Kate lumbered to her feet. "Okay, you win. Lead the way."

"Mind if I come too?" asked Richard.

"Yes, I do mind."

"But there might be a story in it."

"Listen, I'm not doing a double act with the press. See you later."

Lady Kimberley was hovering close to her Audi; keeping, she explained, within hearing of the car-phone in case her housekeeper rang with news of Sir Noah. She had about her the queenly presence, the slightly imperious manner, of the prima donna she'd once been. Yet despite that she possessed immense charm. She was a tall woman of generous proportions, with magnificently expressive eyes. If she gave the impression of always playing to an audience, that was forgivable in someone who was the focus of attention wherever she might be. For this afternoon's ceremony she had chosen a fuchsia-coloured silk dress with trails of floating chiffon, and a huge cartwheel hat. By rights, she should have totally eclipsed Felicity

Moore in her beige tent, but somehow she didn't. Felix carried her own brand of charisma.

Kate had already met the Kimberleys, at a cocktail party. They'd been married only a couple of years; she for the first time, he for the second after a lengthy widowhood. It had been the romantic story of the week in all the Sunday papers. World famous soprano's hand finally won by devoted admirer who for years had trotted the globe just to hear her sing. Dame Vanessa Logan would be renouncing the operatic stage forthwith in favour of domestic bliss as Lady Kimberley. Sir Noah, whom Kate recalled as an ascetic-looking silver-haired man, was a biochemist of high standing in his field. He owned and ran Croptech, a small firm at nearby Little Bedham that researched into agricultural and horticultural chemicals.

As Kate and Felix approached, Lady Kimberley dismissed the inevitable gaggle of admirers with a regal sweep of her hand. She greeted Kate dramatically, in a voice that was husky with emotion.

"Mrs. Maddox, how *extremely* kind of you to come over to me. I dare not leave the telephone, d'you see. *Please* tell me what I should do. I am utterly *distraught*. My darling Noah has *vanished*, and I am dreadfully afraid." The time bell sounded and there was a round of applause, with cheers from the supporters of the winning team. Lady Kimberley seemed totally oblivious.

"There's probably a very simple explanation for your husband's absence," Kate said.

"But what explanation, Mrs. Maddox? What, other than *disaster*, can possibly explain it?"

Skate around the obvious, Kate, and scrape the barrel for a few innocuous possibilities.

"Some arrangement that has slipped your mind. Or perhaps he intended to tell you about it, but forgot. I'm sure it will turn out to be a misunderstanding of some kind."

"But he should be *here*. For the presentation of the trophies." Lady Kimberley coughed and adjusted the trailing chiffon about her throat, lifting it higher. When she continued speaking she was suddenly husky again. "We do it together, you understand. How can he *possibly* have been confused about that?"

"Well, I expect you'll hear from him very soon. It's far too early to start being seriously worried. Tell me, would your husband be driving? Did he take a car, I mean?"

"Well, yes, he must have done. His Saab is not in the garage."

"Can you give me details of his car? The colour and so forth."

"Let me see, it's dark green. And quite new. He bought it about three months ago."

"An F registration, then. Can you remember the actual number?"

"I'm afraid not. Is it important?"

"Never mind. We'll check it out." To damp down further alarmed questions, Kate dispensed soothing syrup. "I'll have all possible enquiries made, Lady Kimberley. You can rest assured that we'll be in touch with you the moment we hear anything." With relief she saw one of the officials was hovering agitatedly. "I think you're needed for the presentation now."

"Oh dear! I . . . I don't know *how* I can go through with it," Lady Kimberley said, one hand pressed to her throat. Then she braced her shoulders theatrically and her voice dropped to a brave whisper. "I suppose I shall have to manage *somehow.*"

The show must go on.

Six paces from her car, Lady Kimberley paused and addressed the crowd at large, supremely confident of being obeyed. "Somebody must stay by my car, and bring me any telephone message at once. *At once!*"

Kate took the chance to escape. Lacking her own transport (they'd come in Felix's sedate old Rover), she walked over to a police patrol car that was drawn up by the ropes further along. The two young officers inside were slumped comfortably in the front seats with their cap peaks tilted forward to shade their eyes. At her approach they glanced up casually, did a double take in unison, and snapped to an upright position.

"Oh . . . Chief Inspector, ma'am. We were just . . ."

"On the alert to quell an outbreak of public disorder? Very commendable. But the crowd here seems fairly placid at the moment, so you can run me to the Chipping Bassett nick instead."

Five minutes later, from the grubby and Saturday-empty CID room at the small police station, she made a call to Divisional HQ at Marlingford.

"Sir Noah Kimberley, the boss of Croptech, seems to have gone missing since last night. You haven't heard anything, I suppose, Bob?"

"Not a whisper, ma'am. Want me to ask around?"

"Well, nothing heavy. We don't want to get too involved in what's likely to end up as just a run-of-the-mill domestic situation. On the other hand, we want to look willing. He was driving an F reg. dark-green Saab. Check the licence number, will you, and see if it's cropped up in any kind of incident."

As she put the phone down, the door opened to admit Sergeant Boulter. Kate was surprised to see him here on a quiet Saturday afternoon, but Boulter didn't look surprised to see her. The man at the desk downstairs had obviously tipped him the wink.

"What devotion to duty is this, Tim? Something new I ought to know about?"

He hefted his broad shoulders moodily. "Nope. I just wanted to get the hell out of the menagerie at home. Half the kids in the street are round at our place, all yelling and shrieking in the paddling pool. I stood it as long as I could."

Did the silly sod imagine that desertion like this would do anything to assist his crumbling marriage? It was the demanding hours of his job that caused most of the friction between him and his wife. Julie Boulter, unlike Tim, had nowhere to run when things got on top of *her* at home. She was stuck there with their two young children, all day and every day, an intelligent young woman smouldering with resentment at her lack of personal fulfilment. But Kate held back from pointing this out to the sergeant. She'd poked her nose into the Boulters' problems once before, and got no thanks for her pains.

"Now that you're here, Tim, there's something I want to ask you. It's about Sir Noah Kimberley. What kind of man is he? Julie worked at Croptech, didn't she, before Mandy was born?"

He nodded. "Lab assistant, she was. She didn't have much contact with Sir Noah, of course, but she always said he was a decent enough old boy. Why, what's up?"

"He didn't come home last night, that's what."

Boulter cocked an enquiring eye at her. "And what makes that a police matter, guv?"

"Nothing, officially. But . . . his wife's upset."

"She'll be a helluva lot more upset when she discovers he spent the night with a lady friend."

"Why should you say that? Is he known as a womanizer?"

"Not that I ever heard. But I'd give you outsider odds it's the explanation."

"That's the trouble with being coppers, Tim, it makes us think the worst of people. Just ask around about him, will you? But discreetly, mind."

"Trust me. My middle name is tact."

"I thought it was Cuthbert." She'd been saving that little gem for the right moment, ever since she'd spotted it in Records.

Boulter paled a few shades. "Who told you?"

"A little birdie."

"Well, for God's sake, guv, don't spread it around."

"Trust me, Cuthbert." She stood up. "Before you do anything else, you can run me back to the Dodford polo ground. Most people will have gone by now, but my aunt and I went there together and she's probably still hanging around in her car wondering where I've got to."

On Sunday evening Kate had a dinner date with Richard Gower, postponed from Thursday owing to other commitments. They usually met about once a week if they could manage to find an evening when both were free. They liked each other, and neither tried to hide the fact. On the other hand, they were allowing their friendship to coast along nice and easy; experience had made both of them only too aware of the dangers of rushing into relationships.

This evening they went to the Black Swan in Chipping Bassett, famed locally for its good food. Their window table overlooked the river, turned now to a thousand golden ripples in the dying sunlight.

"I went to see Lady Kimberley this morning," Richard said as they studied their menus.

Kate felt a prickle of irritation. She asked coolly, "Why did you do that?"

"There might be a story for me, that's why." The look he shot her was challenging; but also, she thought, a mite defensive. "It happens to be the function of the press to provide news, Kate. Lady Kimberley was in a real state about her husband. She still hadn't heard a word about him."

"I know. Felix phoned her earlier. Poor woman, I feel sorry for her."

"Yet there's nothing you can do about finding out what's happened to Sir Noah?"

"I'm doing all I can—which doesn't amount to much, I admit. Just making a few discreet enquiries here and there. But if I tried to utilize police manpower in a big way, my superintendent would have me on the carpet. And he'd be justified. A kid going missing is another matter, but if we set up a major enquiry on every missing-from-home adult, we'd have no time left for anything else. Besides, it's a matter of freedom of the individual. An adult in this country has a perfect right to take himself off if he chooses, without leaving a forwarding address."

"Yeah, sure. But I doubt if Vanessa Kimberley will ever see it. She feels very disgruntled that you seem to be doing nothing about her husband. She muttered about hiring a private detective."

"She might not like the answer he comes up with."

"Do you really believe that the old boy has hopped it with a woman?"

"No, I don't, as it happens. But I'm trying to keep an open mind. I'll tell you one small thing that goes counter to the other-woman theory. Sergeant Boulter's wife used to work at Croptech. He phoned me this morning and said that Julie was adamant that no way could Sir Noah Kimberley be regarded as a skirt chaser. She rather jumped on Tim, apparently, when he took the cynical view. Her ex-boss was always the perfect gent with the female staff, she insisted, and his longstanding devotion to Vanessa Logan was well known. They all thought it was rather sweet."

Richard nodded. "I looked up the Kimberley story in the *Gazette*'s files, to remind myself. They appear to have been a couple of real lovebirds. Still, marriages can quickly go sour—as I well know."

"The explanation for his taking off doesn't have to be a sex-related thing, Richard. It could be anxiety of some kind. About health or money, for instance."

"Neither of which seems to apply in this case. Although . . ."

"Although, what?"

"Lady K. did say that he seemed a bit put out by a phone call he received shortly before she set out for London. That was Friday lunchtime, prior to her charity gala in the evening. She and the housekeeper were busy with her last-minute packing when the phone rang, and her husband answered it. Afterwards, he looked a bit upset and thoughtful, she told me, but when she asked him about the call, he said it was nothing of consequence and he'd explain when she got back on Saturday. Then he went on to wish her good luck with the gala, and she dismissed it from her mind. Now, though, she's beginning to wonder about that phone call."

"She still doesn't know who it was from?" Kate asked.

"Nope. She's blaming herself for not pressing him to tell her. But she was probably too concerned about how her threatening sore throat would affect her performance."

"Sore throat? I noticed she was a bit husky when I talked to her yesterday, but I put that down to emotional strain."

"No, it was the real thing. Laryngitis. Apparently her throat got progressively worse during Friday afternoon and in the end there was no question of her singing. She had to back out of the gala at the last minute."

"Really? How strange she didn't mention that to me. Not even to Felix on the phone this morning. I wonder why."

"She's got something a lot worse on her mind now. What are you eating, Kate? Have you decided yet?"

"Is it my turn to pick up the tab tonight?"

"No, mine."

"In that case, I'll have the filet mignon with scampi."

He chuckled. "Thank God for plastic money. As a matter of fact, I filled in my afternoon by doing a spot of sleuthing on Lady Kimberley's behalf—with her full permission, before you start in on me."

"Oh? Like what?"

"Like talking to various people who work at Croptech. Lady K. had already spoken to most of them on the phone. She was desperate, and rang everybody she could think of."

Kate laid aside her menu and gave Richard her full attention. "What did you discover?"

"Nothing very helpful, I'm afraid. But I know a whole lot more about Croptech than I did."

"Okay. I suppose you might as well tell me."

"Well, first I drove to the Croptech premises and saw the caretaker, who has a bungalow in the grounds. He's an odd sort of chap, name of George Jessop, not at all what I'd have expected in a caretaker. Anyway, he swears that Sir Noah didn't show up at Croptech on Friday evening. He insists he'd have known if he had. And he couldn't suggest any reason for Kimberley's disappearance. Next I went to see Kimberley's secretary, a girl called Sandra English who lives with her parents at Great Bedham. I asked if she'd noticed her boss looking worried on Friday afternoon—or at any time before that. She's a timid sort of girl and I couldn't get much sense out of her. She was very much on the defensive and seemed to imagine that I was accusing her of something."

Kate grimaced. "That's a reaction the police have to contend with all the time. Who else did you see?"

"There are fewer staff at the firm than I'd imagined. Only about thirty-five all told. It struck me that the whole caboodle is very much dependent on Kimberley himself, and even when he takes a vacation he leaves careful instructions about what's to be done. The chief clerk, McEvoy, is a bit of a fussy old woman. An over-precise civil-service type. I got the impression that the thought of taking any responsibility or making a decision scares him half to death. Kimberley's nominal deputy is the senior biochemist in the laboratory. Dr. Gavin Trent. He's a bit of a weirdo, too. Very highly strung, a bag of nerves. He lives in a remote cottage not far from Croptech, and there was no way I could get past his front door. However, it was a different matter with his next in line."

"I'm listening."

"It's a Dr. Miller. Dr. Cheryl Miller."

"A woman?"

"And how! I'd met her once before, actually, at somebody's wedding. She's the sort of woman that once seen a man doesn't forget. Not young, fortyish, and a real looker. Very sexy."

Kate felt slightly miffed. "Are you talking generally, or personally?"

"Sexy is sexy. Cheryl Miller is very passionate on the subject of feminism, and very articulate with it. She had some hard words to say about Kimberley's attitude to women and their capabilities."

"Could be that she has a point," Kate put in dryly. "Did she tell you anything else about him?"

"She had no theory to explain his disappearance—nor did she seem to care a lot. A bit of a hard bitch is putting it mildly. From her I learned that there's a nephew of Kimberley's in the picture. It seems that Croptech was started by Sir Noah's father, who left it to his two sons on a fifty-fifty basis, and the nephew inherited *his* father's share. Name of Aidan Kimberley. But he's making a killing in London as a financial consultant and he's not interested in Croptech except for the profits. He has a weekend home near here, at Inchmere St. Mary, but he's been abroad for the past month. Due back tomorrow from Hong Kong, I gather. His wife has been around, though, but Lady K. couldn't get her on the phone until last evening. She failed to rush round offering solace and support as Lady K. obviously expected, but muttered something vague about having to get back to London first thing in the morning."

"Charming!"

"Actually, I tried to contact her myself a couple of times this afternoon at her London number, thinking that maybe she could tell me more about Sir Noah than she was willing to tell Lady Kimberley. But there was no answer."

"Anyone else you talked to?"

"One or two. Having started probing into the mystery, I thought I might as well stick at it. But as I told you, no one came up with any viable suggestions as to why Kimberley should have gone missing."

Kate could feel her own interest rising and firmly put a damper on it.

"It's all very peculiar, Richard, but like I said, there's nothing to justify police attention." She picked up her menu again, and frowned. "I've gone off the idea of having a steak. I'll try something lighter. Poached salmon, perhaps."

"You *are* concerned about Kimberley, aren't you, Kate?"

"Of course I'm concerned. I'd be damned unfeeling not to be. That poor woman must be going through hell at the moment. Unless . . ."

"Unless what?"

For God's sake, Kate Maddox, must you always dig for dirt? But like it or not, her thoughts raced on remorselessly.

"I've met Vanessa Kimberley a couple of times now," she said slowly. "Once at a cocktail party a few weeks ago, and then at polo yesterday. Both times she gave me the impression of putting on a big performance. I suppose it's in the blood, after all those years on the operatic stage. Every word and every gesture she makes is a lot larger than life. It's probably that she just can't help herself."

"Or?"

"Or . . . your guess is as good as mine. I just got the feeling that things aren't quite as she'd have us believe. But I'm not going to let this business spoil my sleep. There's no case for me here, Richard, and no story for you."

He eyed her shrewdly. "Is there going to be, d'you think?"

"How the hell should I know? I'm not clairvoyant. We'll just have to wait and see."

They didn't, as it turned out, have all that long to wait.

Two

Monday, Tuesday and Wednesday chanced to be quiet days for Kate, while the spell of hot weather continued. Needing to escape from deskwork in her stuffy office at DHQ, she dredged up reasons to visit some of the division's outlying police stations. At least it gave her the chance to get better acquainted with her CID personnel, some of whom she'd hardly more than met as yet. Since her promotion to Chief Inspector and her transfer to the Cotswold Division of the South Midlands force, a heavy workload had kept her under constant pressure. But at last she felt she had time to breathe. As she drove through the Cotswold countryside in her silver Montego, a summer haze lay over the landscape, muting colours and softening the outlines of the hills. *Life could be a whole lot worse, Kate, all said and done.*

Dreamtime ended abruptly not long after she arrived for work on Thursday morning. The report of a suspicious death came in. The body of a man had been found in the woods near Little Bedham on land adjoining the Croptech site. Not Sir Noah Kimberley, though, which scotched Kate's immediate thought. The man had been recognized by one of the attending police officers as Dr. Gavin Trent, a senior scientist at Croptech. Sir Noah's deputy, Kate remembered Richard telling her. Very highly strung, a bag of nerves. Maybe, the thought crossed her mind, he had good reason to be nervous.

On a sudden decision Kate reached for the phone and asked for Sergeant Boulter at the Chipping Bassett station.

"Heard about this man Trent, Tim?" she asked.

"Just this minute, guv. Looks a bit peculiar, doesn't it, what with the bossman having skedaddled the other day?"

"That's exactly what I'm thinking, so I'd like us to be in on this from the start. Get to the scene right away, will you, and I'll meet you there. Is there a wife to be informed?"

"No, he wasn't married. He was known as a real loner. Lived by himself in a cottage about half a mile from where the body was found."

"Better get someone onto tracing his next of kin, then."

Fourteen miles in nineteen minutes. No delighting in the glorious Cotswold landscape this time. At Little Bedham, a short distance along a lost lane that meandered through beechwoods, Kate came across a uniformed officer standing guard by a gated entrance to a woodland track.

"Morning, Constable. Is Sergeant Boulter here yet?"

"Arrived a few minutes ago, ma'am." He swung back the five-barred gate for her. "If you'll just follow the track. It's not too rough."

She bumped her car a further hundred yards and came to a clearing where two other police cars were drawn up. Sitting in the back of one of them were a young man and a girl. Their faces looked shocked and pale.

"Who're they?" she enquired of another uniformed PC.

"They found the body, ma'am. Honeymooners, I gather, staying at the Unicorn Inn. They were out for a morning stroll through the woods, and . . ."

Kate walked over and gave them a sympathetic smile through the car's open window.

"I'm Detective Chief Inspector Maddox. I just want to go and take a look at things, then we'll have a chat. I won't keep you any longer than I have to."

The dead man lay on the bank of a small pond that was ringed with saplings of oak and ash. The clothing—jeans and a thick-knit sweater— was sodden. Sergeant Boulter was crouched down on his haunches, examining the body but not touching it. He straightened at Kate's approach.

"Well, Tim?"

"Drowned is my guess, guv. But the thing that makes it fishy is that when he was found by that young couple he'd already been dragged clear of the water."

"Can we be sure that he didn't struggle out himself, and then collapse?"

"No way. You can see signs here that he was dragged out as a dead weight."

"You're right, Tim. The clothing is only just beginning to dry, so it must have happened quite recently. And look there, a footprint that's still damp. It could have been made by the young man who found the body, of course. Did you happen to notice if he's wearing boots?"

"Trainers, I'm pretty sure."

"Then the footprint was made by our mystery man. We'd better protect it." Kate unzipped her shoulderbag and took from it a silk scarf, which she spread out over the damp marks left by patterned ridges from the sole of a mansize boot. "I wonder who he was, Tim?"

"A mugger who killed Trent for his money?"

"But his wallet is still on him. Would a mugger have bothered to put it back? Let's have it out and take a look."

Boulter removed the wallet from the dead man's hip pocket, touching only one corner. It contained several banknotes, a driving licence and a couple of credit cards.

"Not a mugger, then," said Kate. "Whoever pulled him out, why did they just leave him without informing us? Was it someone passing by who didn't want to get involved with the police? Or is the explanation more sinister?"

"Ah, the doc's arrived," said Boulter, looking up. "He might be able to tell us something useful."

Kate pulled a face. "Not if he can help it, he won't."

The police surgeon and the Detective Chief Inspector were not sympatico. Short, self-important male; tall, self-confident female. Neither missed a chance, within the bounds of protocol, to score off the other.

"Good morning, Dr. Meddowes," Kate said heartily as he walked up to them a minute later.

"Oh, it's you!" He gave her a sour look. "Rather a come-down for you, Chief Inspector, to be attending a simple accident case."

"Accident?"

"That's what I was told."

"We have a dead man, doctor. At least, I imagine your expert findings will confirm the fact that he's dead. The precise cause of death is something we still have to establish."

"What do you suspect?"

"Oh, I shall keep an open mind and allow the evidence to speak for itself."

No reply to that. *Chalk up one point, Kate.*

The doctor put his findings succinctly; reluctant to help the jumped-up female, but too professionally honest to hold back from saying anything that he believed was pertinent.

"Dead. Cause of death, drowning. He was in the water for some hours, judging from the wrinkling of the skin on his hands. Probably overnight."

"Really?" queried Kate in surprise. "But it's obvious he's only been out of the water a short while."

The doctor shrugged. "Didn't whoever found him pull him out?"

"Not so. He was found exactly like this."

"Hmm! I note there are some abrasions and slight bruising on the back of his neck." He tugged down the neckband of the sweater for her to see better. "I wonder how they got there."

Situated where they were, it was difficult to believe the injuries had been accidentally sustained. Kate felt a sharpening of her senses, a conviction that this was a case of unlawful killing.

"As if," she hazarded, "he was knocked on the head and thrown into the water?"

"Isn't that a matter for you to decide, Chief Inspector? Or are you *elevating* me to the CID?"

Okay, that evens the score, Kate. She gave Boulter a glare for daring to grin.

When Dr. Meddowes had departed, Kate took another look at the body. Gavin Trent had been a thin, lanky man, aged somewhere around forty. His hair, now darkened by the water, would be a greying mid-brown and had begun to recede. A small moustache had been grown to conceal, she guessed, his weak mouth.

"This is where he was pulled out, Tim, but not necessarily where he went in. There's a bit of current flowing through this pond, so the body could have drifted. Let's have a look around."

Kate beckoned forward a uniformed PC to stand guard over the body. Then she and Boulter skirted the edge of the pond, examining the ground, taking care not to trample on any possible evidence. Slightly more than halfway round they came to a spot where there were signs of the grass and bracken having been trampled upon recently. Nowhere else around the perimeter was there any kind of disturbance.

"It looks as if this is the place, Tim," she said, returning to the spot. "But nothing suggests that a violent struggle took place here. So *was* he hit over the head and thrown in unconscious? Or . . . it might even be possible that . . ."

Boulter cocked an enquiring eye. He'd learned by now to treat his chief's sudden darts of inspiration seriously.

"Let's try this for size," Kate said. "Trent walked to this spot voluntarily

—or perhaps under threat—then he was taken by surprise and pushed in. When he began to thrash about and no doubt make a lot of noise, his attacker prodded him from the bank with something and held his head under the water. That could account for the scratches and bruising on his neck."

"You'd think he could have fought back, though, or just swam out of reach."

"Suppose the water here is deep and he couldn't swim. A nonswimmer would flounder in panic. Check out both those points, Tim."

"Right," he said.

Kate cast an eye a little farther afield, looking for evidence to support her theory. A few moments later she spotted it, half-hidden in bracken—a length of dead branch. Going closer, she saw it was ten feet long and both ends, where they'd been snapped off, had rough, splintery surfaces.

"How about this? It didn't get here by itself. The trees around here are all saplings and couldn't have shed a branch this thick. And see where some side twigs have been stripped off, as if preparing it for the job. That suggests premeditation."

"A bit farfetched, guv, surely? Isn't it more likely that the branch was brought here by some kids?"

"Maybe, but it's still worth looking into. Get the two ends bagged, and when Scenes of Crime chaps turn up, tell them to take it away for forensic examination."

"Even if it was like you suggest, guv, any blood would have been washed off by the water."

"There still might be some flakes of skin trapped there."

"Huh! When are we ever that lucky?"

"Don't be such a Jeremiah. Now, I want to establish who pulled the victim out of the water. And why. From what the doctor said, it's clear that it happened some hours after Trent's death. I'm going to talk to the young couple who found the body now, and see if they can shed some light. What's their name?"

"Er . . . Carver. Mike and Jenny."

Kate returned to the patrol car and got into the front passenger seat, twisting round to talk to the Carvers. They were over their first horror by now and she could sense stirrings of excitement in them. What a story to beef up their honeymoon! No more than twenty-one, either of them, they sat close together with their hands tightly clasped; it would take a crowbar to separate them.

"All I want at the moment," Kate said, "is to get a general picture. You will be required to make a full statement, of course, but that can be done at a police station. So will you tell me about this morning. You're staying at the Unicorn Inn, I understand, and you set out for a walk after breakfast. What made you come this way?"

"Well . . . nothing. I mean, we've been a couple of times before."

"It's so pretty," the girl said. "With the sun shining through the branches and everything."

"Did you see anyone else in the wood?"

"We did hear a dog barking," she volunteered after a moment. "Sort of as if it was excited. That was just a few minutes before we . . . we found that poor man."

"Was the barking coming from this direction?"

They consulted each other with their eyes. "Hard to say, really," Mike answered. "Yes, I think so. It . . . it *was* an accident, wasn't it?"

"That's what I have to establish. That's why anything you can tell me might be useful. Anything at all. Did you see anyone else after you left the hotel and started on your walk?"

Further non-verbal exchanges, then Mike said, "There was a man driving a tractor in a field. He waved to us. And I remember now . . . there was another man, walking with his dog. He went into the woods just ahead of us, so we took a different path."

Descriptions of things seen through a rosy romantic haze were not usually very informative. The man had been of medium height, medium build, wearing . . . well, ordinary clothes. The dog? Not small. Not big, either. Sort of medium, and brown . . . ish.

"The man had his trousers pushed into his boots," Jenny recalled suddenly. "You know, those green wellies."

As a clue, it didn't amount to a lot. Not a big clue, not small. Sort of medium.

"When you found the body, did you touch it in any way?" Kate asked them.

She sensed hesitation. A flutter of fear. Mike muttered, "I could see he must be dead, really, but I did . . . well, just feel him to be sure. I touched his cheek, and it was absolutely cold. Shouldn't I have done?"

"Yes, of course, don't worry. But that was all—you just touched him? You didn't move him at all?"

"Oh no!" they chorused firmly. "We left him, and ran to find a phone somewhere. But we'd only just reached the road when a police car happened to come along and we waved at it to stop."

Kate thanked them and left the car, beckoning to Sergeant Boulter. "We have to trace a man who walked in the woods with his dog this morning. He was wearing green wellies. Get onto it, will you, Tim. There's a tractor working in the fields over there, and the driver might be able to help."

The nick at Aston Pringle was the most suitable to use as her temporary HQ. It was the nearest one with decent facilities. Unlike many of the local police stations in the division, it was purpose-built. Comfortable, convenient, with smart cream paintwork and carpeting on the floors. Yet it was soulless. Sorting out which of the available rooms she could best use, Kate had a sudden nostalgic vision of the small station in South-East London to which she'd been assigned as a probationer WPC after completing her training at police college. It was on the corner of a street, in a building that had once been a small fur warehouse, and a camphory smell still lingered. There'd even been a station cat, a ginger kitten which had wandered in one cold night, wet through and half-starved. The excuse for keeping her was the totally non-existent evidence of mice under the floorboards, and the stray had grown plump and complacent, pampered by everyone. Even the toughest thief-taker in the nick, a sergeant with a voice like gravel, had once been spotted by Kate feeding the cat scraps of raw liver that he'd brought along wrapped in kitchen foil.

At the start of a murder case one never knew what might be involved. Hopefully, it could be resolved quickly, but it might blow up into a widespread investigation. Kate was on the phone to divisional headquarters, organizing an office manager for the Incident Room, when Boulter turned up. He'd brought in a man for questioning, whom he'd left downstairs with the custody officer while he came to find Kate and fill her in.

"Name of George Jessop, guv. Caretaker and handyman at Croptech. Lives alone in a bungalow within the firm's grounds. Been in the job two-and-a-half years. He's a taciturn sort of character, keeps himself to himself. When I challenged him straight out he admitted to finding the body, but insists that he had nothing to do with Trent's death."

"What was he doing walking his dog in the woods at past nine in the morning?" Kate demanded. "Shouldn't he have been at work?"

"Says he makes his own hours. As long as the various jobs get done, nobody seems to mind."

"Right. I'll talk to him now. I'm going to use the room next door as my office, so bring him along there, will you?"

George Jessop was a formerly handsome man gone to seed. He looked forty-five but was probably a bit younger than that. What had once been black hair was now an unattractive tone of yellowish grey, and untidily long. He wore a lumberjack-type check flannel shirt above bleached blue jeans. His expression was sullen.

"Sit down, Mr. Jessop. I gather that you found the body of Dr. Trent?"

"That's right." His voice was more cultivated than she had expected.

"At what time was this?"

"How should I know?" Then, unwillingly, "About quarter past nine, I imagine."

Kate pretended surprise. "As long ago as that? Why hadn't you notified us?"

"I had to get back to work. The laundry service was due with the overalls delivery and I had to be there."

"For heaven's sake! You know perfectly well you should have informed the police immediately."

"Well, I didn't." He shrugged in resentful justification. "I suppose I . . . well, panicked."

"Why should you have panicked?"

"Finding a dead body. Well, he looked dead but I couldn't be sure. That's why I dragged him out of the water. Then I thought . . . Christ, I'll be done for this if I'm not careful. The best thing, I decided, was to clear off and keep my mouth shut."

Kate regarded him sceptically. No honest and upright citizen this guy. He *expected* to come under suspicion. So . . . did that mean he had a record? She wanted the answer to that question before she talked to him any further. She gave instructions for him to be taken to an interview room to make a statement, more as a delaying tactic than anything.

Meanwhile, Kate made a quick trip with Boulter to the dead man's cottage, taking the bunch of keys found on the body. It certainly was remote, a small two-up, two-downer hiding shyly among the trees, lying at the end of a rutted track leading from a quiet lane with no other dwelling in sight. The surrounding patch of garden was well kept but lacked charm. Vegetables grew in dead straight rows with not a single weed to be seen. Even the flowerbeds looked regimented, and the shrubs had all been trimmed to precise neatness. On a gravelled area beside the cottage stood a black Austin Metro, clean and polished. Locked.

Inside the cottage everything was just as neat. The front door opened directly into a decent-sized living room. It was a masculine room. The furniture, Swedish-style, dated from the fashion of a few years back. The carpet, wall-to-wall, was a good quality plain beige Wilton. The stereo equipment was of superb quality, with a collection of classical tapes and compact discs methodically filed in a cabinet beside it. Set between the speakers for optimum effect was a comfortable leather armchair. It looked as if music was high on the agenda of a lonely life. The other armchair had a little-used look about it. Everything was clean and tidy. Did he have a woman come in to clean for him? Kate told Boulter to check that point. A cleaning lady might be a useful source of information.

She pointed to a whisky bottle on a small table, a quarter full, with a used glass beside it.

"Was he a solitary drinker, Tim?"

He shrugged. "Looks like it."

The adjoining kitchen was also neat and tidy—a designer job with expensive fitments. And why not? Dr. Trent must have been earning a good salary, with only himself to spend it on. The back door was beside the sink unit. There was a keyhole but no key, and the bolt was drawn back. Touching only the shank of the handle, Kate found that the door was unsecured. It opened onto a small area of concrete slabs where the refuse bin stood.

"Carelessness?" she said to Boulter. "Or what?"

They climbed the narrow, boxed-in staircase. A smart bathroom . . . towels on the heated rail neatly folded, the soap placed squarely on the basin. The first of the two bedrooms was clearly little used except as a place for storage—an empty suitcase, a portable electric heater and several grocer's cartons full of books. Trent's own bedroom was a good deal larger and adequately if unimaginatively furnished. A blue-striped duvet was spread tidily across the bed and there was nothing an inch out of place. Even the piled-up scientific journals, presumably his favoured bedtime reading, were squared off with fussy precision.

They returned to the living room and gave it a more careful scrutiny. A wide teakwood unit was set against one wall. In addition to bookshelves it held the television and video recorder, with drawers and cupboards underneath. Kate glanced at the books for clues about Trent's taste in literature. Mostly they were works of reference with a few scientific biographies and a handful of classic novels. The only video tapes as far as Kate could see were of TV programmes that had been recorded for keeping or retiming, each one meticulously labelled. In one of the drawers were various papers neatly banded together. Receipts, catalogues . . . nothing out of the ordinary. A few letters from friends or acquaintances working in the same field as himself, it seemed, with very little in the way of personal chat in them. There were several letters and a few picture postcards from someone signing herself Fiona. They mentioned a husband and children, chatty accounts of domestic life. Trent's sister, Kate guessed. She handed them to Boulter.

"She's very possibly the next of kin. Or she could put us on to who is. Lives in Preston, I see. Have her informed. Better take his address book away with us, and that list of phone numbers too."

"Will do, guv."

In a cupboard under the drawer were a few bottles, cans of beer and glasses. The usual standard drinks . . . gin, sherry, martini, mixers, some white and red table wines. And another bottle of whisky, a different brand from the one Trent had been drinking from. What immediately struck Kate was that the whisky had been opened and was about three quarters full. It bore the price sticker of a supermarket in Marlingford, as did all the other bottles in the cupboard.

She glanced across at the whisky bottle on the table. No price sticker on that.

"Why would Trent open a new bottle when he had an already opened one in the cupboard? A tidy-minded man like he obviously was."

The sergeant bit his thumbnail. "A visitor brought it? Trent wouldn't like to produce his own bottle, in that case."

"But only one glass!"

"The other person didn't drink, perhaps."

"And Trent sank most of the bottle all on his own? He'd have been legless. No, Tim, there's something a bit out of kilter about this. Get Scenes of Crime to check for fingerprints and so on. Now, it's time we got back to the nick to see what's turned up about George Jessop. Better slip the bolt on the back door to prevent anyone getting in."

Quite a lot of information had turned up. Criminal Records reported that Keith George Jessop had been charged with manslaughter, nearly five years previously, in Leicestershire. He'd served two years in gaol before his release.

The name "Keith George Jessop" struck a chord with Kate where George Jessop hadn't. Details of the case came back to her as she scanned the report.

"Do you remember it, Tim?"

"No, guv."

"It was a nasty one. He was a schoolteacher and the dead boy was one of his students, a seventeen-year-old. Jessop denied that there had been anything sexual between them, but a couple of other boys in his class gave evidence that Jessop had rewarded them for sexual favours. Anyway, on the evening in question, Jessop and the dead boy had been seen together outside a pub, quarrelling fiercely. Later they were spotted on a railway footbridge, still arguing. A man living nearby reported hearing a scream, followed by running footsteps, and another witness saw Jessop, still running, in an adjoining street. Next morning the boy's body was found beside the railway line by a platelayer. Under cross-examination Jessop admitted having been with the boy when he fell, but insisted that it had been accidental. They'd been struggling and the boy had fallen back against the wall and toppled over—it had already been established they'd both been drinking. Jessop then panicked and ran for it—without even checking whether the boy was dead or alive. That really stuck in the public's gullet, plus, of course, the fact that he was regarded as a monster for corrupting the lads in his charge."

"What was the quarrel supposed to be about?"

"Jessop claimed he'd been trying to help the boy with extra coaching for his A-levels, and they'd been arguing about the amount of work he needed to put in if he hoped to pass. The prosecution tried to make out that the boy had been trying a spot of blackmail, threatening to expose Jessop to the education authority if he didn't cough up more money. But none of that could be proved. The public was furious that the jury brought in a verdict of manslaughter. They reckoned that Jessop had got away with murder—literally. There was an outcry when he was only given a three-year sentence."

Kate had Jessop brought back to her for further questioning. He stuck grimly to the story he'd already given . . . that he'd had nothing to do with Dr. Gavin Trent's death except for coming across his body in the pond and dragging it out to check that he was dead. Confronted by Kate's knowledge of his prison record, Jessop declared it was precisely because of what had happened before that he'd wanted to avoid getting involved with the police.

"They wouldn't believe me then," he said bitterly, "so what hope had I of anyone believing me now?"

"We only want to get at the truth, Mr. Jessop," said Kate. "If you're innocent in this matter you have nothing to fear, and you won't help yourself by concealing evidence. Now, you live alone, I gather?"

"That's supposed to be a crime, is it?"

"You're not married?"

Jessop gave her a dark look. "Separated."

"Did you and Dr. Trent have a sexual relationship?" Kate asked.

"No, nothing like that." He almost shouted it.

"Was Dr. Trent homosexual?"

"How am I supposed to know? I'm only the caretaker at Croptech."

"Very well, Mr. Jessop. I'll be wanting to talk to you again, so I must ask you not to leave the district."

"Where the hell would I go?"

"Just so long as you understand that I mean what I say."

Kate and Boulter adjourned to the Half Moon across the street for lunch. Kate ordered a half of lager and a slice of pizza; Boulter a pint of bitter with a Cornish pasty, and as an afterthought, a ham roll and a pork pie. The way he demolished food, Kate reflected, he'd end up with a paunch before he was many years older.

"My money's on Jessop," he said as he broke open the pasty and smothered it with tomato ketchup. "He did it all right."

Kate sipped her lager. "According to Doc Meddowes, Trent died last night. Yet the evidence at the scene supports Jessop's story that he dragged the body out of the water at around nine-fifteen this morning. If he was the killer, why should he return to the pond next morning?"

"Making sure that Trent was dead." Boulter took a massive bite and chewed.

"He'd hardly have needed to pull him out to confirm that, after so many hours."

"He might've been scared that something we'd find on the body would incriminate him—if there really was something going on between the two of them. A letter he'd written to Trent, something like that."

"It's a possibility, Tim."

"There's a big 'but' in the way you said that, guv."

Kate nodded her head. "I don't go for it. What did Jessop tell you about his movements last night?"

"That he knocked off just after six and went across to his bungalow for his supper. About eight o'clock he made his usual round of the premises, checking that everything was locked up and nobody had left any lights on.

Then he went back and watched telly for the rest of the evening . . . he was able to tell me which programmes. Says he went to bed around eleven-thirty."

"And there's just his word for all that?"

"Yep. He's a real loner, all right. Just like the Trent character." Boulter took another large bite of pasty and spoke through it. "Come on, guv, it has to be him."

Kate cast a speculative eye at her sergeant. "If the canteen at the nick missed a plateful of doughnuts, would it be fair to immediately point a finger at Tim Boulter as the obvious culprit?"

He grinned back at her sheepishly.

"A straightforward enough case, wouldn't you say, Chief Inspector?"

Kate had driven over to Marlingford to report to her superintendent. Whenever she had an audience with her chief, it had become something of a ceremony that tea and biscuits were served to them in dainty bone china. "Jolly" Joliffe seemed to imagine that this little gallantry would go down well with a female officer. In fact it did the exact opposite, singling Kate out as an oddity. She'd far rather her superintendent treated her as he did the male officers under his command and invited her to have a friendly drink at the local now and then. But tea with biscuits was her lot, and she'd grown wise enough never to offend by a refusal.

"Straightforward, sir? I don't think so. We have no real leads at the moment. But considering that Dr. Trent and Sir Noah Kimberley are both top-ranking people at Croptech, that has to be our starting point."

A frown appeared on the lugubrious face. "Now don't let us get too concerned about Sir Noah Kimberley. His recent disappearance is probably sheer coincidence. It's Dr. Trent's death we have to concentrate on."

"But we must take Kimberley's disappearance into account. There may very well be a connection."

"Possibly. But tread carefully, won't you? We don't want to go chasing after red herrings, my dear."

For God's sake, Kate, you've got to put a stop to this bloody my-dearing. But this wasn't the moment. Next time, she promised herself.

"You've set up your Incident Room at Aston Pringle, I hear," Jolly continued.

"Yes, sir. It's the most convenient station, with the best facilities. But I shall also ask Croptech to put one of their offices at my disposal. It looks as if we'll be doing a lot of interviewing there."

"I suppose that's a good idea." A tortured smile gave forewarning of an equally tortured witticism. "No doubt the brilliant Chief Inspector Maddox is aiming to dazzle us all with a speedy solution."

"If I don't, sir, it won't be for want to trying."

By God, she was going to try. Another case briskly solved might put an end to the patronising attitude she'd met with from her superintendent and all the rest of the bloody male establishment ever since her promotion. But as she left Jolly's office, a stray thought made her wonder if putting her on her mettle wasn't the old bastard's deliberate intention. He hadn't got where he was without being astute.

She grinned to herself wryly. What the hell?

Three

The Kimberley residence was separated from the pretty village of Radlett by the breadth of two meadows and a grove of young oaks. Belonging to the village community, but nicely set apart from it. Wide and low-built, the house was English domestic architecture of the cry-your-eyes-out-with-envy variety. Elegant, gracious, charming, a picture of serene tranquility. Its creeper-clad stonework had weathered over centuries to that unique Cotswold tawny-grey. At one side, French doors stood open to a paved terrace and smooth, sunlit lawns. A Chief Constable might have afforded such a house at a pinch, Kate reflected, but never, ever, a mere Detective Chief Inspector.

Her ring was answered by a pink-overalled woman so tiny that at first glance Kate almost took her for a flaxen-haired child. Far from it. Her silver-white hair and seamed face betrayed three score and ten; her bright blue pebble eyes looked alert and wily.

"I'm Detective Chief Inspector Maddox, to see Lady Kimberley," Kate announced. "I telephoned to say I'd be coming."

"Oh dear! I'm afraid Dame Vanessa isn't ready for you yet. She's been doing a bit of gardening this afternoon, you see, to occupy her mind, and she's upstairs now getting showered and changed."

"Don't worry. I know I'm a little earlier than I said to expect me. You'd be her housekeeper, I imagine?"

"That's right. Mrs. Dorothy Byworth. Dame Vanessa always calls me Dotty. I was her dresser for years and years, went everywhere with her. Then when she married Sir Noah and retired from the stage, she wanted to keep me on, so I came here. And thankful I am to be with the poor love at this dreadful time."

They were standing in the hall, where sunlight made diamond patterns on the red turkey carpet. Antique oak shone with the elbow grease of generations of Dotty Byworths.

"Such a terrible thing to have happened," the little woman ran on. "The phone's hardly been quiet for a single minute, and people keep calling round all the time. They mean to be kind, of course, but all these anxious enquiries only upset poor Dame Vanessa still more."

Throwing open a door, she ushered Kate into the drawing room. It was pleasantly spacious and cool-looking, plainly two of the original rooms of the house made into one. The oak-beamed ceiling was low, but not uncomfortably so, the walls painted pristine white. A full-size grand piano occupied one corner of the room, leaving ample space for the three large cushioned sofas in deep rose velvet. Above the carved stone fireplace was a portrait of a much younger Dame Vanessa as Violetta, painted by Annigoni.

"If you'll just take a seat, Chief Inspector, I'm sure Dame Vanessa won't keep you long."

Kate seized this opportunity. "Before you go, Mrs. Byworth, I'd like a word with you. About Sir Noah, I mean. In the period of time before his disappearance, did anything strike you as unusual? Did he seem at all upset? Or worried about anything?"

"Oh, yes. Dame Vanessa told me since that he was really out of sorts about a phone call he took just before she left for London."

"And how about you, Mrs. Byworth? Did you yourself notice anything unusual in his manner?"

"Well, I can't say I did, not particular. I just put it down to him not being very happy about Dame Vanessa being away. But if she said it was the phone call that upset him, that's good enough for me."

"What other phone calls were there that Friday?" asked Kate.

She considered. "Only the one other, that was just before dinner."

"Who was it from?"

"I don't know. I was in the kitchen, dishing up, and Sir Noah called to tell me not to bother, he'd answer the phone."

"And afterwards, did he seem upset, preoccupied . . . anything like that?"

A shake of the head. "Like I said, he wasn't very cheerful, with Dame Vanessa being away. Leastways, that's what I thought it was. He ate his dinner—not very much, I seem to remember, even though it was one of his favourites. Steak and kidney pie and butter beans. I thought it would comfort him, like. I cleared the dishes and gave him his coffee, and a bit later on I heard him leave the house and drive off."

"He didn't tell you he was going out?"

"No." She stiffened, her pride at stake. "There was no reason why he should have done. I'm off duty after dinner."

"Yes, I understand. But perhaps, while you were serving the meal, Sir Noah might have said something about his intention of going out later."

"Well, he didn't. Not a word."

"Could you make a guess where he might have gone?"

"It could have been anywhere. Sometimes of an evening he'd go back to his office at Croptech to finish something he was working on. I don't know."

"Did Sir Noah take any clothes or personal belongings with him? His shaving things?"

"No, nothing. I looked special, next morning, when I realized he'd never come back home. And Dame Vanessa has looked, too. There's nothing gone, nothing at all. Just the clothes he stood up in."

"What was it he was wearing that evening?"

"Oh, one of his grey suits. A pinstripe." She screwed up her face, remembering. "White shirt . . . he always wears a white shirt, and his tie was . . . red and black, striped. He's a neat dresser, Sir Noah. He doesn't care much for casual clothes."

"You said just now that he wasn't very cheerful when you served his dinner, which you took to be because his wife was away. It's well known that he used to travel all over the world to hear her sing, so I'd have thought he would have gone with her to London."

The bright blue eyes clouded over. "I thought we'd all three be going, as per usual. But Dame Vanessa said no, Sir Noah was staying home this time, and I ought to be here to look after him. She could easily manage dressing herself this once, as it was just going to be an evening gown she'd be wearing."

"Did Lady Kimberley happen to say *why* Sir Noah wasn't going with her?"

Her mouth tightened. "She just said it wasn't convenient." Clearly the woman felt hurt and resentful about her exclusion. Possibly she still hankered for the days when her mistress had been an international star, and this gala would have been a highlight in the quieter life she now led. Kate found it curious that Lady Kimberley wanted neither her husband nor her dresser to be with her that evening.

"Going back to that phone call earlier in the day, Mrs. Byworth, just before Lady Kimberley left for London. Is there anything more you can tell me about it?"

"Well, not really. I did hear the phone ringing, just as Sir Noah was about to fetch the car round the front for Dame Vanessa . . . he was always like that, so attentive. But I was busy with last-minute packing for her, so he answered it."

"And you've no idea who the caller was?"

"No idea at all. Could have been anyone. He gets lots of phone calls."

"Thank you, Mrs. Byworth, that's all I want to ask you. Perhaps you'll just make sure that Lady Kimberley knows I've arrived."

Sitting alone in the silent room, Kate had an odd feeling of being on stage, waiting for curtain up. After a couple of minutes came the sound of firm footsteps on the stairs, then Lady Kimberley made her entrance. She was wearing black velvet trousers and a marigold yellow top with a cowl neck and floppy sleeves. Her hair and make-up were immaculate.

"Chief Inspector, I am so sorry to have kept you waiting," she said graciously, in her richly beautiful voice. Her face changed, with anxiety showing in every line of it. "You said on the phone that you have no word of what has befallen my husband, but in that case why are you here? Is it bad news? Please, you *must* tell me the truth. Without any *prevarication.*"

"No, really, Lady Kimberley, I have discovered nothing to explain Sir Noah's disappearance. It is, in fact, more about Dr. Trent than your husband that I wish to speak to you. No doubt you have heard of his death? That we suspect murder?"

"I have heard." The magnificent figure sank down onto a sofa, with a gesture inviting Kate to resume her seat. "Has the same horrible fate overtaken my darling Noah . . . that is the thought which *terrifies* me."

"There is no evidence to suggest that, and I sincerely hope not. However . . ."

"However?"

"I have to consider the possibility that Dr. Trent's death and Sir Noah's disappearance might be in some way connected." Kate paused a moment, then asked quietly, "Lady Kimberley, why didn't your husband accompany you to London for the gala?"

A sharp gaze from her fine violet eyes met Kate's briefly, then slid away. "It was . . . decided that he shouldn't, on this occasion."

"By your wish? Or his?"

"Really, what *does* it matter? I thought you said it was about Dr. Trent that you wished to speak to me."

"But first, please bear with me and clarify this point. Wasn't it normal for your husband to go and hear you sing, wherever it happened to be?"

"Good heavens, it isn't an *invariable* rule. We just decided that this time he would remain at home."

"I believe, in the event, that you didn't actually sing. You were prevented by a sudden throat infection?"

A fraught silence stretched through fifteen seconds. Then, "That is true."

"But you still stayed overnight in London?"

"Well, yes. I thought it would be unwise to drive back at night, in the circumstances. Besides, it would have seemed discourteous towards Lord Balmayne, the organizer of the gala. I was a guest at his home in London. He has been a very dear friend of mine over many years." A tiny pause. "A dear friend of us *both.*"

Tuck that pause away for future consideration, Kate.

"Now, Lady Kimberley, about Dr. Trent. How well did you know him?"

"Naturally I met him from time to time as he was in a senior position at Croptech. My husband had a high opinion of his professional competence."

Kate scented an evasion. "And as a person?"

"Dr. Trent was a man who kept himself to himself, Chief Inspector. He possessed none of the social graces. To be frank I found him somewhat *boorish.*"

"Your husband, too?"

"In many ways, I think, Gavin Trent was a disappointment to Noah, though he tried not to admit it. He'd been hoping to see qualities of leadership emerge in Gavin, ready for the day when he himself relinquished the reins. But Gavin never showed any signs of that. Somehow he couldn't inspire liking or even respect in the people working under him. On the contrary, he usually managed to *antagonize* them."

"I see." That widened the field of possible suspects. "Can you think of any disagreements or upsets occurring recently that might throw some light on Dr. Trent's death?"

Both hands played in the air in protest. "How could I?"

"Your husband might have mentioned something to you."

She shook her head. "Croptech is like any other organization, I suppose. There are personal differences, little *undercurrents*. But nothing, I am sure, that could account for anything so dreadful as . . . as . . ." She baulked at uttering the word.

"Can you fill in some background for me, to get a clearer picture in my mind. The people who worked most closely with Dr. Trent, for example. Who are they, and what sort of relationship did he have with them?"

"Surely you should address that question to his colleagues on the staff."

"I would greatly value your views, Lady Kimberley."

She sighed on a descending note. "I will do what I can, of course. Let me see . . . the only person of comparable rank working with Dr. Trent would be Cheryl Miller." Was there a touch of distaste in her voice?

"Dr. Miller is also a biochemist, I believe?"

A nod. "Noah would not normally have engaged a woman in such a senior scientific position but he said that *academically* her qualifications entirely justified it. They were higher than any of the other applicants for the vacancy."

"When was she appointed?"

"Oh, you'll have to consult the records. About six or seven years ago, I'd say. She worked under Dr. Lintott, who afterwards took up a post in the United States. Gavin Trent was engaged in his place . . . *much* to Cheryl Miller's fury. She thought that she was altogether better qualified than he was for the senior post."

"But your husband wasn't willing to appoint a woman to such a top position?"

"Noah believes"—her voice wobbled noticeably over the tense of that verb—"that women are *emotionally* unsuited to a career in the sciences. When it comes to the arts, of course, it is an *entirely* different matter."

"And does Dr. Miller still feel resentful, do you think?"

"Definitely. She never misses an opportunity to make that plain."

The telephone rang outside in the hall. *On cue, Kate, like a stage effect.* Why did that thought come to her? There were muffled sounds of the housekeeper answering it. Then the door opened and the child-size woman peered in.

"It's Lord Balmayne, Dame Vanessa, phoning from Paris. Shall I plug the phone in here for you?"

"Er . . . no, Dotty, I'll take it outside." She rose to her feet, pridefully elegant. "If you'll excuse me, Chief Inspector."

The door, though, was left ajar. Accidentally or on purpose? Whichever, Kate could hear every word uttered by Lady Kimberley.

"Oh, my dear Gerald! Yes, it's too *dreadful* for words. I wondered if the news would reach you. No, there's nothing further been heard of Noah . . . *nothing*. I am quite *distraught*. Oh, but I cannot expect you to . . . well, if you *insist*. You are such a dear, kind man. I admit that having you near at hand just now would be a *great* blessing." The talk gushed on in similar vein for several more minutes.

Lady Kimberley returned, closing the door this time. She resumed her seat. "I apologize for the interruption, Chief Inspector. Lord Balmayne is an old and very dear friend of ours, as I've said."

"I believe I heard it mentioned that Lord Balmayne has a country home near Cheltenham."

"Yes, indeed, a *beautiful* house. He is in Paris at present, on business, but he telephoned because news had only just reached him that poor Noah was missing. He is returning at once . . . so *extremely* kind of him, so as to offer whatever help he can at this terrible time."

"Lady Kimberley, I know this is very distressing for you, but in view of what has happened, I want you to answer very carefully. In the past few days have you been able to think of anything that could explain your husband's disappearance?"

"No, no, it's a complete mystery."

"You and he hadn't had any kind of quarrel? Or disagreement?"

"Noah and I? We have *never* quarrelled. *Never!* We are utterly devoted to one another."

"And you can't suggest any reason to link his disappearance with Dr. Trent's death? Any possible reason at all."

"Certainly not," she said disdainfully. Then she put a hand to her mouth, stifling a sob. "But somehow I feel even more fearful about Noah now. Please, Mrs. Maddox, can't you do *something* to find out what has happened to him?"

"I will do all I can," Kate promised, knowing how little that could be. Jolly Joliffe had warned her off pursuing Sir Noah Kimberley's disappearance too ardently. Despite her own instincts, she still lacked sufficient evidence to justify a widespread search for Sir Noah.

"Can we go through exactly what happened that last day," she went on, "so that I have the details clearly in my mind? I understand that when Mr. Richard Gower came to see you at the weekend, you told him that just before you set out for London after lunch on Friday, your husband received a phone call that seemed to upset him."

"That is correct. But Noah said I wasn't to worry and that he would explain all about it when I got home. And as I was already somewhat later setting out than I'd intended, I didn't press him. If only I *had.*"

"You still don't know who the caller was?"

"I haven't the *faintest* idea. I've phoned everybody I could think of, to ask."

"What time was this phone call, exactly?"

"It must have been . . . somewhere between twenty and a quarter to two. I'd intended to leave at half-past one, d'you see."

Kate kept her talking, probing her memory for details, but little more emerged than she'd already learned.

"Before I leave, Lady Kimberley, there is one other point. With things as they are, who will be in charge at Croptech during Sir Noah's absence? Will Mr. Aidan Kimberley step in? I believe he is an equal partner in the firm."

"That is true, yes. But Aidan has never played an active part in the business."

"Might he not have to now, though, with Dr. Trent dead? Decisions will need to be taken, and someone must assume the responsibility."

"I see what you mean." She frowned, looking burdened by this new anxiety. "How much time Aidan could spare I really don't know. He is only just back from a month in Hong Kong. He's an investment counsellor in the City, you know, and he told me on the phone that he's simply up to his eyes with a backlog of work. And on top of that his wife has flu. But Aidan did promise to come down to see me the moment he can get away."

"When was it he telephoned?" Kate asked.

"Er . . . Monday evening. Paula . . . that's his wife, had gone back to London on Sunday, d'you see, to get their flat in Sloane Street ready for his return. They have a weekend cottage at Inchmere St. Mary, and she'd been staying there for most of the time Aidan was away. She's an interior designer, which means she can continue with her work—quite a lot of it, anyway—wherever she chooses to be." Lady Kimberley sighed. "It would have been nice if Paula could have stayed on down here, so I'd have someone in the family near me. She knew how desperately worried I was about Noah, because I told her so on the phone on Saturday evening. To be candid, Mrs. Maddox, I felt rather *hurt* that she didn't even offer to come round to see me on Sunday before driving back to London. However, from what Aidan said she was already sickening for flu then, so I suppose Paula didn't feel up to it. Of course she told Aidan what had happened the moment he arrived home from the airport on Monday, and he rang me straight away. He was *most* upset about Noah. He has phoned me each day since, to enquire if I've had any more news."

"Have you informed Mr. Kimberley about Dr. Trent's death?"

"Well, no. He hasn't phoned yet, today."

"When you do speak to him, will you please say that I shall want to talk to him sometime in the near future."

"To Aidan? For what reason, may I ask?"

"In pursuing my enquiries I shall need to talk to everyone who is even remotely connected with recent events."

"Oh, yes. I see."

"Lady Kimberley, another thing Mr. Gower mentioned to me was that you were considering engaging the services of a private investigator. Have you done so yet?"

The question seemed to take her by surprise. "Well . . . no, I thought I would leave that . . . for the moment. You had said, had you not, that you would do everything possible to discover what had happened to my poor Noah. And . . . well, Mr. Gower promised to ask in his newspaper for anyone with information about my husband to come forward. It was in the *Gazette* today. Did you see it?"

"I did. Let's hope that it produces something useful."

From the Kimberley house, Kate headed for the Croptech premises, where Boulter had gone ahead of her to make arrangements for interviews. The narrow by-way meandered, dipping and rising through the wooded countryside. Amber sunlight slanted down through branches that met and tangled overhead. Who but a disillusioned copper would see death and villainy lurking beneath the surface of this tranquil landscape?

She almost shot past the entrance to Croptech Agricultural Research and Development Limited, only at the very last moment catching sight of a discreet bronze name plaque on one of the two stone pillars that flanked a pair of particularly fine wrought iron gates. These, newly painted black and tipped with gold leaf, stood open to allow free access. A tarmac driveway was flanked by wide grass verges. On either side lay test grounds sown with crops, bordered by miniature box hedges.

The drive ended at a group of buildings linked by paved walkways. Architecturally non-attributable, Kate gauged, but easy on the eye. Nothing stark, nothing vulgar, everything low key.

Boulter's dark blue Escort was parked outside the office block at the end. As Kate drew up beside it, the sergeant's stocky figure appeared at a doorway and he came over to meet her.

"Did you get anything useful from Lady Kimberley, guv?"

"Precious little. I'll fill you in with the details later. Did you manage to see Sir Noah's doctor and his bank manager?"

He nodded. "You said they wouldn't be very forthcoming, and you were dead right. But I think we can take it that Kimberley has no serious problems, healthwise or financial, that would have caused him to head off into the blue yonder."

"If he went voluntarily, how is he living? Is the bank manager going to tip us the wink if Kimberley cashes any cheques or uses his credit card?"

"Cheques, yes—he agreed reluctantly, with much persuasion from me. As for credit cards, it seems the old boy has never possessed one. Doesn't hold with them; says they encourage thriftless spending. Lady Kimberley has several, but apparently her husband always carries largish sums in cash to cover his day-to-day expenditure. He cashed a cheque for three hundred the day before he disappeared, which was his usual sort of amount."

"Three hundred wouldn't last him long. He'd need to cash further cheques quite soon. Unless the disappearance was premeditated, of course, and he'd salted cash in readiness. Or is he being staked by someone? Or—and I feel increasingly certain of this—he didn't disappear willingly. Either he's being held somewhere against his will, or he's dead. Now, Tim, what have you done here so far?"

"I've fixed a room for us to use for interviews. It's Kimberley's secretary's office. She's moving out, pro-tem."

"Right. His secretary could be very useful to us, regarding both men. What's she like?"

"Younger than I'd have expected, hardly more than twenty-two, and she's worked for Kimberley for just under eighteen months. Sandra English. Lives with her parents in Great Bedham. She's not what you'd call overflowing with zip and competence."

"Did she have anything useful to tell you?"

"Not really. She was a bit on the defensive, but that could have been just nerves. The last she saw of Kimberley was when he left at five on Friday. He said goodnight and wished her a pleasant weekend, though when I pressed her she did think he'd seemed rather preoccupied all afternoon, as if he had something on his mind."

"The result of that mysterious phone call? We've got to find out who it was from, Tim. *Was* it a woman?"

"Sandra seemed horrified when I hinted that maybe Sir Noah had woman trouble. He was always the absolute gentleman, she insisted, just like my wife said. Sandra's not bad looking in a quiet sort of way, and I put careful feelers out that he might have made a pass at her now and then. She got quite upset at the mere suggestion. As for Trent, she hadn't really seen him all this week, though her boyfriend told her he'd been in an even worse mood than usual these past few days."

"Her boyfriend?"

"Roger Barlow. He's one of the scientists in the lab."

Kate nodded. "I hope you've made it clear, Tim, that nobody is to leave the premises this evening until I give the okay?"

"Crystal clear, guv."

"So lead the way and we'll get started."

The secretary's office was small, but adequate for their purpose. The girl behind the desk jumped to her feet as they went in, and seemed about to slip away in silence.

"Thank you for giving up your office, Miss English," said Kate pleasantly. "Another police officer will want to take a written statement from you sometime, probably tomorrow. If I need you for anything, where do we find you?"

Boulter was right about her. She was pretty ordinary, or ordinarily pretty, with undistinguished features. Nevertheless there was a certain glow about her. The glow that came from being in love, perhaps. She had a clean, wholesome look, with neat fingernails and even teeth. Her newly washed hair, a warm mid-brown, she wore fluffed around her face almost like a halo.

"I'll be in the general office. Extension five." She pointed at the intercom on the desk, a typed list on a card beside it. "You can get through to anyone else you need, too. The numbers are all there."

"Thank you. I gather from the sergeant here that you can offer no suggestions about what might have happened to Sir Noah?"

"No." Her expression became sombre. "It's a complete mystery. Do you think he's all right?"

"Let's hope so, Miss English."

In addition to the typist's chair that went with the desk, two others had obviously been brought in . . . one placed the same side, one opposite. There was very little spare room left. Kate sat down and took a notebook and pen from her shoulderbag. The sergeant also prepared himself for taking notes.

"Who's first?" asked Kate.

Boulter studied a list he'd made. "The chief clerk, I'd say. Name of Duncan McEvoy."

"Right. Buzz for him, will you."

McEvoy answered the summons immediately. An extremely thin man, his narrow bone structure made him look rather taller than he really was. He was as precise in dress as in manner . . . a charcoal grey suit, white shirt and dark tie. Pale blond hair was brushed flat against his head, and he wore half-lens spectacles with thin gilt frames.

He glanced around the small room with a critical frown. "If I'd been given warning, Chief Inspector, I could have accommodated you somewhere better than this."

"This will do very well, Mr. McEvoy. Won't you sit down?"

He did so cautiously, lowering his narrow frame into the dead centre of the chair. Kate sat quietly while her sergeant dealt with the preliminaries. Duncan Alexander McEvoy lived with his wife and two teenage daughters in one of those prim and proper semis that lined the Cheltenham Road in Marlingford. A prim and proper little family, by the sound of it. He'd worked at Croptech from the time he left school, edging his way up from junior clerk to his present position.

"What was your relationship with Dr. Trent?" Kate intervened briskly.

"My *relationship?*" The word seemed to shock him, offend him. "Why, I hardly knew the man, except just for work. And I had very little contact with him even here. He and I worked in quite distinct departments.

Normally, I had little reason to speak to Dr. Trent at all, apart from saying 'Good morning' and so on."

"It sounds to me as if you didn't like him very much."

"Well, nobody . . ." McEvoy stopped short, and after an embarrassed pause, continued, "I neither liked nor disliked Dr. Trent."

"When did you last see him?"

"Er . . . yesterday evening. I passed him at the gates as I was driving out. That would have been about ten past five."

"You passed him? He was walking, you mean?"

"Yes. He always walked. Once when it was raining I stopped and offered him a lift, but he was quite short with me. He'd have used his own car to come to work, he said, if he'd wanted to drive."

"So when did you last see Dr. Trent to speak to, Mr. McEvoy?"

He didn't need to search for an answer. "On Tuesday. He came to my office demanding to know what was happening about a new centrifuge he wanted for the laboratory. I told him that Sir Noah hadn't yet given his authorization, and that for such an expensive item of equipment I couldn't possibly act without it. That should have been quite obvious to Dr. Trent, but he wouldn't listen to me. He became very angry and called me a petty-minded bureaucrat. He said what made me think Sir Noah was ever coming back. We just had to accept what had happened, and carry on without him. And we might just as well get a few sensible things done like ordering new equipment before his successors or whoever moved in and started wanting to reorganize everything."

"Did Dr. Trent tell you why he didn't think Sir Noah would be returning?" Kate queried. "Had Sir Noah said something to him?"

"No, I'm sure he hadn't told him anything, but Dr. Trent just seemed to take it for granted he wouldn't be coming back. That's what annoyed me, his whole attitude." McEvoy drew himself up and went on with an air of prim satisfaction, "I told him that unless we all adhered to the correct procedures we might as well hand in our resignations. Sir Noah had entrusted me to conduct things in a proper manner and I intended to go on doing so. In fact, Sir Noah would be most upset were he to return and find that we had deliberately flouted his ruling. So until I received further instructions from Sir Noah himself or some authorized person acting for him, there would be no question of ordering a new centrifuge or anything else."

"So Dr. Trent retired defeated?"

"Oh, yes! Oh, yes, indeed!" His eyes glinted behind the half lenses.

"Do you have any ideas about who might have killed Dr. Trent?"

McEvoy came down to earth again from his flight of virtuous triumph. "No, of course not. How could I?"

"Think about it, will you? And let me know immediately if anything occurs to you."

"Oh, yes, I most certainly will." He half rose, assuming the interview was at an end.

"Would you mind telling me what you were doing last evening?" Kate said.

McEvoy slumped back into the chair, his pale face whitening. "Why . . . why? You can't possibly suspect me of killing him."

"My question implies no suspicion," she explained. "It would merely be helpful for me to know your movements last night for elimination purposes. I shall be asking everybody the same question."

"Oh . . . oh, yes, I see." McEvoy struggled to regain his composure. "I'm sorry, you just took me by surprise, and I thought it meant . . . Of course I don't mind telling you. Not a very interesting programme, I'm afraid. My wife and I lead a quiet life and go out very rarely. So last night I went home as usual, had my tea, and spent the evening quietly with my family. Oh no, I was forgetting. It was my younger daughter's night for guides and I went to the church hall to collect her afterwards. I don't like her to walk home alone, not these days. You can't be too careful, can you? That was at seven forty-five."

"Thank you. And now, Mr. McEvoy, there's the question of Sir Noah's disappearance. Have you any theory to explain that?"

He shook his head. "None at all. It's most disturbing."

"You must have come to know Sir Noah well in the course of your work here. He'd have relied on you, I imagine, to keep him *au fait* with the week-by-week financial state of the company."

"Well, yes. I *am* the chief clerical officer here."

"That's what I meant. So you would know better than anybody if he had any business worries. Was he at all concerned about how things were going?"

"Absolutely not! Croptech is in a very healthy state—as it has been for a number of years." He spoke with stiff pride, as if he alone were responsible.

"Can you think of anything else that might have so preyed on Sir Noah's mind as to make him behave irrationally? Was he at all preoccupied or visibly upset just lately?"

"On the contrary. He was very pleased with the way things were going. Though I must admit he was a trifle short-tempered on Friday afternoon. As a matter of fact the question of the centrifuge came up then, and he told me that Trent would have to wait for a decision on that. He just wasn't prepared to authorize such expenditure on the laboratory at the moment without being convinced that the need was justified."

"Is Sir Noah usually cautious about expenditure?"

"Not at all, when he can be shown the justification for it. Last year, for instance, when I put up a plan to computerize our whole accounts system, he was perfectly ready to agree, and that involved a very large sum indeed."

"So how do you explain his different attitude about laboratory equipment?"

The prim mouth pursed. "He would know that he could rely on me not to suggest any expenditure that wasn't totally justified."

"But not on Dr. Trent?"

"I didn't say that, Chief Inspector," he said, flustered.

"You implied it, though."

McEvoy shrugged. "I suppose scientists live in a different world. They can easily get carried away by their enthusiasms."

"Sir Noah himself is a scientist."

"Oh yes, of course. But he's a practical businessman, too, and Trent would never have been that."

"You don't think so? I rather understood that Dr. Trent was seen as Sir Noah's ultimate successor."

McEvoy took a while to answer. "If Sir Noah ever regarded that as a possibility, I'm sure he has long abandoned the idea."

Kate leaned back in her chair. "That's all for now, Mr. McEvoy. I may need to have a further talk with you tomorrow."

Now that he was free to leave, he seemed oddly reluctant. "Er . . . if Sir Noah doesn't return soon, Chief Inspector . . ." He dithered to a halt, and Kate prompted him. "What is it you want to say?"

He gestured around in a vague sort of way. "I've been wondering. Suppose Sir Noah doesn't ever come back, what will become of Croptech? He's been away before, of course, on holiday, but he's always left me my instructions. But now, with Dr. Trent gone too, I don't quite know what I should do. Do you think the firm might be sold?"

"Would Croptech readily find a buyer, Mr. McEvoy?"

"Well, I imagine so. Not at its true value, though, not without Sir Noah at the helm."

"Perhaps Mr. Aidan Kimberley will step in and run things here," Kate suggested, watching his face.

McEvoy shook his head from side to side, looking dismayed and at a loss. Clearly he was a man who liked routine, and any kind of change disturbed him.

Boulter said as the door closed behind him, "He obviously hated Trent's guts. Could he be our chummy, guv?"

"He certainly took fright when I asked him about last night." Kate was thoughtful as she glanced down at her list. "Let's have Dr. Miller in now, and see what we make of her."

Four

Cheryl Miller made quite an impression the moment she walked into the room. A professional woman of Kate's age and Kate's height—but there the resemblance ended. Cheryl Miller positively exuded sexuality. Richard Gower had commented that she was the sort of woman whom once seen was never forgotten. She had dramatic green eyes, full sensual lips, and a voluptuous figure that was clearly evident even beneath her starched laboratory coat. Her mass of hair, a subtle shade of auburn (an expensive tint job?), was drawn back into a tortoiseshell clip. Kate guessed that a single practised flip would send it tumbling sexily about her shoulders. Boulter, on his feet in a flash, seemed to be steaming slightly.

Cheryl Miller spared the sergeant one direct glance, then totally ignored him. Her green eyes, sparking with hostility, were fixed challengingly on Kate as she dropped into the chair provided and crossed her legs

. . . long, shapely legs that terminated in a pair of high-heeled black court shoes.

"About bloody time, too. At least you're a woman," she added with grudging approval. "That makes a pleasant change."

Amused, Kate asked, "This isn't the first time you've been interrogated by the police?"

The green eyes narrowed in anger. "I just meant it makes a change to see a woman in any position of authority. Not that you'll climb much higher, I hope you realize. Detective Chief Inspector is about as far as they'll ever let a woman get, the bastards."

"You seem to have a low opinion of men, Dr. Miller."

"Oh, they have their limited uses. Though even in bed they seem to imagine they're God's gift to us women. You must have found that."

"Since you've been kept waiting," said Kate dryly, "perhaps we'd better get on with the business in hand."

She let Boulter handle the routine details and his voice sounded definitely husky. Cheryl Miller's arrogance could be forgiven, Kate thought, if this was the instant effect she had on a man.

Kate took over with a foursquare question. "Who might have wanted Gavin Trent out of the way, do you think?"

"Me, for one."

Smothering her surprise at this blunt answer, Kate asked mildly, "Because you resented his having been appointed to the job you wanted?"

"Aha! Someone's been talking, I perceive. Yes, I resented Gavin, damn right I did. Wouldn't you resent a man who was less qualified than you getting promoted over your head?"

"Did you kill him, Dr. Miller?" It could have been a woman who'd held Trent beneath the water till he drowned. It wasn't so much strength that had been needed, but cool cunning and ruthless determination. And Cheryl Miller was probably capable of both.

"Oh, for God's sake," she snapped. "Of course I didn't kill him."

"Maybe you know who did? Or can guess?"

Kate received a hard stare. "I'm beginning to wonder about you, if this is the best line of approach you can think of."

"Please answer the Chief Inspector's question," intervened Boulter automatically.

"It's all right, Sergeant," said Kate. "Dr. Miller has already answered me, in her own way. But we'll need to have an account of your movements at the relevant times, Dr. Miller, just so you can be formally eliminated."

"What are the relevant times?"

"From when Dr. Trent left the laboratory on Wednesday evening until say 3 A.M.," Boulter told her.

Cheryl Miller considered unhurriedly, then announced in a casual tone, "In that case, you'll have to *formally* retain me on your list of suspects. Actually, I knocked off yesterday about half-past four—much to dear Gavin's annoyance. He was always so puritanical about sticking to proper hours, but I wanted to catch a boutique in Marlingford to pick up a skirt I'd bought which they were altering for me."

Boulter noted the name of the shop and the times she'd have got there and left.

"And after that?" asked Kate.

"After that, nothing. I had a drink and a bar snack at the Dolphin, then I drove home and stayed home, curled up with a good book." Home, they had already established, being one of the flats in the converted Old Rectory at Lower Aston.

"Do you live alone, Dr. Miller?"

"Yes, I do. From choice. How about you? Do *you* live alone?"

Kate ignored that. "Did you have any visitors during the evening? Any phone calls?"

A hesitation, slight but definite. "No, I didn't, as it happens."

Kate wondered about that hesitation. Was she shielding some man . . . and if so, why? Or did she just hate having to admit that she'd been left to her own devices for the space of an entire evening?

"Tell me, Dr. Miller, was your resentment of Dr. Trent purely from a professional point of view? Or did you dislike him on a personal level?"

The green eyes half closed in speculation. "Tell me, Chief Inspector, what would your attitude be towards a senior officer, a superintendent say, who you knew bloody well was less competent than yourself, but who'd been given the job that should have been yours solely because he was male? Wouldn't it make you hate his guts on a personal level?"

Kate wished that Boulter hadn't been present, ears twitching. "I hardly think this is relevant, Dr. Miller."

"Oh, yes it is, totally relevant. And you know it."

No, let it pass, Kate. This wasn't the moment for trotting out her grudges against the male hierarchy.

"What did other people in the lab think of Trent?" she enquired.

"You'd better ask them that."

"I intend to. Right now, I'm asking you."

Cheryl Miller shrugged. "He treated Roger like a snotty-nosed kid. Well, he isn't much more, I suppose, but he does have quite a good degree which deserves a modicum of respect."

"Roger Barlow? He's Sandra English's boyfriend, I believe?"

"For the moment. Though what a good-looking stud like him sees in someone so insipid, I can't imagine."

Stud? Was that said on the basis of personal experience? Cheryl Miller would probably consider anything male as a challenge, to be captured, used, then cast off. Had she ever tried it on with Trent?

"Was there a woman in Dr. Trent's life?"

"You've got to be joking."

Kate raised one eyebrow. "Are you saying there was a *man?* Or men?"

"The mind boggles."

"Let me understand you, Dr. Miller. Are you suggesting that Dr. Trent lived a celibate life?"

She looked amused. "It's an intriguing question, I must say. There's a certain mutuality demanded by sex, isn't there, and I can't see dear Gavin sharing a bloody thing with anyone."

Kate nodded and jotted down a note. "Thank you, Dr. Miller. I won't keep you any longer just now."

For the first time Cheryl Miller looked slightly thrown. "You haven't said a word about old Kimberley."

"Do you have something to tell me about him?"

"No, I was hoping you could tell me. I just want to know what the hell's going on. It's been chaos here these past few days with the boss missing, and now . . . God knows what's going to happen if he doesn't turn up soon."

"Believe me, Dr. Miller, I'm just as keen as you are to know what has happened to Sir Noah. So if anything occurs to you that might possibly throw some light on his disappearance, you can include it in the statement we'll be requiring from you tomorrow. That's all for now."

Boulter sucked in a breath as the door closed. "Christ, what a woman!"

"She'd eat you for breakfast," Kate observed dryly.

He rolled his eyes. "But what a way to die."

"Cool it, Cuthbert. Let's have the next one in."

Roger Barlow, ranking number three in the laboratory, was a tall, well-built chap who only just missed being very good-looking by having a slightly overlong nose. He had the bloom of healthy youth and the arrogance of a young male about to conquer the world.

"I'm sorry to have kept you waiting, Mr. Barlow," said Kate. "Please sit down."

As he did so, he smiled deep into her eyes. Just to show how totally at ease he was. A cover, Kate realized, for considerable *unease*. What did Roger Barlow have to fear from her? What might he be hoping to keep hidden? She sat waiting quietly while Sergeant Boulter handled the preliminary formal questions, then she winged in with an uppercut designed to shake him.

"I understand that you heartily disliked Dr. Trent?"

Barlow stared at her, his jaw slackening. "Why should you say that?"

"Are you denying that it's true?"

He looked down fixedly at his hands, and began picking at the quick of one finger. "Well . . . nobody liked him that much. Nobody. He had a way of always acting superior, and sneering at people all the time."

"At you in particular?"

Barlow flickered his eyes up to meet hers again, and Kate tried to read the look that lurked in them. Guilt? Anger? Or just plain fear at being treated like a suspect? He seemed about to say something, something explanatory, then changed his mind and resumed the keen study of his hands.

"No, not really," he muttered.

"When did you last see Dr. Trent?"

"Packing up time yesterday. Five o'clock."

"You left the lab before he did?"

"As it happens, yes." He glared defiance. "Any reason why I shouldn't?"

"And you're sure you didn't see him again after that?"

"I already told you."

"Someone, Mr. Barlow, someone who didn't like Dr. Trent, *did* see him last night. Someone called at his cottage, perhaps taking a bottle of whisky designed to look like a placatory gesture—after a quarrel, it could be. That someone then managed to persuade Dr. Trent to accompany him into the nearby woods, and there pushed him into the pond to drown. Could it have been you, I wonder?"

She watched every trace of colour bleach from his face. "It wasn't me. No way. I had nothing to do with his death, nothing at all. I wasn't anywhere near Trent's cottage last night."

"Then all you need to do is to prove it by telling me *where* you were."

"I was with my girlfriend."

"That's . . ." Kate glanced down at her pad as if for the name. A display of formality could often be unnerving to an interviewee. ". . . Sandra English?"

"That's right. Sandra and I . . . we spent the whole evening together. I picked her up outside the office block after work and we drove over to Oxford."

"Oxford? Any special reason?"

"That was where I went to university. Nuffield College. I promised to show Sandra around sometime, and it was a fine evening."

"Did you meet anyone you knew?"

"No, I didn't."

"So you looked around your old college. What then?"

"I suggested going to a pub for something to eat."

"Which pub?" asked Boulter.

"The Cricketers' Arms at Boscombe." This was a large and popular hostelry, invariably packed with customers on a summer evening. "We had spaghetti bolognese."

"You're known there, are you?"

"Not exactly. We've been there once or twice before."

"What time did you arrive?"

He shrugged. "About nine, I suppose."

"Did you speak to anyone? Would any of the bar staff remember your being there? The waitress?"

"They were all pretty busy."

"Did you see any friends while you were there?"

He shook his head. "No, we didn't."

"So what it boils down to is that you and Sandra can only vouch for each other. What time did you leave the pub?"

Another shrug. "Closing time. Eleven o'clock."

"What did you do after that?"

Barlow gave her a defiant glare. "D'you want me to spell it out? She and I were . . . together, right up until late. Then I dropped Sandra off at her home."

"Where exactly were you together until late?" she enquired dryly.

"Over by Ampney-on-the-Water. There are places there where you can pull off the road."

"And just how late was it that you left Sandra at her home?"

"It must have been a few minutes before one-thirty. I got to my digs just after then."

"Can anyone confirm that?"

"You can ask my landlady if you want to. She was watching some late show on television in her bedroom, and I called out goodnight as I passed her door."

"Then you went to bed yourself and stayed there?"

"That's right."

"Hmm! I'd like to talk a bit more about Dr. Trent. His personal life. What friends did he have?"

"Why ask me? I had nothing to do with him except just for work."

"But surely . . . the odd overheard remark, a telephone call he made or received while you were around."

Barlow shook his head. "He didn't seem to have any friends."

"Oh, come now," said Kate, and added sententiously, "No man is an island."

"Well, Trent was—as near as anyone could be."

"Did he never socialize at all? Never have a drink with anyone?"

A shrug. "I can't say. I saw him in the local now and then . . . not to talk to, I mean, I always took care to avoid him. I think Gavin wanted to be accepted as one of the regulars, but he always put everyone's back up. He bragged about how he belonged to Mensa, and he just couldn't stop acting as if he had a superior brain to the rest of us."

"How about women?" asked Kate.

"He never talked about anyone." A smirk. "My guess is that he had to pay for it."

He'd deliberately spoken crudely, Kate guessed, to get a reaction from her. But she just asked mildly, "Have you any evidence to back up that guess?"

He shrugged a no.

"That will be all, then, Mr. Barlow. We'll require a written statement from you, but tomorrow will do for that."

As the door closed behind him, Kate instructed Boulter, "Go and fetch Sandra English in here, before Barlow has a chance to square their stories about last night. Quickly, Tim."

When the secretary arrived, she looked scared. Kate smiled pleasantly to put her at her ease. Off guard.

"There's something I should have asked when I spoke to you earlier, Miss English. Could you please tell me about your movements yesterday evening. I'm asking everybody, just for the record."

Sandra, unlike most people faced with such a demand, was ready and eager to answer. "I went out with Roger . . . Roger Barlow."

"Tell me about it."

"Well, at five o'clock when we finished work, Roger drove me to Oxford. I'd asked him to show me his old college. Then afterwards we came back to a pub at Boscombe for supper. We had spaghetti bolognese."

"What did you each have to drink?" Kate tossed in.

"Er . . . I had a glass of white wine."

"And Roger?"

"He had bitter. A pint of bitter—I think."

"Did either of you have another drink?"

That had thrown her. She swallowed hard, then said, "I . . . I can't really remember. I think we had the same again."

"And after you left the pub? What did you do then?"

"Well . . . we drove on a bit, then we stopped and . . . and chatted."

"I get the picture," said Kate dryly. "How long did you . . . chat?"

Colour flooded to her face. "I don't really know. It was well past midnight when I got home. After one, I think."

"You're very fond of Roger, aren't you?"

She met Kate's eyes proudly. "Yes, I love him."

"Well, thank you, Miss English. That will be all for now."

To Boulter, when they were alone, Kate said vexedly, "We were too late, weren't we? The story tripped off her tongue, just as Roger had agreed it with her. Except for the drinks they had, they'd forgotten to fix that, so she had to improvise. Those two have something to hide about last night, but whether it was murder remains to be seen."

It was getting late. Kate decided that she would interview only the laboratory assistants who had worked most closely with Gavin Trent. The remainder would be seen by other detectives on her team. There were two women involved. The first, Rachel Pye, a bubbly dark-haired girl of about twenty, was agog with the drama of it all. The disappearance of the head of the firm, then a murder, and now a police investigation with her as an important witness! However, she had nothing useful to tell Kate.

The other woman was in her mid-fifties, Mrs. Violet Sneddon, and Boulter remembered her by name as being something of a colourful character from the days when his wife had worked at Croptech. She was a little round tub of a woman, with dead straight greying hair chopped off short just below the ears. Her plump wrinkled face was defiantly devoid of make-up. One shouldn't speak ill of the dead, she said piously to Kate, but it hadn't been a change for the better when Dr. Lintott had gone off to America and Dr. Trent was appointed in his place. Very fussy, Dr. Trent was . . . had been. A bit over-fussy, if she told the honest truth. All the same, though, who'd want to kill him? It gave you the shivers to think that someone around these parts—possibly someone you actually knew—was a killer. Nobody deserved to be brutally murdered, not even a bad-tempered man like Dr. Trent had been.

"Bad tempered?" Kate prompted.

"Oh, well . . . he could be. Only now and then, mind. Most of the time he was just sort of standoffish, as if he thought you were beneath him. Then all of a sudden, out of the blue, he'd sort of explode and start shouting. Mind you, in the past it had never been as bad as it was last Monday."

"What happened on Monday?"

"He'd been a bit odd all morning, from when he first arrived. Specially odd, I mean. He hardly spoke a single word to anyone, and when he did it was only to snap at them. Then just before lunchtime I was helping Roger . . . Roger Barlow, to set up some equipment for a new experiment, and one of those big glass retorts got smashed. It was a pure accident, I was carrying the thing and Roger turned suddenly to speak to me and knocked it flying right out of my hands. It smashed to smithereens on the floor. Dr. Trent went nearly berserk, screaming at Roger and calling him a great clumsy oaf. It was horribly unfair, because it wasn't really anyone's fault. Just one of those things that happen now and then in a lab."

"What did Roger Barlow say?"

"Not much. He started to, then he gave a shrug and walked away. Showing his contempt very plain, you know, and I didn't blame him one bit. Poor Roger had an awful lot to put up with from Dr. Trent. For one thing, he never got the credit for developing a new technique for testing for toxicity which will save the firm thousands . . . well, he reckons it will. He went and complained about that to Sir Noah, but *he* seemed to side with Dr. Trent. I don't know the ins and outs of it all, but it did seem very hard on poor Roger. He's a nice lad. A bit of a devil, but young men always are at that age, aren't they? I know my two sons were. Still, when they meet the right girl they usually settle down. I've got three lovely grandchildren now, and another one expected any day."

"When did this occur, about Roger developing the new technique? How long ago?"

"I can't rightly say. It must be some weeks ago now, and Roger's been grumbling about Dr. Trent ever since. And Sir Noah, too, about the unfairness of it all. Mind you, on Monday, I think Dr. Trent realized afterwards that he'd gone too far about that broken retort, because he muttered a sort of apology to me later on. He said that he'd had a bad migraine over the weekend, and it had left him feeling washed out."

"Did he suffer regularly from migraine attacks?" asked Kate.

"Well, not that often. But now and then we'd see the signs, Rachel and me, and we'd take special care not to upset him. Once or twice he even felt so bad that he had to pack up early and go home."

"Thank you, Mrs. Sneddon, you've been extremely helpful."

Her heavy features registered alarm. "Oh . . . I do hope I haven't been talking out of turn. I mean, I wouldn't want to get Roger into trouble."

"Don't worry. If everyone spoke as frankly and truthfully to the police as you have, our job would be a great deal easier."

Before heading for home, Kate looked in at the newly set up Incident Room at the Aston Pringle station. A preliminary report from Scenes of Crime was on her desk concerning their investigation of Gavin Trent's cottage. She and Boulter scanned it together, he reading it over her shoulder. Fingerprints other than Trent's own had been found which were as yet unidentified. A notable fact, though, was that the whisky bottle and the glass on the table were devoid of prints. They'd been wiped clean. As had the back door handle, both inside and out.

"What are we to make of that, Tim?"

He scratched his ear. "The killer had handled those things, so he made sure we wouldn't find his prints."

"But see what it says, no sign of a struggle at the cottage. I reckon we were on the right track in thinking that Trent had a visitor that night who drank whisky with him, then somehow persuaded him to walk with him to that pond in the woods. After the killing, the assailant then returned to Trent's cottage to remove any evidence of his previous visit."

Boulter was looking excited. "So the guy had it all worked out in advance, even to slipping the bolt on the kitchen door so he could get back in without having to take the keys off Trent's body."

"It's a theory that fits the evidence, Tim. Do we know if Trent had a woman to do his household cleaning? Have you sorted that out yet?"

"Yep." Boulter flicked through a sheaf of papers, then handed one to Kate. "He used one of those domestic cleaning services. Apparently they send in a pair of cleaners to give the whole place a thorough going over. Not necessarily the same ones each time."

Kate ran her eye down the report. "Last cleaned on Tuesday. Get the two cleaners interviewed to see if they can come up with anything useful. And you'll need to get their prints to eliminate them. The same goes for everybody else who's been sent there to clean. Now, what about Trent's sister? Has she been informed of his death yet?"

He shook his head. "The Lancashire police tell us she's away on holiday with her family. Caravanning. They're trying to track her down."

"This'll put a damper on the holiday. Anything else?"

He was checking through the reports once more when the door opened and a PC looked in.

"Just to let you know, ma'am, that Mr. Richard Gower has been trying to contact you all day. He wanted to know where you were."

"Huh! It's not my job to feed information to the press. He'll have to be content with official handouts, the same as the rest of them."

As the door closed again, Boulter glanced at Kate curiously. He hesitated a moment, then ventured, "Maybe he just wants to make a date, guv. You could do with a relaxing evening after a day like today."

"And you could do with minding your own business, Sergeant."

You bloody idiot, Kate! Why the hell did she have to slap him down like that when he was just being friendly? *Admit it, you like it when Tim fusses over you a bit.*

Although the burly sergeant had initially been resentful about acting sidekick to a female—and probably still was, deep down—Boulter had reconciled himself to the inevitable, and he worked with her conscientiously. He was a fine detective and together they made a good team. Once, she walked in on one of those "that bloody woman" harangues at the Chipping Bassett nick. It had instantly dried on her entry, but she'd known that Boulter had been defending her. Exactly as he might loyally have sprung to the defence of his guv'nor, if male, but with maybe a touch of chivalry, too. And she hadn't minded that. In her daily work she demanded (and was rarely granted) total equality with her male colleagues. But she *was* a woman, for God's sake, not some tough-as-old-boots unisex creature.

"Sorry, Tim. But Richard Gower is after getting a story out of me. He still acts as a stringer for the national daily he used to work for, and he'd pick up a nice fee for any inside info. on the Trent murder."

"Well then, d'you feel like having a drink with me instead? I reckon we both deserve one."

She could certainly use a drink; but more than that, it was good strategy to accept the well-intentioned invite from her sergeant.

"Okay, just the one. And then it's off home for us both. Tomorrow's going to be another heavy day."

Even though they stayed only twenty minutes at the pub, it was past nine when Kate got back to Stonebank Cottage. Her aunt was in the living room, talking on the phone.

"Well, you're in luck this time. She's just walked in the door." Felix held out the phone to Kate. "It's Richard. The third time he's rung in the past hour."

"Damn! Tell him I can't talk now."

"Tell him yourself, girl."

"Oh, all right." Kate took the phone. "Now look here, Richard, it's not a bit of use your pestering me. I haven't anything to tell you."

"I suppose it never occurred to you, Detective Chief Inspector Maddox, that *I* might have something to tell *you.*"

"Oh! Well then, out with it."

"Where do we meet?"

"No, Richard. If you've something to tell me concerning the Trent case, get on with it. Don't play about."

"It's nothing to do with Trent. Remember the piece I printed in today's *Gazette* about Sir Noah Kimberley going a'missing?"

"What about it?"

"It's borne fruit, that's what."

"How?" She felt a mixture of both excitement and dread.

"Meet me at the Wagon and Horses in ten minutes and I'll reveal all."

"No, I—"

"See you," he said, and hung up.

"Bloody man!" Kate muttered darkly.

"What's up, girl?"

"He says he's got some information, and he wants me to meet him at the pub."

"Nothing wrong with that. Have you found time to eat this evening?"

"Not yet."

"Well, they do nice bar meals at the Wagon. I'll contain my curiosity until you get back."

Richard was at the bar, chatting to the landlord. "Whisky?" he queried as he turned to greet Kate.

"Just a small one. I've already had a drink with Tim Boulter. Now then, what's this all about, Richard?"

"I shall want a *quid pro quo.*"

"What you want and what you get are two different things."

He grinned at her. "Wait till you hear. This'll soften your hard police person's heart. I had a call this lunchtime from Giles Lambert. He's a car dealer in Marlingford. I know him quite well. He's a regular advertiser in the *Gazette.*"

"Get on with it."

"Have patience! Giles read my piece about Kimberley and it jogged his memory. Last Friday night, sometime after midnight, he and his wife were driving home from some trade do or other. The roads were pretty deserted, but at that T-junction where the road from Great Bedham joins the main Marlingford road, he came up behind another car. Taking the turn, the driver ground the gears horribly, which made Giles look more closely. He couldn't see a lot, but his headlights showed it was a woman at the wheel."

"So?"

"It was Noah Kimberley's car, Kate . . . the dark green Saab that Giles had sold him only three months ago."

"How could he be sure of that? One dark green Saab is very like another."

"The number plate told him. It was one of the batch of registration numbers allocated to his firm."

"I'll buy that. Was the woman alone in the car?"

Richard nodded. "Not a vestige of Sir Noah."

"Have you told Lady Kimberley this?"

"No. I thought you should be the first to know. And if you hadn't been dodging me all day, you'd have known it hours ago."

Five

First thing Friday morning Kate went to see the car dealer. Checking by an early call to his home that he'd be at his showroom by nine o'clock, she drove straight to Marlingford and managed to arrive on the dot.

The showroom was immaculate. Selling both new cars and quality used cars, Giles Lambert had built himself a reputation in the district. A sleek young salesman who'd been alerted to look out for Kate's arrival escorted her directly to the boss's office.

Giles Lambert was a smooth businessman, but not so smooth as to make her doubt his honesty. His dark grey suit was discreetly expensive, his shirt and tie total perfection. He was maybe ten years older than Kate. A slightly thickening waistline was kept in check with, very likely, energetic games of squash. She found herself liking him. As they shook hands, he met her gaze with a pleasing candour, with no hint of the male condescension she encountered so often in her job.

"Good morning, Chief Inspector. Do please sit down. You drive a Montego Mayfair, I noticed. Quite a nice motor car. I trust you'll be coming to me for its successor."

"I'm not in the Saab bracket, Mr. Lambert. Not yet."

He smiled at that, then became serious. "You want to talk to me about my seeing Sir Noah Kimberley's car on Friday evening?"

"Mr. Gower passed on to me what you told him, but this could turn out to be very important so I'd like to hear it from you myself."

"I understand." He leaned forward attentively from his executive chair, fingers laced together on the desk top. "A wretched business about Sir Noah. And now this murder of his top scientist."

Kate took him through the details of his sighting, establishing the exact spot at which it had happened, the time as precisely as possible. "You said it was a woman driving. It was dark, so how can you be sure?"

"It certainly wasn't Sir Noah. At the time I took it to be Lady Kimberley. I remember thinking he'd be horrified at the way she'd crashed his gears. It was only yesterday, when I read in the *Gazette* about her staying in London the night he went missing, that I realized it couldn't possibly have been Lady Kimberley."

"You're quite positive it was a woman?"

"Oh, yes." He spread his hands apart in an assessing gesture. "How is it one can be positive of such a thing? She had longish hair, quite a lot of it, though I can't say as to the colour."

"This may sound silly to you, but is it possible it could have been a man wearing a wig? Or a man with long hair, come to that."

Lambert shook his head. "There was something more than just the hair that conveyed the feminine to me. The set of the shoulders, perhaps, the way she held her head. I don't know exactly, but I *am* sure it was a woman."

"You said she was alone in the car. But if there'd been a passenger, are you certain you'd have seen him? Or her?"

"Unless they were deliberately hiding, I would have."

"I know your headlights would have helped you, but you could only have got a fleeting glimpse."

Lambert ruminated a moment, running his thumbnail along his lower lip, then he nodded with conviction. "There's an illuminated traffic sign at that point. As the Saab passed it the light shone clean through the car's side windows. I saw a silhouette of the driver, and no one else."

"Your wife was with you, I understand. Would she be able to confirm any of this?"

He smiled ruefully. "I'm afraid not. When Barbara and I go out for an evening, we take turn and turn about to either drink or drive. In my trade I've seen the result of too many accidents to think it's possible to do both —as doubtless you have too, Chief Inspector. It was quite a party we went to that night, someone's retirement, and on the way home my wife was . . . well, let's say inclined to be dozy."

Corroboration would have been useful. All the same, Kate felt sure that Lambert was a reliable witness. He'd told her what he'd seen, and what impression it had given him, without any embroidery.

"Thanks very much, Mr. Lambert," she said, making to rise.

"Won't you stay for a cup of coffee?"

"I'd love one, but I can't afford the time."

Lambert escorted her out to her car. "You're quite a subject of conversation, you know, in the local watering holes."

"Oh? Why is that?"

"Come, come." He wagged a finger at her. "A woman, and a damned attractive woman if I may say so without offence, in such a high-ranking position! You've put more than a few noses out of joint, I hear, and it's whispered that you're running rings round some of your male colleagues. Sides are being taken, Mrs. Maddox."

"And which side are you on, Mr. Lambert?"

He threw back his head and laughed at her. "My wife, whom I love most dearly, is no old-fashioned *hausfrau* herself. She runs her own business, and a thriving concern it is, too. I daresay you've noticed her shop here in town, Acme Office Supplies. In addition to the retail sales, she handles typewriter servicing on a contract basis—including, in fact, for the local police. The motor trade has its ups and downs, but with Barbara there's only one way—up! I think you and she must be two of a kind, Mrs. Maddox, so there's no need to ask me which side I'm on."

Kate looked in at divisional headquarters on her way to Aston Pringle, to see what had accumulated on her desk there. She dealt quickly with a couple of routine matters, and then, as she was on her way out of the building, she bumped into Superintendent Joliffe in the corridor.

"Mrs. Maddox!" He sounded suspiciously jovial. "Just the person I wanted to see. Come into my office."

Inside the spacious room with windows overlooking the municipal gardens, he indicated that she should be seated. He didn't, on this occasion, ring for tea to be brought.

"I have a little job for you," he said. "Milford Grange was broken into this morning. You probably don't know the place, as you haven't been working long in this division. It's a large rambling house on the outskirts of Milford belonging to Mr. Justice Tillington and his wife."

Kate waited in silence, reserving judgment.

Jolly Joliffe rubbed his hands together, a rare sign of nervousness in him. "You're aware, of course, that Judge Tillington has considerable influence. He's renowned for speaking his mind, and his quotes get a good deal of media attention. Anyway, he and his wife are away just now on a lengthy visit to their married daughter in New Zealand. The judge is convalescing after major heart surgery."

"Whom have you sent there to handle things, sir?" Kate could scarcely believe the way things were pointing.

"Well . . . Inspector Trotton is at the scene. But where people like Mr. Justice Tillington are concerned, it is prudent for us to show action at a higher level. So I'd like you to look in at Milford Grange this morning, to see what's what and nudge Don Trotton in the right direction.",

"Sir, can it have escaped your attention that I'm just at the start of what looks like becoming a major murder enquiry? Surely I can't be expected to drop everything and go haring off on some piddling little break-in?"

His expression grew pained. "Hardly piddling. We suspect that a number of valuable items have been stolen. The trouble is, with the owners away we can't know precisely what *is* missing. Look, I'm not suggesting you should waste a lot of time on this. Just drop in and wave the flag a bit. You know the sort of thing I mean, my dear."

My dear! Kate's fuse had burnt too short to snuff it out. She exploded. "I'd be grateful, *sir*, if you'd stop patronising me with that expression. I have a name, and I have a rank. Address me as you wish, formally or informally . . . Mrs. Maddox or Kate, I don't mind which. Or Chief Inspector."

The superintendent was gaping at her. "What on earth are you talking about?"

You went over the top, Kate, but you can't back down now.

"You are always calling me 'my dear,' sir. I find it very offensive. It's sexist."

His eyes were cold with anger. "You're making rather a fool of yourself, Mrs. Maddox, over a mere trifle."

Trouble is, Kate, the man's got a point there. If you go and lose your cool over something small like this, you're giving him ammunition for claiming that you're not sufficiently balanced emotionally for the rank you hold. She'd won a Pyrrhic victory. Jolly wouldn't call her "my dear" again in a hurry, but it wouldn't upgrade his respect one iota for her.

Fortunately, Superintendent Joliffe (wise man that he was) decided to make a joke of the incident. With a hollow little chuckle, he went on, "If I were to call you by some of the ripe epithets I use on your male colleagues, you'd have reason to complain. Now then, Mrs. Maddox, about this break-in. Just pop in for half an hour, so Judge Tillington can be informed that there is high-level attention being given to this case. Believe me, I'd go myself if I could possibly manage it. But I'm completely tied up today. I'm just about to leave for a CID symposium at Scotland Yard—a gathering of superintendents and upwards, organized by the Home Office."

Oh, what the hell. "I hope it's a slap-up lunch, sir."

He smiled thinly. "They usually do us quite well on these occasions. We'll have a talk about the Trent case tomorrow. Hopefully, you'll have some progress to report by then."

Kate went back to her own office upstairs and rang the Incident Room at Aston Pringle to tell them where she'd be. Then she headed her car for Milford Grange. Okay, she understood that Jolly Joliffe felt obliged to send the highest ranker available to the scene of the crime. Otherwise, he'd have the Chief Constable breathing down his neck. Under the law of the land, everybody was equal. And a judge would be the last person to demand favourable treatment . . . but he'd still expect to get it. So a mere murder investigation would have to wait its turn.

As a residence, Milford Grange wasn't in the same enviable category as the Kimberleys' house. Standing in grounds of two or three acres, shielded from its neighbours on either side by woodland, it was in the worst tradition of Victorian Gothic Revival . . . quaint and rather amusing in a town, perhaps, such an edifice looked ridiculously out of place in a rural hamlet. It could be that Mr. Justice Tillington felt at home there because it reminded him of London's Law Courts.

A young uniformed PC at the gates saluted alertly as Kate turned into the driveway. A second PC ambled lazily down the front steps to meet her as she got out of the car. He owed it to his male dignity, she guessed, not to kow-tow to a bloody woman. A cigarette was (barely) concealed in his cupped palm.

"Good morning, Constable. Is Inspector Trotton here?"

"Er, yes, I think he's somewhere upstairs."

"Well, fetch him down, please," she said briskly. "And put that cigarette out. If I ever catch you smoking on duty again, my lad, you'll be in for it."

In the arched and columned hallway Kate waited impatiently until the tall figure of Don Trotton appeared at the head of the staircase. He came running down to her lightly, the performance of a man who wanted it noted that he was in the peak of condition.

"Aha! The brains have arrived." He came up to where she stood, quite close, and treated her to a slow smile. "Not that brains are all you've got to offer a grateful world, Kate, my sweet. There's a delectable body hiding beneath that severe item of ladies' suiting you're wearing."

"Now where did I last hear that line? Oh, I remember, a sixth-former at my school who thought he was being a real devil."

Don wasn't the least abashed, not that he let show. "Co-ed school you went to, then? Mine was boys only. What a time those lads must've had, the lucky swine."

This was standard routine to Don Trotton. A year or two younger than Kate, undeniably good-looking, he cherished the firm conviction that there wasn't a woman alive who wouldn't instantly come running if he crooked his little finger at her.

"Let's get on, shall we, Don?" she said tiredly. "Put me in the picture about what's been happening here."

"Amateurs!" he said contemptuously. "The alarm was set off at nine-eleven this morning, reported by neighbours on both sides. Looks as if chummies just grabbed what was handiest, then scarpered. They smashed open a splendid antique desk, presumably looking for cash. If they'd taken away the desk itself, it would have made more sense. Bleeding amateurs! A blue Peugeot estate seems to have been their vehicle . . . one was seen careering through the village a few minutes later, two youngish chaps inside. Poor descriptions, though."

"I gather from Jolly that there's difficulty establishing exactly what was taken."

"Sure is. The Tillingtons are in New Zealand, and we can't contact them at the moment. They're touring with their daughter and son-in-law in Mackenzie country, wherever that is."

"South Island," Kate informed him. "It's remote highland country where there are more sheep than people. Keep trying, Don. What about other relatives here in Britain?"

"None, apparently, according to our local chap. The Tillingtons shut up house completely for the twelve months they reckoned to be away. There's a part-time gardener comes in to keep things tidy. The two cleaning women aren't expected to do anything until just before the owners return, when they'll come in and get the house ready for them."

"That must mean those two women have access to the house," said Kate sharply. "Are they in the clear?"

"They're being investigated. But if they were in on it, wouldn't chummies have known there was an alarm? Obviously they didn't. They broke a window to gain entry, which set it off."

"Good point, Don."

"Oh, I'm not just a gorgeous hunk, Kate."

Ignoring that, she continued, "Can't the cleaning women help over what's missing?"

"They're upstairs right now, we fetched them straight away. But they're a dead loss. They can't seem to agree about anything."

"There must be friends of the Tillingtons who could help us. Or their solicitor. There's most likely an inventory somewhere, for insurance. We've got to show some brisk action on this one, Don, or heads are going to roll."

"There's no need to get heavy with me, Kate," he said sulkily.

She cocked an ear, listening. From upstairs there came a faint mumble of voices, but everything was quiet on the ground floor, except for a low-pitched humming sound, very faint.

"What's that, Don?"

"What's what?"

"That humming noise. Seems to be coming from the rear of the house."

"I can't hear anything."

Kate's own hearing was very acute. She'd noticed before that she responded to sounds that other people didn't pick up. She walked across to a door at the back of the hall and opened it. "It's coming from here, all right. Surely you can hear it now?"

Don Trotton listened a moment, then gave a bright smile. "That's the deep-freeze. You probably noticed when the compressor motor cut in."

She frowned. "I don't understand."

Patiently, he explained technicalities to the feminine mind. "When the temperature inside the deep-freeze cabinet rises above a certain level, there's a thermostat which automatically switches on the current. The compressor starts operating and hey-presto, the temperature is brought down again."

"I meant," Kate said irritably, "why is the freezer left on when the owners are away for such a lengthy period?"

He still didn't get her drift. "If it wasn't left on, the stuff inside would have thawed out and gone bad."

"But a lot of freezer foods don't keep indefinitely. Not without deterioration. Most people going away for a whole year would empty the freezer beforehand. Use up the contents, or give it away to friends."

"The Tillingtons obviously didn't."

"I think we'd better take a look," said Kate. "There's something odd here."

"Is this your idea of brisk action?" he enquired derisively, then hefted his shoulders. "Okay, you've got the pips. Let's go open the box."

Don led the way to a small utility room down a passageway leading off from the kitchen. The freezer was set against one wall. It was the chest variety, six feet wide with access from the top. As they entered the room, the thermostat cut out with a soft click. Don laid a hand on the lid, and paused for effect.

"What'll it be, a packet of fish fingers, or a nice bit of fillet steak?"

"Open it, Don."

He did so with a flourish, smirking with delight because this damned female DCI was about to look foolish. Glancing down casually, he did a double take.

"Christ Almighty!"

Kate said the same thing, but inaudibly. Crammed into the otherwise empty freezer was the hard-frozen body of a man.

Six

Did you have a premonition, Kate?

The body, prone and fully clothed, was that of Sir Noah Kimberley. He'd been a tall man, and to fit him into the confined space of the freezer, his head had been twisted on its neck, so that the fine grey eyes stared up at her in mute agony. His silver-grey hair was dishevelled, frozen now in grotesquely icy spikes.

Instantly, automatically, Kate had switched into action. Orders were issued and delegated down the line; due processes were set in motion. Dr. Meddowes arrived and superfluously confirmed that life was extinct. As people came and went, Kate overheard every possible variation of the "frozen stiff" sort of wisecrack. To the general public they'd have sounded unfeeling, but she knew that such jokery was a safety valve for men who had a difficult and unpleasant job to perform. In this instance, though, she found their flippancy hard to take. She had met Sir Noah socially, and she had liked what she'd seen. He'd impressed her by his dignified bearing, by his somewhat old-fashioned charm as a host, by his obvious devotion to his wife. Now, she had to make an effort to appear calm and detached, for any sign of emotion on her part would be regarded as feminine weakness.

Dr. Meddowes remarked morosely, "He's going to take hours to thaw out enough for a post-mortem to be performed."

"We could always pop him in a microwave," a Scenes of Crime man quipped over his shoulder. "Set it to Defrost."

As soon as Kate felt able, she left the scene. Her next task was to obtain authority to enlarge her murder squad to cope with this second killing. With Superintendent Joliffe away for the day, this entailed contacting the Assistant Chief Constable. She then had a conference with the office manager of the Incident Room to get things set in motion. She was glad to have Inspector Frank Massey working with her again. A former colleague on Wye division, Frank was thoroughly capable and reliable, with the necessary streak of toughness running through his mild manner. Unambitious for further promotion himself, he bore no resentment of Kate's senior rank. In that, he was damn nearly a one-off policeman.

Just as she was due to leave for Radlett to break the news to Lady Kimberley, a call came through from London. Sir Noah's nephew, Aidan Kimberley, was asking to speak to her.

She picked up the phone. "Good morning, Mr. Kimberley. I expect you're calling me because Lady Kimberley told you I'd be wanting to speak to you. Is that right?"

"Yes. I was talking to her last evening and she told me the shocking news about Dr. Gavin Trent's death. Murder, she said. Can that be true?"

"That is what we believe."

"It's quite appalling, especially coming on top of my uncle's disappearance. My wife and I feel we should be with my aunt at this distressing time, and of course there is Croptech to be considered. I'll get away as soon as I possibly can, but I've been abroad for the past month and—"

"Mr. Kimberley," Kate cut in, "you had better come at once. I am afraid there has been a further development."

"A further development," he echoed faintly. "How do you mean?"

"I am sorry to have to tell you that your uncle, too, is dead."

There was a shocked silence. Then, "You are presuming he's dead, I take it you mean, now that so many days have passed without news?"

"No, I don't mean that. Sir Noah's body has been found. This morning."

"His body? But . . . but where? How?"

"I won't go into that on the phone," she said. "I'm just this minute setting out to break the news to Lady Kimberley. I think it's important that you should be with her as soon as possible."

"Yes, of course. Of course. I'm at my office, but I'll collect my wife and we'll drive down right away. But you must tell me, Chief Inspector, how did my uncle die? When?"

"Those facts are still to be established. I must go now. I'll be in touch later."

Fortunately, Kate still reached Lady Kimberley before anyone else had got to her with news of her husband's death. That was evident from Mrs. Byworth's demeanour.

"Oh yes, Dame Vanessa is in. She's hardly left the house these last few days, poor thing. She's still hoping the phone will ring and it will be Sir Noah. Oh dear, I wonder if it ever will be."

Kate made no comment.

"She's got Lord Balmayne with her just now," the little woman went on. "Oh, he's been such a comfort to her in her hour of need. He's a good friend, always has been, and now he's rallying round something wonderful. I'll just go and tell Dame Vanessa that you're here, Chief Inspector."

Kate wasn't left to wait in the hall for more than a few seconds before the statuesque figure of Vanessa Kimberley appeared at the drawing room door.

"Chief Inspector! What brings you? Is there news? Come in, do come in."

A tall man standing by the open French windows swung round as Kate entered. Though elderly, in his mid-seventies, he held his lean frame erect. Kate hadn't matched a face to his name when it first cropped up in this case, but now she recognized him from newspaper pictures. He was attired (the word seemed to fit him) in lightweight grey suiting, and he sported a blue silk bow tie. His eyes were bright and piercing, and both his hair and his small pointed beard were elegantly white.

Vanessa performed hasty introductions, and asked again, "*Have* you news, Chief Inspector?"

"I think perhaps we should first sit down, Lady Kimberley."

She looked bemused, as if wondering whether she was being criticized for lack of courtesy, but Kate saw that Lord Balmayne had instantly grasped the significance of her suggestion. Crossing swiftly to Lady Kimberley, he took her arm and led her to one of the sofas. With a gesture inviting Kate to be seated wherever she chose, he sat down himself beside Vanessa Kimberley, holding one of her hands in both of his.

"Yes, Lady Kimberley," Kate said. "I do have news of your husband. Bad news, I'm afraid. I have to inform you that Sir Noah is dead. We discovered his body this morning."

Lady Kimberley gasped a juddering breath and her whole body slumped. Lord Balmayne, also seeming deeply shocked, supported her as best he could, slipping an arm around her shoulders.

"There, there, my dear. You must be brave." He glanced across at Kate. "You had better tell it all, Chief Inspector. The . . . the details. How did poor Noah die?"

"We don't know that, sir, not yet," she said, watching both their faces carefully.

This was something Kate always hated, the need at such a moment to reserve a degree of suspicion concerning people who probably merited nothing but the deepest sympathy. But it had to be so. In a case of murder, the spouse was automatically suspect. And in this instance, the question mark had to include the "dear old friend" of that spouse. She'd have to get someone to probe into their past association, to try and establish if there'd ever been anything closer than friendship between them.

"What led you to make this discovery?" he asked.

A slightly odd question? More natural, surely, would have been to ask *where* the body had been found. That had been the immediate reaction of Aidan Kimberley when she'd spoken to him on the phone earlier.

"It was pure chance, Lord Balmayne. We were investigating an entirely unrelated matter. A break-in at a house in the locality."

Perhaps he'd had time to pull himself together. He reacted now more as one would expect from a self-confident man of considerable standing in the world.

"Come, Chief Inspector, you appear to be making a mystery of this. Please speak plainly, and tell us everything you know."

Kate had deliberately been giving the information piecemeal in order to observe and assess their reactions. Now she told the full details. "As I said, the police were called to the scene of a break-in. It was at Mr. Justice Tillington's house at Milford . . . he and his wife are away on a lengthy trip. Whilst we were there, we found Sir Noah's body. It was concealed in a large chest freezer."

"Good God! Are you saying that the burglars had killed him and put him there?"

Kate glanced uneasily at Lady Kimberley. She had shed no tears but was sitting still and utterly quiet, leaning her whole weight against Lord Balmayne. Kate couldn't decide whether or not she was taking in any of this conversation.

"No, sir, that isn't possible. The break-in occurred only this morning, but the body had been in the freezer for some while. Long enough to be totally frozen."

"Some while?" he repeated dazedly.

"We can't establish for how long, I'm afraid, until it's possible to conduct a post-mortem. In the circumstances, this will be somewhat delayed."

"I see." Lord Balmayne nodded his head gravely and went on nodding for several seconds, as if forcing himself to accept this fearsome knowledge. Then he said slowly, "Have you no clues as to who it might have been, whoever put Noah there?"

"We are pursuing our enquiries, sir."

His handsome features darkened with anger. "For heaven's sake, spare us your officialese. Can't you give a plain answer to a plain question? Do you have any idea who the perpetrators may have been?"

"At this stage, none."

Was it relief in his face? Or just acceptance of the bald fact?

Addressing Lady Kimberley, Kate went on, "Just before leaving to come here, I had a telephone call from Mr. Aidan Kimberley. I told him the news about your husband, and he promised to come and see you straight away. He and his wife should be here later today."

She raised her head, and turned a tragic face to Kate. Speaking with grave dignity, she said, "Thank you, Mrs. Maddox. It will be a comfort to have Aidan and Paula close at hand."

Lord Balmayne looked slightly pained. "You have me, my dear. You know that I will not desert you at a time like this."

With her free hand Vanessa Kimberley patted the veined hand that still held her right one. "Oh, my dear Gerald, *of course* I know that. I do *so* appreciate having you here. And," she added, "my poor darling Noah would have been glad to know that you were with me at this terrible time."

Hmmm! thought Kate. She said, rising to her feet, "I'll be going now. But later, Lady Kimberley, when you've had a chance to recover a little from the shock, I'd like to talk to you again."

A hand lifted and flapped weakly, signifying agreement to anything. *Anything* that was demanded of her.

Back at the Incident Room, Kate found that extra recruits to the murder squad were already beginning to assemble. The small police station seemed to be bursting at the seams as more space was demanded. Kate had another short conference with the office manager, fixing to hold a general briefing of the squad at the end of the afternoon. Then she closeted herself with Sergeant Boulter.

"The only possible starting point, it seems to me, is to assume a direct link between the two murders. So the chummy we're looking for had a reason for killing the two men. That ought to narrow down the field, but I doubt if it'll make our job that much easier. Let's run through everybody we can think of who knew both Kimberley and Trent—or had some kind of connection with both of them—and we'll check their alibis closely. We know there was a woman involved in some degree, since a woman was seen driving the Saab, but I don't think that a woman alone could have manhandled Kimberley's body into the freezer cabinet. Any more than it's *likely* that a woman on her own drowned Trent."

"Which means that we're looking for two people acting together. A man and a woman."

"Or it could be two women. There's no definite evidence of a male being involved, as yet. So who do we have? Relatives first. For the moment I think we can leave out Trent's sister, but we must certainly look closer at Lady Kimberley . . . and Lord Balmayne could fill the role of accomplice. Then we'd better check on the nephew and his wife. There could be a strong financial motive there. Aidan Kimberley is supposed to have been out of the country when Sir Noah disappeared, of course. That's easily verifiable. Then there are the people at Croptech who had dealings with both the victims. First, George Jessop . . . with his record he's got to be a major suspect. Plus a female accomplice. Roger Barlow and Sandra English—they'd make a team. As for McEvoy, he could have enlisted his wife. Cheryl Miller mustn't be left out—together with some mystery man or woman. Is there anybody else?"

"I suppose we can forget about those two lab assistants, Violet Sneddon and Rachel Pye?"

"Oh, I think so. There's another point we've got to consider, Tim.

Who was on such familiar terms with the Tillingtons' house as to be able to switch off the alarm system before going in and dumping Kimberley, and then resetting it. And *how* did they make their entry without leaving signs of a break-in as our chummies of this morning did? And when? The body had obviously been there for some time before we discovered it, to have become so completely hard frozen. Specially remembering that the freezer wouldn't have been on to start with, and it takes quite a few hours to bring the temperature down. We'll have to await the post-mortem before we get any clear information about the timing of his death. Even then, I doubt if it's going to be very precise."

Boulter pulled a long face. "This case is going to be a tough one, guv."

Damn, she'd been letting her own uncertainty show. Part of her job was to maintain morale in every member of the murder squad.

"We'll crack it, Tim," she said briskly. "I want you to put someone onto re-interviewing all the men or women who did cleaning at Trent's cottage. See if they come up with anything useful about Trent's manner of life, and evidence of callers—that sort of thing. Then there's the landlord and customers of the local pub he frequented, according to Roger Barlow. And the people working in the shops where he bought his food. The filling station he used, news agent, dry cleaners, whatever. And every single person on the payroll at Croptech. We've got to start building up a picture of how the lives of those two men interreacted. Mutual friends, mutual acquaintances. And especially, mutual enemies."

George Jessop had been fetched by car from Croptech. Kate held the interview in the cold severity of an interview room. She sat facing him across the small table, bare apart from a tape recorder, with Boulter just visible to him from the corner of his eye. Kate went through the preamble of time and place for the sake of the recording, then plunged in.

"Mr. Jessop, we are now investigating the murder of Sir Noah Kimberley, in addition to the murder of Dr. Gavin Trent."

He was surly, his fleshy face set against her. "I heard about it."

"What did you hear?"

He shrugged. "The rumour flying around is that you found him in the freezer of some big house over Milford way. Belonging to a judge."

If only, Kate thought ruefully, this sort of leak could be avoided. She'd likely have learned a lot more if she could have confronted Jessop with a surprise. Or a nasty shock. As it was, he'd come prepared.

"You want to nail me for this one, too, I suppose," he groused. "That's the way the police mind works, isn't it? Just because I've got a record."

"*Did* you kill Dr. Gavin Trent and Sir Noah Kimberley?"

"No I did not."

"Then you should have no difficulty accounting for your movements at the relevant times."

Jessop shrugged again, and waited. Kate, having little idea what the relevant times were, made a stab; meanwhile watching the man's eyes for a betrayal of . . . something. Joy that she'd got it wrong, perhaps? "So will you tell me where you were last Friday evening, Mr. Jessop, from say eight-thirty onwards."

"That's easy," he said promptly. "I was at the pub. The Holly Tree. I always go there on Fridays for a couple of pints and a game of darts."

"When did you arrive at the pub," asked Boulter from the sidelines, "and when did you leave?"

"I set out round about half-past eight, I suppose, and I left the pub at closing time. Just after eleven. You ask them."

"We will," Kate said. But it would answer nothing. If only she knew with some exactitude when Kimberley had been killed. And when he had been placed in the freezer. "You went home and spent the night alone? Is that right?"

"What else?"

Thinking of the woman seen driving Kimberley's car at past midnight on Friday, Kate suggested, "You might have had a . . . friend with you."

"Well, I didn't."

"We've only your word that you went home."

"You could always ask the dog," Jessop said facetiously. He was getting too sure of himself.

"What was your opinion of Sir Noah Kimberley?" she asked.

He spread his palms. "He was my boss."

"You've worked at Croptech for some two and a half years. How did you get the job in the first place?"

"The usual way. I applied for it, and got taken on."

"You used to live in Leicestershire. How did you get to know there was a caretaking job going in this part of the country?"

"I . . . I heard about it."

"From whom?"

He hesitated. "I can't remember."

Kate let that pass. "Did Sir Noah know about your prison record?"

"Yes, he had to know."

"And yet he took you on for a job that included security duties. That was very trusting of him, wasn't it? Very public spirited, giving employment to an ex-convict."

"There are a few decent people around."

"So you liked Sir Noah Kimberley? You had no reason to feel any antagonism towards him?"

"He was always all right with *me*." But there'd been a slight hesitation before he spoke, plus an emphasis on the final word.

"Who wasn't he all right with?"

"Listen, I don't know. He was the boss and I'm only the lowest of the low at Croptech. We only ever spoke when he gave me instructions, or just to pass the time of day."

"Very well, Mr. Jessop. You'll be taken to another room now where you'll be required to give a detailed statement to one of my officers about your movements from last Friday up until this morning."

He glared from beneath his tawny brows. "I thought you said Kimberley was killed on Friday night."

"I didn't say that. And aren't you forgetting Dr. Trent?"

Jessop departed, and Kate and Boulter returned to her office, where a PC brought her a sheaf of various reports. Of the numerous fingerprints found at the Tillington house there were three sets of very recent ones. Two men were reported as having been seen in the burglars' getaway car, so who did the third set belong to? A couple of other items—a footprint on a flowerbed outside the window through which entry had been gained, and some fresh spots of blood which doubtless came from a hand cut on the broken glass—would be useful in nailing the thieves when they were tracked down. The freezer cabinet had been carefully wiped clean, so no help there.

The body of Sir Noah Kimberley had by now been eased out of the freezer, and the clothing had thawed sufficiently to extract his wallet, which contained two hundred and sixty pounds in banknotes. That, plus the expensive Rolex watch and gold signet ring he was wearing, ruled out theft as the motive for the killing.

"Tim, I want you to gather all the information you can about what cash Sir Noah spent on Thursday and Friday after drawing three hundred pounds from the bank. I've got a hunch we might learn something useful from that."

The door opened and a PC looked in. "Roger Barlow has just been brought in, ma'am, as you instructed."

"Right, thanks. I'll see him in a minute. Tim, I want you to shoot straight off to Croptech and talk to Sandra English. We must make sure those two don't have a chance to put their heads together again so she can adjust her story to fit anything Barlow may have let slip to me. Go easy with her at first. Try a spot of your famous charm on her before you play it heavy."

"I'll do my best," he said with a grin. "But she's not my type."

"Oh, and Tim, on your way out tell someone to fetch me a sandwich—cheese will do—and a cup of coffee."

She kept Barlow waiting while she rapidly consumed her snack. When he was brought in, he looked pugnacious; a cover, Kate surmised, for extreme nervousness.

"What do you want me for? I know nothing about what happened to old Kimberley. How could I?"

She regarded him calmly. "Sit down, please, Mr. Barlow. I want to discuss your reasons for feeling bitter towards the Croptech management."

He looked startled. "Who told you that?"

"Never mind who told me. As I understand it, you claimed to have developed a new laboratory technique, and you felt that you hadn't been given due credit for it by the firm. Is that correct?"

"Suppose it is?"

"What were you expecting? A large rise in salary?"

"Wouldn't *you?*" he demanded. "The firm is saving thousands through me."

"I am informed that Dr. Trent didn't agree with that view. And that when you appealed to Sir Noah, he referred you back to Dr. Trent."

"The mean old bastard wouldn't even hear me out," he said sourly, and then did a double take. "Listen, you aren't seriously suggesting I'd kill the two of them just because I felt cheated out of a pay rise?"

"Are you saying there was more to it than that? Something I don't know about?"

"No! You're twisting my words. I had nothing at all to do with those murders. Nothing whatsoever."

"Then we ought to be able to prove that fact." She surveyed him closely. "Where were you when Sir Noah was killed?"

"You mean Friday evening?"

"*Was* he killed on Friday evening?"

"Well, naturally, I thought . . . I mean, that's when he disappeared."

"So tell me how you spent Friday evening."

"Sandra and I went to a disco in Marlingford. The Friars' Cellar."

"You were there from when until when?"

He thought. "Round about eight-thirty till one A.M."

"Were you there the whole of that time?"

"Yes, we certainly were."

"Were you with friends? Is there anyone who could vouch that you didn't leave the hall for any appreciable time?"

"Sandra could."

Kate veered off at a tangent. "Can Sandra drive?"

"What's that got to do with it?" Barlow asked, staring at her in bewilderment.

"Just answer the question, please."

"Well, she hasn't taken her test yet. But I've been teaching her in my car."

"How's she getting on?"

He still stared, sensing a trap. "All right, I suppose."

Perhaps still at the stage of crashing the gears in a strange car?

Kate noted that Roger's pugnacity had vanished. By now he was looking as scared as hell, but she was accustomed to that in people questioned after a serious crime. The very knowledge that one was under suspicion could bring out all kinds of uncontrolled emotions—anger, hostility, fear. To her, Roger Barlow was just one of several suspects, with a not particularly strong motive. She gauged that he was a hot-tempered young man, who might conceivably kill in the heat of the moment. But *two* murders, was that conceivable? Unless the second had followed as a direct consequence of the first, made necessary to avoid detection.

She jotted a few notes on her pad while these thoughts ran through her mind. Looking up at him suddenly, she asked, "Have you ever visited Milford Grange?"

"You mean, where . . . where Sir Noah's body was found? No, of course I haven't."

A slight flicker in his eyes made Kate ask, "You're quite sure about that?"

He started to nod confirmation, then thought better of it. "Well, last Christmas my girlfriend persuaded me to join a carol singing group to raise money for charity, and it was one of the houses we went to."

"That was Sandra?"

He coloured a bit. "No, another girl. I don't see her now."

Kate nodded. A changing love-life was only par for the course at his age. "Did you go inside the house?"

A slight hesitation came before the admission. "We did, as a matter of fact. The judge's wife asked us in for mince-pies and hot punch. We didn't stay long, though."

Long enough, perhaps, for a man with a scientific bent to suss out the burglar alarm system?

"You knew that the Tillingtons were away for a long period?"

"What if I did? So did most people around here." A touch of pugnacity was returning. *He knows you're scratching in the dark, Kate.* Best to terminate the interview for now. Once she established the time of Kimberley's death—if ever!—she could really put the screws on Roger Barlow for a precise alibi.

Just a measly cheese sandwich and a cup of coffee! Tim Boulter marvelled that the guv could keep going on so little. He'd take a bet it was the first sustenance she'd had since breakfast; which, he'd also take a bet, was only the muesli and black coffee variety. He himself, since his bacon and eggs and toast and marmalade, had snatched a couple of doughnuts with his elevenses. Even so, Boulter felt faint with hunger by now. He restored his metabolic balance at the dive bar of the Half Moon before driving to Croptech to interview Sandra English.

"The Chief Inspector has a few more questions to put to you, Miss English, and she was intending to send for you. But I pointed out to her that as I was coming this way I could save you the trouble of having to go to the police station. I expect you must be very busy this afternoon."

She smiled at him nervously. "Thank you. But I'm not very busy, actually. Everything's at sixes and sevens here, you see, and I don't really know what to get on with. We're all of us most dreadfully upset about Sir Noah." She was looking pathetic, wan, totally unnerved. "Er . . . you can't seriously think that Roger . . . well, had anything to do with . . ."

"No more than we think *you* did," Boulter assured her ambiguously. "The only way we'll ever get to the truth is to ask lots and lots of questions and gradually build up a picture of what happened."

"Oh, yes, I see."

"That's why we want you to tell us everything you know that could possibly be helpful. By the way, while I think of it, do you drive?"

She looked puzzled, as well she might. "Drive?"

"Drive a car," he explained. "Can you drive a car?"

"Well, not really. I . . . I'm still learning. Roger's teaching me."

Boulter jotted down a note. "Now, Miss English, to get this out of the way, you've already told us what you were doing on Wednesday, the night Dr. Trent was killed. But what about last Friday evening?"

She said at once, "I went out with Roger that night. To a disco at Marlingford. The Friar's Cellar. We were there all evening, until well after midnight."

Very pat! Boulter had a feeling it would precisely match the alibi that her boyfriend would most probably by now have given to the guv.

"Is that what Roger told you to say?" he asked in a conversational tone.

Sandra seemed totally at a loss to understand him. She wasn't such a bad looker, Boulter conceded, if only she hadn't been so insipid. What did she have that attracted a guy like Roger Barlow? Had he found the trigger which could turn her into a hot number? It was hard to imagine.

"Listen," she said, as if suddenly galvanized, "really and truly Roger had nothing at all to do with Sir Noah and Dr. Trent getting killed. He . . . he just isn't the sort of person who could do something wicked and horrible like that. Besides, he was with me both times. Honestly."

Boulter gave her a smile that was warm and friendly and understanding; what Kate Maddox called turning on his sickening charm. "You're in love with Roger, aren't you? You've told us that already."

"Yes, but . . ."

"So maybe you'd tell lies to protect him."

She was silent, staring at him in dismay.

"Do you two plan to get married?" Boulter persisted.

He caught a glint of tears before she looked down at her lap. She was hoping like hell they would be getting married, but she felt none too sure about the depth of Roger's feelings for her. She, poor girl, would do anything for Roger. She'd lie and perjure herself for him if the need arose. He could make use of her all he wanted, just so long as he loved her back. Loved her a little bit.

Risking a technique he'd seen Kate Maddox use so often, Boulter lobbed in a chancy remark designed to throw Sandra into a panic and hopefully give something away.

"It's time you told us about it, Sandra . . . the thing you're trying to hide."

She looked back at him dumbly, her pink and white complexion turning the colour of pallid dough. "I . . . I don't know what you mean."

"Yes, you do. You're covering up for Roger, aren't you?" He paused a moment, and added weightily, "It's a very serious matter, you know, impeding the police in their enquiries."

Sandra shook her head, wildly, vehemently. "Leave me alone. I haven't done anything. Nor has Roger. Just leave us alone."

"Is he really worth landing yourself in deep trouble for?"

Her look of tormented love-at-bay hit Boulter like a smack on the jaw. Then Sandra burst into tears, and he found himself going to her embarrassedly, patting her heaving shoulders to try and comfort her. Why did he feel like a heel? He was only doing his bloody job, for Christ's sake.

"Is the guv'nor free?" Boulter asked, walking into the Incident Room at Aston Pringle nick.

A WPC looked up from her table. "Sure. And here, Tim, you can take these in with you." A bundle of yet more reports. Boulter scanned them quickly so as to be *au fait* with the contents before entering the DCI's office.

"How'd it go, Tim?" she asked, as he went in.

They traded stories, concluding that Roger Barlow and Sandra English were no more in the clear, and no more suspect, than they'd been before.

"They're hiding something, all the same," said Boulter doggedly.

"But is it murder? A great many people have unsavoury secrets they'd hate to come out."

"But what, in this case? It can't just be that they hit the sack together. Roger was more or less boasting about that yesterday."

Pointing to the reports in Boulter's hand, Kate asked, "What's come in, Tim?"

"There's one thing that's going to please you, guv. The forensic on that tree branch by the lake, and the couple of little wood splinters found in Trent's neck. They match exactly. So you were spot on about how he was done in. Held under until he drowned."

Noting her sergeant's triumph at this result, Kate recalled wryly that when she'd first mooted the idea, he'd thought she was off her trolley.

"And another bright idea of yours seems to have paid off," he went on breezily. "That one about trying to account for what money Kimberley spent after going to the bank on Thursday. For starters we had a stroke of luck. Just after lunch he had his car filled up, and when he went to pay he mentioned to the garage man that he was down to his last fiver. Then later that afternoon, after he'd drawn the three hundred, he put a twenty towards a wedding present for one of the garden hands at Croptech. On his way home that evening he stopped off at the florist's in Little Bedham for a big bunch of roses. Fifteen quid, they cost. Then on Friday morning he called in to pay the weekly paper bill on his way to work, as he always did. Another eleven quid went on that. So there we are, down to the two hundred and sixty pounds in his wallet when you found the body. Which is a definite pointer to his having been killed on Friday night."

Kate mused, "Do we know who the flowers were for?"

"Oh, his wife. He said so in the shop. They also mentioned that buying her flowers was a regular occurrence. Seems he was that kind of husband."

It fitted. Kate remembered having seen a vase of longstemmed white roses at the Kimberley house that had clearly come from a florist rather than from the garden.

"I wish we could get something really definite on the time of death," she said. "Where the hell is Kimberley's car, Tim? What's being done about tracing it?"

"We've already had an intensive throughout the South Midlands area. Now we're widening the search."

Kate nodded. "Good. I'll ring Richard Gower and ask him if he can get the registration number printed in some of the national papers tomorrow."

"That ought to help a lot, guv. A Saab isn't one of your two-a-penny motors. Unless it's been taken off the road and hidden away, somebody's sure to spot it."

In a leafy suburban road in Cardiff, Detective Constable Elwyn Williams stopped his clapped-out Austin Allegro a few yards along from the neat little house, the end of a terrace of four, that had once been his pride and joy. Walking in at the gate, he surveyed the patch of front garden critically. Megan was letting it go, sod her! She'd rather spend her time dashing around with her new fancy-man in his flashy red MG. There the bloody thing was now, parked bang outside for all the world as if he was the one who paid the mortgage. Got it jammy, he had, the lucky bleeder. All the fun and none of the responsibility. It was Elwyn Williams who had to keep the place going as a home for the kids. Elwyn Williams who had to feed and clothe them, plus having to cough up the rent of a bed-sitter for himself.

The front door opened before he reached it, and Gordon and Kim bounced out to greet him fondly. A fondness that was partially bought, Elwyn acknowledged ruefully, with the money that he couldn't really afford but that he nevertheless splashed out on them during his access days—Saturday one week, Sunday the next. Megan stood in the doorway, leaning against the jamb with her arms folded, watching him sardonically as he bent to kiss the children.

"You actually managed to make it today, El, for a change."

"Last Sunday wasn't my fault," he protested. "Something came up at work that I couldn't get out of. I explained all that."

"Oh yes, bloody work always comes first with you, doesn't it? It didn't worry you that all my arrangements were messed up. Garry was furious. Had to take the kids along with us, didn't we?"

"You'll have me crying my eyes out," said Elwyn savagely, and spoke more sharply than he intended to the children. "Stop messing about, you two, and get in the car."

He had to slam the door twice before the latch held. Gordon, eight years old to his sister's six and a half, said cheerfully, "Why don't you get a super car like Uncle Garry's, Dad? It doesn't half go. Vrmmm, vrmmm!"

His father didn't deign to reply as he eased his ancient Allegro away from the kerb. To think that once upon a time he'd been happy, in love with his wife and thinking that life was great. God, what a laugh!

"Where're we going, Dad?" asked Kim.

"I thought we'd try the airport." It was getting harder and harder to find things to interest them. Things that didn't cost too much.

"Will we go up in an airplane?" she asked excitedly.

"Well, no. Not today. But you'll find there are heaps of things to do and see."

"I want to see Concorde," declared Gordon.

"Concorde won't be there. It doesn't fly from Cardiff."

They both lost interest, and started squabbling amiably about who was cleverest.

Twenty minutes later Elwyn Williams found a vacant space at the airport's short-stay car park. On one side was a bloody great Merc. Sod-all chance of him ever owning a motor like that. On the other side was a more attainable-looking car . . . a Saab, wasn't it? On his income as a DC, if he hadn't been lumbered with bloody maintenance payments, he could almost afford a motor like that. Not a new F reg. like this one, but maybe a Y or an A. What a sodding rotten deal he'd had out of life, with Megan turning out to be such a bloody bitch.

It took no more than forty-five minutes for the kids to exhaust the possibilities of the airport. They were starting to whine. Their father steered them towards the buffet, to try and buy a few minutes' contentment with Cokes and ice-creams. On the way he bought a paper, plus a couple of comics.

They found a vacant table and all sat down. Blessed quiet! The coffee was good and hot. The page three girl was really something. Mind you, though, Megan had a figure that put her in that class. Bloody memories. Always coming back, they were. Never left a guy in peace.

He turned a page, idly scanned a story about vice in Britain's cities, but quickly lost interest. He saw more than enough of that on the job. Down at the bottom of the page was a small headline. *Have you seen this car?* To do with the double murder that South Midlands had on their plate. A Saab, dark green, F registration. It quoted the number.

"Da-a-ad," Kim began.

"Just a minute."

No, it *couldn't* be. Luck was something that happened to other people. He screwed up his eyes, trying to visualize the number plate of the car parked next to his. F reg., definitely. God almighty, he really thought it was.

"Come on, you two," he said, jumping to his feet.

"But Dad, I haven't finished my Coke." This was Kim. Gordon had been making sucking noises through his straw for ages.

"Bring it with you," he snapped impatiently, and made them run all the way back to the car park. But once there, he was almost scared to look. Did he actually imagine that he, Detective Constable Elwyn Williams, had stumbled upon the car wanted in a murder case? Still, there was one consolation if he was wrong, he'd never have to breathe a word about it to a living soul.

But he was right. He checked again with the newspaper, just to be a hundred per cent sure. Then he grabbed both children by the hand.

"Come on, hurry up, I've got to find a phone."

Seven

"Cardiff Airport?" Kate raised her eyebrows at the report that had just been brought in to her by Sergeant Boulter. "Does that mean our chummy has flown out of the country, I wonder?"

"Looks like it, guv."

Kate thought quickly. She was at her desk in the Incident Room. Saturdays were no different from any other day during a major investigation. The whole murder squad was on duty, and would be tomorrow.

"I think you'd better go to Cardiff straight away, Tim. Take a DC with you. Get Wales to fingerprint the car for us and give it a careful once-over. Then one of you can drive it back here. Find out, if you possibly can, how long it's been parked there and if anyone remembers seeing the driver. And check along the way, too. The most likely route from here would be over the Severn Bridge, so see if anyone at the toll gate remembers a dark green Saab that night—or since, come to that. Driven by a woman on her own, presumably."

Boulter pulled a long face. "I should think the trail's gone pretty cold by this time."

"You never know, you might strike lucky. Meanwhile, I want to talk to Lady Kimberley again, and Lord Balmayne. And there's also Sir Noah's nephew to see, Aidan Kimberley. He must have arrived by now. So let's get on to it, Tim, and we'll liaise later."

Already this morning Kate had re-interviewed Dr. Cheryl Miller, who'd arrived in a bad mood, especially displeased at having been summoned to the police station on a Saturday.

"I've already told you everything I know," she'd grumbled, when Boulter brought her into Kate's office. "And that's virtually bugger-all."

"You drive, of course?" queried Kate.

"As in motor cars? Yes, I did manage to scrape through my test. But what's that got to do with anything?"

"I'd like you to account for your movements around midnight on Friday of last week."

Cheryl Miller appeared to be scanning her memory, then she chuckled throatily. "I was tucked up in bed by then."

"Your own bed?"

Another chuckle. "Now, now, Chief Inspector!" She indicated Boulter with a lazy finger. "Don't shock sonny-boy. Yes, my own bed. My very own."

"And were you alone?"

"You *are* being inquisitive."

"Believe me, Dr. Miller, it might turn out to be very important for you to have someone to vouch for where you were at that time. A slight embarrassment is a small price to pay."

"Huh, who's embarrassed?"

"Then what possible reason can you have for not being frank with me?"

"That's an exceedingly naive question. I can think of several reasons."

"Each one of them innocent?"

"It all depends," she drawled, crossing her legs and hitching her skirt to display the shapely curve of her calf, "on what you mean by innocent." Boulter showed signs of restlessness—exactly as she'd intended.

Kate clung to her patience. "What do you know about Sir Noah Kimberley's death?"

"Nothing, apart from what everybody's talking about. I must say it's intriguing, popping the old boy in the freezer like that."

"You don't appear to have liked Sir Noah any more than you liked Dr. Trent," Kate observed.

"He was a pompous old ass. I'll give you a little vignette of him, shall I, as a bonus. A good biochemist, but dated. He was scared out of his hidebound masculine mind that a woman might run bloody rings around him. Which I could easily have done, if he'd promoted me instead of bringing in Gavin Trent."

She'd handed Kate a chance to get under her skin. "I wonder you stayed at Croptech, after that. Surely you could have found a position elsewhere that would be more suited to your talents?"

The green eyes flickered, then she said with a shrug, "Oh, well . . . it suits me here, I suppose. The countryside is pleasant, and I have a nice place to live."

"So you were willing to put up with a lot of aggro from your male bosses?"

"Don't worry, I gave as good as I got."

"Or better, eh? Perhaps you decided to remove them from the scene of combat."

Cheryl Miller had recovered her poise by now; the off-balance moment was already history. "That, Detective Mrs. Chief Inspector, is your job to find out, isn't it?"

"Which I will, I promise you. You can go now, Dr. Miller."

"Oh! Isn't your good-looking sergeant going to handcuff me?"

"I have a distinct feeling that if he tried to," Kate said, "he'd be the one to end up in cuffs. Metaphorically speaking, of course."

The two women grinned at one another guardedly. It was odd, Kate thought, but there was a kind of liking between them. Certainly a mutual respect. The respect of two females tough enough to have made their own way in a male-dominated world.

As Cheryl Miller departed, Boulter let out a whistle. "My God, she's a cool one."

"Sultry, I'd have said. You look distinctly warm, Sergeant."

"The way she slammed into both the dead men, you'd think she was asking to be charged with murder. It's almost as if she doesn't care a damn."

Kate pressed the retractor button on her ballpoint. "Or is it double-bluff, Tim?"

Tim Boulter found himself thinking about Dr. Cheryl Miller as he headed for the motorway and Cardiff. In the passenger seat sat DC Clutton, a few years younger than Boulter and still blessedly single and unattached. Jack Clutton, the lucky sod, was free to have a crack at any attractive woman who crossed his path. He'd win some, lose some, but what the heck? There were always plenty more. Jack Clutton had no ball and chain anchoring him to the path of virtue. Boulter heaved a heavy sigh for the glorious freedom he'd lost so long ago.

Clutton shot him an amused glance. "What's eating you, Sarge?"

"Life, that's what. Bloody life."

"Is the DCI giving you a hard time?"

"What's that supposed to mean?"

"Well, you know . . . frustrated widow and all that."

"You're a dirty-minded bastard, Clutton."

"Hey, it's not just me. All the lads reckon she must be more'n ready for it."

Tim felt outraged. "They'd better not let Kate Maddox hear them talking like that. She'd chop their balls off in ten seconds flat."

They drove on in a moody silence. At the Severn Bridge the sergeant pulled up at the toll gate.

"Who'd have been on the graveyard shift last Friday?" he asked the man in the kiosk, flashing his warrant card. "Just the one, I take it?"

A nod. "I'll have a look. Oh yes, Charley Blaisdale. Why, what's up?"

"I want to ask him if he noticed a particular car come through round about 1 A.M.-ish."

"What, a week ago! Do me a favour, chum."

"A dark-green Saab," Tim went on. "F reg."

"Hey, just a minute! Charley mentioned her when I took over from him. She shot away like a bat out of hell as soon as she'd paid. The stupid cow hit the railing over there and careered away swerving all over the shop. Pissed out of her mind, he reckoned."

"Tell me where I can contact Charley. I need a description of this woman."

"You'll be unlucky, then. In this job you don't look at the faces."

The car behind them hooted impatiently. Sticking his arm through the window, without bothering to glance round, Jack Clutton made a rude gesture. Boulter took down Charley's address. Another lead to be followed that would finish at a dead end. Charley would remember nothing more than they'd got already.

At Cardiff Airport they were directed to where Elwyn Williams was standing guard over his find. He'd long since disposed of the two children, phoning Megan and asking for them to be collected . . . to her blind fury at having her "free" Saturday spoilt. Elwyn led the two South Midlands men to the Saab and they strolled around it, noting a dented offside wing. Another job for someone in forensics, checking that the damaged paintwork matched possible traces left on the railing at the Severn Bridge. Boulter had no doubt in his mind about that, though.

"Got anything on the driver for us?" he asked Williams.

The Welsh DC spread his hands. "Wha'd'ya expect. There's no way of knowing when the car came in, not even which day. The driver might have taken a plane; equally he might have caught a bus out. Or switched cars here. Or just walked away. If you could give us a name . . ."

"Can't. All we know is that it was most likely a woman."

"Now that really narrows it down," Williams said sarcastically.

The local forensics circus had already been along and photographed the car from all angles, fingerprinted it and given it a pretty thorough going over. There'd be nothing more to learn by keeping it in situ, Boulter decided, so he told Jack Clutton to drive it back to DHQ at Marlingford.

"I'll follow on a bit later," he added. "There'll be one or two things to attend to here first."

Clutton winked, a touch ruefully. "Have a pint for me while you're about it, Sarge."

"All right, all right. On your way, Jack."

When he'd driven off, Williams said to Boulter, "I know a little place where the beer's sheer nectar. Brewed on the premises."

"Lead me to it, chum."

In the cosy pub, the two men talked companionably. They were approximately the same age; and both, it emerged, had a couple of kids. Williams explained how it was he'd come to the airport.

"My access day."

"Divorced, are you?"

"Mmm. A year ago. Bloody women!"

"Bloody *wives*," corrected Boulter. "You're free as air again, then, you lucky bugger."

"Bad for you, is it, at home?"

"Oh, Christ! Nag bloody nag morning till night. I can't remember the last time I did something right in her eyes. If it wasn't for the kids, I wouldn't have stuck it this long."

"Well, take my advice and hang on in. If you don't, you'll lose those kids. Lose 'em to some slimy git. You'll end up in a grotty bedsitter, while he helps himself to what's rightly yours . . . bed and board, the lot, all at your bloody expense."

"It's a question of how much more I can stand," Boulter muttered.

"Let me tell you something," Williams said, in his singsong Welsh lilt. "If I could turn the clock back, I'd stick it out. Has your missus got another bloke already?"

"Not one that I know about," said Boulter grimly.

"How about you?"

Boulter shook his head, baring his teeth in a humourless grin. "Some of these sexy pieces you see around . . . I get so I could rip the clothes off 'em."

"You mind what I say, now." Williams sounded quite severe. "Come on, I'll fill you up with the best fish and chips you've ever tasted, before I wave you on your way."

At the fish bar a few doors along, they sat at a cramped, plastic-topped table. Boulter had a double portion of cod, and extra chips served in a separate dish because they wouldn't all pile on his plate.

Williams remarked, "I hear you've got a woman DCI handling this murder case."

"Right. I've worked with her before."

"What's she like? A real old battleaxe?"

Boulter forked up a nice crispy bit of cod and chewed it before replying. "No," he said at last, as if surprising himself, "she's okay."

That morning, after Boulter departed for Cardiff, Kate had asked the office manager to telephone the Kimberley residence to say she wanted to see Lady Kimberley again and, if convenient, would be coming along at once. Lord Balmayne had taken the call, and he'd announced his firm intention of being present at the interview. Kate didn't object to this; in fact, it suited her very well. It would suit her even better, she decided, if the nephew and his wife, Aidan and Paula Kimberley, were also present. Seeing all four together would help to keep the atmosphere informal, which was what she wanted at this stage.

Just as Kate was about to set out for Radlett, a call was put through from one of the house agents she'd been in touch with in her search for a new home.

"Mrs. Maddox, I've found just the property you're looking for. It's at Ingram's Green, nicely within the area you specified. A modern house, but built traditionally, and with a small, manageable garden that's well matured. Two bedrooms, a large living room, kitchen and bath." He named a price that didn't make Kate gasp too alarmedly.

"Sounds wonderful, Mr. Hampton. I'm terribly busy just at the moment, but I'm sure I could manage to get along to view it one day next week."

"Sorry! It's got to be today. We've already had a firm offer, and the owner wants a quick sale as he's been posted abroad at short notice. I do urge you to view this house, Mrs. Maddox, because I'm certain you'd want to snap it up. You only have to top this offer by a small amount, and it's yours."

Kate sighed. Much as she longed to find a place of her own, she could do without this sort of pressure right now. It wasn't just the time needed to view the property, but all the hassle of dealing with the paperwork that would follow a successful offer. She'd never forgive herself, though, if she let the place go by default; she'd kick herself every time she drove past it.

"All right," she agreed grudgingly, "I'll be out there today." Ridiculously, she almost hoped that the house would prove unsuitable, so as to be a problem off her mind.

"What time shall I tell the vendors to expect you?" he pressed, after giving her the address.

"What time? Oh, I really don't know at the moment. It's just a matter of when I can get away."

"Shall we say some time before three-thirty? After that, I can't promise the property won't be gone."

"All right, then, before three-thirty," she said, and put down the phone.

Driving to the Kimberley house, Kate's mind tussled with the problem of how to fit in the house viewing. Even without that, she still had an overloaded schedule. Normally on Saturdays, when she wasn't engaged on a major case, she and her aunt dropped in at the Wagon and Horses in Chipping Bassett for a pub lunch—and sometimes Richard Gower joined them. She'd already warned Felix that their pleasant little ritual was out of the question today, but now it looked as if she'd be lucky even to find time to gobble down a sandwich at her desk.

The Aidan Kimberleys, as Kate had hoped, were also there. All four present were standing around sipping a pre-lunch aperitif when Kate was shown into the drawing room.

"Please join us in a drink," Lady Kimberley invited. "What will you have, Mrs. Maddox? Sherry? Gin and something? Whisky?"

"A dry sherry, thank you."

"Gerald, my dear, would you be so kind?" she asked Lord Balmayne, with a regal wave of the hand. She turned to introduce her late husband's nephew and his wife.

Aidan Kimberley was a tall, impressive man; a man, Kate guessed, who was accustomed to dominate. His dark hair, greying about his ears, was loosely wavy, his forehead high, his slatey grey eyes intelligent and penetrating. He was wearing lightweight slacks and a tailored short-sleeve shirt. Consciously dressed for summertime in the country.

Paula Kimberley looked the sort of woman a wealthy, successful man would expect his wife to be. In her twenties, she'd probably been outstandingly attractive, and now in her early forties she wasn't making a bad job of keeping her looks. She had a long, oval face that was framed by a mass of golden blond hair, and huge almond-shaped eyes. Tallish and slender, she wore a white pleated skirt and peach-coloured silk-knit sweater with considerable elegance. At the moment, though, suffering from the aftermath of flu, she looked pale and drawn, ill-at-ease.

As she shook hands with Kate, her softly mellow voice was laced with self-reproach. "Oh, Chief Inspector, I feel so dreadfully guilty that I wasn't here with poor dear Vanessa when she most needed me. Of course, at the time—last Saturday—I had no conception that Noah was dead. I thought . . . I imagined that he was just delayed somewhere."

Her husband laid a hand on her forearm. "There, there, darling, you mustn't blame yourself. Vanessa understands." Yet despite the gentleness of his words, there was a hardness in his tone. Kate sensed anger between them.

"Yes, of course I understand," Lady Kimberley concurred, though somewhat unconvincingly.

Kate said, "I gather, Mrs. Kimberley, that you went back to London on Sunday so as to be there when your husband returned from the Far East?"

"Yes, I wanted to make sure our apartment was ready. But of course, Vanessa's needs would have come first. Aidan would have *wanted* me to put her first, if only I'd realized it was really serious."

Her husband was frowning, Kate noted, as if he thought all this self-reproach was a bit overdone. Lady Kimberley, too, was looking thoroughly impatient with it.

"Do let us all sit down," she said, with an inviting sweep of her hand.

Kate avoided taking a seat in one of the deep sofas. Instead, she chose a higher, tapestry-covered armchair from which she could more easily stay in command of the situation.

"I have various questions to put to you all," she said, after sipping the sherry Lord Balmayne handed her. "Can I take it that you are happy to speak in one another's presence and don't wish to be interviewed separately?"

Head shaking and low murmurs of assent indicated that no one had any objection.

Setting her glass down on a small table, Kate took her notebook from her shoulderbag and became briskly professional. "First of all, I need to establish the whereabouts of each one of you at certain specific times. Most importantly, on the evening of yesterday week, and the evening of Wednesday last."

She had expected a barrage of horrified protest. Instead, they all seemed shocked into silence. Then Aidan Kimberley said quietly, "I'm sure you understand, Chief Inspector, that it's somewhat dismaying to be faced with the need to prove one's innocence in these appalling circumstances. But I for one do accept that the police are obliged to ask these questions. Let me see, last Friday I was still, of course, in Hong Kong . . . a fact you can easily verify. On Wednesday of this week I was in London with my wife. We spent the evening at our apartment in Sloane Street."

"Did you have any visitors?"

"Er . . . no, though we do very often have people in for drinks or dinner. But Paula was still feeling groggy from her bout of flu, the poor love."

"I see. Is there anyone who can confirm this?"

"My wife can," he said sharply.

"I meant, anyone else?"

"How could there be? I told you, we spent the evening alone."

"Did you make or receive any phone calls, for example?"

He looked annoyed. "I really can't be expected to remember. Very possibly. I spend a lot of time on the phone."

"You telephoned me, Aidan, if you remember," Lady Kimberley interjected.

He considered a moment. "Yes, of course I did. What time would that have been, Vanessa? Somewhere between nine and ten, wasn't it?"

"It was just after ten you phoned that night, I seem to recall."

"And that was the only phone call you made or received?" Kate persisted.

"The only one I can recall just now. If anything further occurs to me, I'll let you know."

"Please do. By the way, just for me to be quite clear, when was it exactly that you arrived home from Hong Kong last Monday?"

"My plane was dreadfully late getting in," he said critically. "We didn't land at Heathrow until thirteen hundred hours. I took a taxi, and reached the flat just before three o'clock."

"And you telephoned Lady Kimberley at once, when your wife told you the news about Sir Noah's disappearance?"

"Naturally I did. I was most distressed."

Lord Balmayne cleared his throat with a sharp hrrmph. It was an effective way of commanding attention. "Pity you didn't get in touch with me at the same time, Aidan."

Kimberley turned to look at him in pained protest. "You move around so much, Gerald, one never knows where to find you."

"Any one of my staff could have told you where I was."

When the little spat had subsided, Kate resumed her questioning. "Mr. Kimberley, how well did you know Dr. Gavin Trent?"

"How well? I'd met him once or twice, at this house, but beyond that I didn't know the chap at all."

Kate raised her eyebrows. "Even though he was your uncle's deputy at Croptech? I understand that you have a half share in the firm."

"That's true, but I've never had any hand in the running of things there. I always left all that to my uncle. Though now, of course . . ." His sentence was left hanging.

"I was hoping, you see, that you might be able to suggest a reason why somebody should have wanted Dr. Trent out of the way."

The puzzlement on his face darkened to anger. "I thought you were here to discuss the tragic death of my uncle, Chief Inspector."

"The two deaths, I believe, are closely linked."

A strangled gasp came from Lady Kimberley. But she said nothing, just sat staring at Kate with horrified eyes. It was Lord Balmayne who spoke.

"Have you any foundation for that theory, Chief Inspector?"

"It would be too great a coincidence, sir, if it were not so."

"But you have nothing to link the two deaths beyond the mere fact of coincidence?"

"Not at the moment, no." She returned her gaze to the other man. "Well, Mr. Kimberley, can you think of any possible explanation for Dr. Trent's murder?"

"Absolutely none. How could I know anything?"

"And you, Lord Balmayne?"

"Good heavens, no. As far as I know I never even met the fellow."

Kate turned to Mrs. Kimberley. "Now perhaps I could have details of where *you* were."

The question was greeted with a look of shock and sheer amazement. "My husband has already told you that we were at home alone."

"Not Wednesday. I was referring to last Friday."

"Last Friday? Well, I was here—at our cottage, I mean. You know that."

"You didn't go out at all?"

"No, I didn't." Paula Kimberley seemed to think this required an explanation. "I was doing some of my packing, you see, ready to return to

London. I'd spent most of the month Aidan was in Hong Kong here, so I had a fair bit of stuff with me. Besides, although I didn't realize it then, I was already sickening with flu. I was in no mood for seeing other people."

"I understand. Can you remember any phone calls?"

She began to shake her head, but her husband intervened. "I phoned you, darling, from Hong Kong, to confirm my travel arrangements."

"Oh yes, of course you did."

"What time would this have been, Mrs. Kimberley?"

She looked vague, and her husband helped her out once more. "It was first thing Saturday morning Hong Kong time, about 7 A.M. That would make it about 11 P.M. British time. I wanted to catch Paula before she went to bed."

His wife's face cleared. "Yes, that's right, Aidan. Just a few minutes after eleven. I remember now. I was watching 'Newsnight' when you phoned."

Kate scribbled down a note. "I take it that you also had met Dr. Trent, Mrs. Kimberley?"

"Why, er . . . yes. On the same occasions as my husband did. And I saw him once or twice in the village and so on. Just to say hallo to."

"Do you know the Tillingtons at all?"

"We went there to dinner once," said her husband. "They're too pompously formal for my taste. We never returned the invitation."

"But you know them quite well, Paula, don't you?" put in Lady Kimberley. "I recall running into you and Marjorie Tillington having lunch together in Marlingford. I rather gathered that you saw a fair bit of each other."

Paula frowned at her. "We have a few things in common, that's all. She's interested in interior design, too."

"You'd never think so," said Kimberley with a scornful laugh, "to judge from that ghastly house of theirs."

"That's all her husband's choice, darling. The judge is a lot older than she is, don't forget, and he's a man of very fixed ideas. But I only know Marjorie Tillington slightly. She's not what I'd call a *friend* of mine."

"I seem to remember you brought her to polo at Dodford once," Lady Kimberley remarked.

Paula stared at her blankly, as if trying to recall the occasion. "Oh yes, that's right. I'd happened to mention that Aidan was playing on the Saturday and Marjorie said that she'd never seen a polo match, so I invited her along."

Kate said, "You weren't at Dodford last Saturday, I believe? Do you not bother to go when your husband isn't playing?"

"Well, I suppose I do go to polo usually. But as I said, I was busy packing last Saturday, and I wasn't feeling very bright." She gave an apologetic laugh. "I still don't feel up to much, I'm afraid. Sorry if I don't seem very with it."

"I hope you'll soon feel better." Kate addressed Lord Balmayne. "Now you, sir, if you don't mind. Those two evenings . . ."

He said with stiff courtesy, "I was in London last Friday, Chief Inspector, for my gala."

"So . . . if you could give me a detailed account of the evening, sir, say from eight o'clock onwards."

"Very well. As Dame Vanessa has explained to you, I believe, at the very last moment she was most unfortunately unable to perform."

Kate nodded. "A throat infection, she told me."

"Yes, poor lady. I persuaded her to remain at my home in Paddington, where she was staying overnight, while I put in an appearance at the theatre."

"She was left alone?"

"No, no. My man Jefferies was there. I made excuses and left the theatre at the interval so I was home by soon after nine, because I felt concerned about her. We spent the remainder of the evening quietly together, listening to music on the gramophone. Dame Vanessa retired to bed a little before eleven-thirty, I think it was, and I did so myself shortly afterwards."

"All of which, presumably, your manservant will be able to confirm?"

"If you feel it necessary to question him," he replied, affronted.

"I believe you were also expecting to have Sir Noah as your overnight guest, and Mrs. Byworth was due to come, too?"

"Yes, it was indeed Sir Noah's original intention to come to London for the gala, but then he decided against it. And Dotty had to remain behind to look after him. I knew beforehand of the change of plan."

"From Sir Noah himself, or from Lady Kimberley?"

"Really, are these questions of any relevance? If you must know, it was Dame Vanessa who telephoned me, on Friday morning."

"Did she give you a reason for Sir Noah's change of plan?"

He hesitated briefly, with a glance at Lady Kimberley. "I think you should ask Dame Vanessa herself, not a third party."

"I'm sorry to press you, sir, but I'd like you to answer the question, if you please."

Again he glanced at Lady Kimberley. There seemed to be a query in his eyes. She looked back at him mutely, a wisp of lace handkerchief pressed to her lips.

"She didn't go into details. She merely said that Noah had things to attend to at home so he thought he'd give the gala a miss on this occasion."

"Was this the first time he'd missed one of his wife's charity performances?"

He gestured vaguely. "Perhaps. I really cannot say."

"Lady Kimberley?"

She looked startled to be addressed. "Er, yes . . . Noah did miss one other occasion. A few months ago, when I was singing for Famine Relief, he had to go up to Scotland at the last moment."

"But this time there was no such definite reason?"

"No, I, er . . . I suppose not."

Paula Kimberley burst out, "If only Uncle Noah *had* gone with you, Vanessa, this dreadful thing would never have happened."

"Oh, how I wish he had," Lady Kimberley agreed in a piteous voice. "How I wish that my poor darling Noah had come to London with me."

The other three shifted uncomfortably in their seats as people do when faced with a display of emotion. Lord Balmayne reached for Lady Kimberley's hand and patted it consolingly.

"This morning," Kate announced into the momentary silence, "we found Sir Noah's car."

They seemed stunned, all of them. Then Aidan Kimberley asked, "Where did you find it?"

"At an airport. In a car park there."

"An airport? Which airport, for heaven's sake?"

"Cardiff. One of my officers is there at this moment, investigating. I hope to have more information shortly."

"Does this mean that whoever drove the car to Cardiff has flown out of the country?" asked Lord Balmayne.

"We have no means of knowing that, sir. Not yet, anyway. Lady Kimberley, did you ever drive your husband's Saab?"

She hardly seemed to absorb the question, and Kate repeated it.

"No, I . . . I never did. I'm used to an automatic gearbox, you see, and I find the other kind difficult to manage."

"But you have been a passenger in the car?"

"Yes, naturally. Quite often."

"Then I shall have to trouble you for your fingerprints. Perhaps you'll come to the police station at Aston Pringle later today to have them taken. You see," she went on quickly, "if your fingerprints are possibly somewhere on the car, we need to have specimens in order to discount them. This will permit us to concentrate on any other prints we find in addition to yours and your husband's."

Lady Kimberley nodded her understanding. "Of course, Chief Inspector. I am ready to do *whatever* is required of me."

"There is one other thing. A formal identification of your husband's body is necessary. If you don't feel up to it yourself, then perhaps Mr. Aidan Kimberley will take your place."

"Naturally I will," he agreed readily.

"No!" Lady Kimberley held up one hand in a dramatically brave gesture. "It is for *me* to perform this last act for my poor darling Noah. I shall not *shrink* from it."

Kate had delayed requesting an identification until now in view of the hard-frozen state of the corpse when it was found. She felt it would have been unseemly, and there had been no doubt about the identity. However, she'd been told before leaving the Incident Room that the body had by now thawed out sufficiently for a post-mortem examination to be held quite soon, possibly later in the day if the pathologist was available.

The break-in at Milford Grange was still on her plate, a niggling extra problem. Superintendent Joliffe, damn him, would expect her to be able to report some developments on this. Kate seized on a fortuitous chance that had come her way. To Paula Kimberley, she said, "It's possible that you could assist me in quite another matter."

"Me?"

"We've been unable so far to discover exactly what is missing from the Tillington residence. Clearly, the thieves snatched just what they could easily lay their hands on while the burglar alarm was sounding. You, with your trained eye for antiques and so on plus your personal knowledge of the house, might be able to assist us in making a list of missing items and their approximate value. The inventory, according to their solicitor, is locked in the safe at Milford Grange, so we can't get at it."

"But . . . but I could never remember what was there," she protested. "I told you, I don't know the Tillingtons or their home all that well."

"If one of my officers escorted you round the house, perhaps it would jog your memory," Kate persisted.

"Oh, no! Oh, no, I couldn't do that."

Kate wouldn't have judged Paula Kimberley as overly modest in professional matters, and she found this reluctance puzzling. So, it seemed, did her husband.

"Of course you could, darling," he said easily. "I'll come with you, if you like."

Taking Paula Kimberley's agreement for granted, Kate stood up. "I won't trouble you any longer, you'll be wanting your lunch. We'll be in touch, Lady Kimberley, regarding the identification. And someone will contact you, Mrs. Kimberley, to fix a convenient time for you to go to Milford Grange."

The two men had also risen, and Dame Vanessa. Paula Kimberley remained seated on one of the sofas. She was still looking deeply troubled.

At the door Kate paused a moment, then asked with an air of apology at having yet one more bothersome question, "By the way, Lady Kimberley, on the Friday evening when you were staying at Lord Balmayne's, did you call in a doctor to look at your throat?"

Silence for a count of four. Then, "No, I didn't bother. There seemed no point. I felt sure it was nothing serious. Er . . . why do you ask, Mrs. Maddox?"

"Simply for the record," Kate said smoothly, with a little smile. "I'm sure you understand that in cases of serious crime the police have to try and corroborate every statement made to them. If you *had* called a doctor in that night, then he would have been able to give us the required confirmation of your statement."

And, she thought, confirmation that Dame Vanessa Logan really did have a throat infection. It would be good to be totally certain of that fact.

Eight

It was already past one o'clock when Kate headed back to the Incident Room. Less than two and a half hours to the deadline for seeing the house at Ingram's Green. She'd see what had come up for her, then arrange her afternoon to leave an hour free to drive there and view the place. Not a clever way to go about making a decision regarding her future home, but it was the best she could manage.

As it turned out, she couldn't manage even that. A message greeted her arrival at the police station.

"Superintendent Joliffe rang to say he's coming over to see you, ma'am."

Oh, bloody hell! Her face said it, not her vocal cords. Why couldn't Jolly behave like any other superintendent and harmlessly amuse himself playing golf on a fine Saturday afternoon?

"When was this, Brian?"

"Quarter of an hour ago, ma'am. He should be here any minute now."

"Heard anything from Sergeant Boulter?"

"Not a dicky bird."

Damn Tim, she thought unfairly, she could do with him here right now. She had to keep up a certain front with her sergeant, of course, but not so much of a front as with the rest of them. To Tim she could have voiced a moan about superintendents who descend on you at the most inconvenient times.

In her office, she hastily recorded a few notes about her interviews at the Kimberley house while it was all still fresh in her memory, and passed the notes out for typing up and cross-indexing. She buzzed Inspector Massey and told him, "When Jolly leaves, Frank, I want to have the next hour free for some personal business. Important business. So keep things clear for me, will you?"

A sheer waste of breath, if only she'd known. Three minutes later Jolly was ushered in, wearing his version of a warm smile.

"Have you had lunch yet, my d—Mrs. Maddox?"

"Not yet, sir," she admitted, unwisely. "I've not had time."

"Good, good. There's no reason why we shouldn't have our little discussion over a meal. Where do you suggest?"

This was transparently an attempt to sweeten things between them after yesterday's little upset. And if she declined, Jolly would never understand. Were she to tell him the truth, that she wanted to dash off to view a house she might just possibly want to make an offer for, she'd give him new grounds for thinking she was too irresponsible by half. In the cause of female coppery in general, if not in her own best interest, she smiled sweetly and thanked him.

"How about the Half Moon across the road, sir?" The advantage of this pub, as well as being close at hand, was that it wasn't the sort of place where one could linger in comfort over a meal. The food was ordinary, and the small tables were jammed together. But Jolly knew that too. His long face registered distaste.

"No, I'll tell you what we'll do, we'll drive over to the Spotted Trout at Hadleigh. They always do one very well there."

During the drive to the restaurant, Kate filled him in about the discovery of Sir Noah's body. Jolly was all sympathy.

"When they told me about it, I thought at once, Poor Mrs. Maddox! What a nasty shock it must have been for her. Pity it was you who should have discovered the body. But full marks to you, my er . . . for being so astute as to latch on to the significance of the hum of that freezer. Ah, here we are. Nice place this, don't you think? And it lives up to its name. Best trout for miles around."

He fussed over parking his Rover, near to the entrance but out of the hot sun, fussed over holding the swing door open for Kate, and fussed over being ushered to the table that best befitted his dignity. Once drinks were served, there followed a lengthy debate with the waiter about just how the trout should be cooked. At last he leaned back in his chair.

"Well, er . . . Kate, it was a very interesting day I had yesterday. I have quite a lot to impart to you. But more of that later. You haven't yet mentioned any progress on the break-in aspect."

One deep breath. Another. "There's very little to tell you, sir. We're having a problem working out what exactly was taken. Just this morning I lined up a friend of the judge's wife who has agreed to try and help us. That's Mrs. Aidan Kimberley—he's Sir Noah's nephew."

"Well done! Keep up the good work. We've managed to track down Mr. Justice Tillington in New Zealand, and he's been on the phone to the Chief Constable. The wires were humming, I gather." Jolly sipped his chilled Tio Pepe savouringly. "Among a number of other things, the judge said we'd better get that freezer cabinet cleared out of the house before they arrive home, or his wife would have nightmares."

"That's hardly a police responsibility," Kate observed in a dry tone.

The superintendent regarded her severely. It was clear that he thought she needed a few lessons on the diplomacy of policemanship.

"We can always remove the freezer and hold it as an exhibit. Yes, that's what we'll do. Have it seen to, will you?"

"Very well, sir."

Their starters were served. Cantaloupe melon for Kate, wild duck pâté with wheaten toast for Jolly.

"Sad about Noah Kimberley," he intoned in a token expression of regret. Then he went on, quite cheerfully, "Still, at least we now know what fate befell him. We have something to get our teeth into, so to speak. It shouldn't take too long to pin down a common enemy of him and that man Trent—and there you are!"

"I don't know about that, sir. There seem too many complexities in this case."

He grimaced at her across the table. Meant to be a winning smile, it came over as a leer of condescension. "I have more confidence in you than you have in yourself, my dear . . . oh, er . . ."

Let it go, Kate. The old blighter's trying, and it's costing him.

When she'd finished her trout, she lifted the cuff of her blazer for a surreptitious glance at her watch. Twenty past two already. "If you don't mind, sir, I think I'll skip dessert. I do have rather a heavy schedule today."

He looked distinctly pained. "But I haven't yet got around to telling you about yesterday's symposium. We had a team of senior officers from the New York Police Department to address us. Naturally, they let it be known that compared to the problems they face on a daily basis everything over here is like a church outing. But we gave them something to think about." He sighed. "It's a great shame I didn't know then that we have a *double* murder on our quiet little patch. I say, Kate, what a magnificent dessert trolley today. Sure you won't change your mind?"

Why not? Anything to soothe her frazzled nerves. "Perhaps a few raspberries and cream, then."

The superintendent nodded to the waiter. "I think I'll have the same. No, on second thoughts, I'll try a slice of the strawberry shortcake. And the clotted cream looks tempting. Now then, to get back to what I was saying . . ."

When he finally dropped Kate off at the Aston Pringle nick en route to his home, it was—hell's bells!—twenty-five minutes to four. Kate dashed up to her office and grabbed the phone. She had to wait a couple of minutes before the estate agent's negotiator came on the line.

"Mr. Hampton, it's Mrs. Maddox here. Listen, I'm sorry I've not been able to get out to Ingram's Green before this, but I'm just on my way."

"I'm sorry, too," he said in a doom-laden voice. "But it *is* past the agreed deadline, Mrs. Maddox. I've just this second put the phone down from telling the other party that their offer is accepted. So you see . . ."

Kate hung up on him without saying a word. Sod the bloody man, sod Jolly Joliffe, sod this job. Sod everything! After that it was damn near impossible to give her attention to the pile of reports on her desk. When her door opened several minutes later after a perfunctory knock, she glared up at the intruder with hostility.

"What do *you* want, Don?"

"No need to snap my head off, Kate love." Inspector Trotton smirked at her, looking pleased with himself. "I'm the bearer of glad tidings."

"Oh? What?"

"Case solved," he said, sliding a file aside and perching on the edge of her desk. "Our little break-in yesterday. We've nabbed the chummies responsible. They hadn't even unloaded the haul from the back of their car, the silly beggars."

"You've been able to identify it as definitely coming from Milford Grange?"

"Sure thing. That woman you sent was able to give us a good description of a number of articles she reckoned were missing, and they tally with what we found in the car."

"Woman?" Kate said. "Do you mean Mrs. Kimberley? That was quick work. I only asked her just before lunch today."

"She came with her husband. He said it was a convenient time and that they'd be busy later. She had a good look round the house and made a list for us."

"Oh, well, I'm glad it's worked out. Listen, Don, go and ring Jolly. He'll be at home by now. It'll be the cherry on the top for his weekend. Never mind small trifles like a couple of unsolved murders."

"I'll do that thing." He slid off the desk, then paused. "You sound really pissed-off, Kate. What's bugging you?"

Don Trotton wasn't her choice as a confidant, but he had the virtue of being on hand.

"I've just lost the chance of a house over at Ingram's Green that sounded perfect for me. And all because Jolly wanted to pontificate over a lengthy lunch about comparisons between American police methods and our own. I had a three-thirty deadline on the house and I couldn't meet it."

"What filthy luck, Kate. I'm really sorry. I know what it's like trying to get somewhere to live. I was a hell of a time finding my present place."

"Well, keep your eyes and ears open for me, Don." This was a reflex remark with Kate these days. Who knew where a lucky break might come from?

"Sure I will. Well, I guess I'd better go and gladden the heart of dear old Jolly. See you."

When Tim Boulter arrived from Cardiff half an hour later, Kate was still feeling bloody-minded.

"Where d'you think you've been all this time, Sergeant?" she demanded. "DC Clutton arrived back with the Saab ages ago."

"Well . . . I had things to see to, guv."

"You had a stomach to fill, you mean."

Colour flamed his face. "From what I hear I wasn't the only one doing that," he muttered.

"What did you say?"

"Oh, nothing."

"Well, you'd better get cracking, now you've finally condescended to put in an appearance. Trent's sister is on the way here from Preston. She should be arriving any time now. Have her brought straight in to me." Belatedly, she asked, "What do you have to tell me about Cardiff? Apart from the quality of the beer."

Boulter filled her in. "That Saab was definitely driven across the Severn Bridge sometime between one and two on the Saturday morning. And there's strong eye-witness evidence that it was driven by a woman. Beyond that, mighty little. What happened to the driver once she'd parked at the airport, God knows."

"If she's someone living around here," said Kate, "how did she get back? Especially at that time of night."

"A second car?" Boulter hazarded. "One driven by someone else, or one that she'd left ready parked at the airport for her to use. It may be she hung around till the morning."

"Doesn't help much, does it?"

Trent's sister arrived around seven o'clock, and was brought in to Kate. She was thin-framed, like her brother, with no surplus flesh. A couple of years younger than Gavin, perhaps, she'd lost whatever looks she might once have had. Dark, hollow eyes made her long face look gaunt, and her vaguely mid-brown hair hung lankly. But for God's sake, the woman had recently had news of her brother's murder; had interrupted her holiday to drive the long way down south to Oxfordshire.

Kate rose and went round the desk to shake hands with her. "Good evening, Mrs. Chapman. Sit down, won't you? Sergeant, will you organize a cup of tea for Mrs. Chapman?"

Though fairly tall, she looked a small woman seated in the chair opposite; crushed, defeated. Kate told her the circumstances of her brother's death as gently as possible, then went on, "Did you come straight here? Or did you stop off to book in somewhere for the night?"

"No, I er . . . I haven't yet."

"Perhaps you'd like us to fix some accommodation for you? Right, I'll get that seen to. You're on your own, are you, Mrs. Chapman? I expect your husband had to stay at home to look after the children?"

"Steve *would* have come, he offered to. His mother could have taken Wayne and Peter. But I said no. Better not. He and Gavin never got on, you see, so . . ."

"Why was that?" Kate asked.

"Oh, the fault was all on my brother's side. I don't blame Steve one bit. He's just a local government officer, you see, in the finance department, and Gavin . . . well, he didn't think much of that, and he never tried to hide it." The woman gave a sigh that told of years of split loyalties. "Poor Gavin, he couldn't help it, I suppose, being so clever himself, but . . ." Her voice trailed off.

"So he and your husband didn't see much of each other?"

"They only met a couple of times since we got married, which is thirteen years ago. At my mother's funeral, and then at our cousin Angela's wedding. It was best that way. I visited Gavin on my own now and then, just to keep in touch. Mum would have wanted us to."

A young WPC came in with two cups of tea on a tray. Kate thanked her, and said, "Carol, would you please book accommodation for Mrs. Chapman? A single room, and she'll probably want to stay a few more days. Try the Willow Bank guest house. That will be nice and near for her."

As the WPC withdrew, Kate went on, "Before we go any further, Mrs. Chapman, I'd like to ask if you'd mind if I tape-record our talk."

"Tape-record?"

"It would be useful. You might tell me something, perhaps a seemingly unimportant little detail about your brother, that could later prove helpful in finding his killer."

"Oh yes, I see. Well, I suppose that's all right, then."

Kate switched on and verbally identified the occasion. "Now, Mrs. Chapman, I'd like you to tell me when you last saw your brother."

Like most people, Fiona Chapman cast an uneasy glance at the tape recorder before answering.

"It was just a few weeks ago, at half term. The children were away at camp, and I thought it was a good opportunity."

"How was he then? Did you notice anything different from usual about him?"

"Not really," she said, frowning a little. "Except, perhaps . . ."

"Except, perhaps?"

"Well, Gavin was always pleased to see me. Always. I think I was about the only person he could get on with. I understood him, you see. He was my big brother, and I was terribly proud of him. I knew how hard he'd had to work to get to university, and then all that studying for his degree. A first class degree, it was. Anyway, when Gavin and I got together we used to chat about the old days, when we were kids, and he seemed to really enjoy that. But this last time . . . I don't know, but it was almost as if he was waiting for me to leave. I was only planning to stay for two or three nights anyway, but several times he asked me if it was really okay for me to be away from home for so long."

"What did you make of his attitude?" Kate asked.

She lifted her shoulders. "I didn't know what to make of it. I felt a bit hurt, but then I thought maybe I was imagining things. When I was going, Gavin gave me an affectionate hug, just as usual." She looked at Kate imploringly. "Haven't you any idea who it was who killed him? I realize he couldn't have been popular, but I can't imagine anyone hating him enough to murder him."

"We have a number of potential suspects," Kate told her. "But as yet there's no clear indication of who was responsible. That's why talking about your brother could be so helpful. For instance, I'd like to know anything he might have told you about the people he worked with at Croptech. The people under him in the lab, say."

"Well, there was a woman he didn't like. She was Dr. something . . . Millet or Miller, I believe. Gavin said she was a prize bitch, and he reckoned she had an inflated idea of her ability." Fiona Chapman made a rueful little moue with her lips. "To tell you the truth, I don't think my brother rated women very highly, especially in the scientific field."

Kate nodded. "Was there anyone else he mentioned to you?"

"Well, yes, but I don't remember his name. That last time I stayed with Gavin I remember that he was in a filthy temper one evening over a row he'd had at the lab. Apparently this chap claimed that Gavin was taking the credit for some kind of discovery he'd made. I'm sorry I can't remember his name."

Normally, Kate would avoid prompting. But this time she felt it was justified. "Roger Barlow?"

"Yes, that's right. Why?" Her face changed. "You don't think he was the one who . . ."

"I don't think anything at this stage," Kate said. "I'm just gathering all the information I can. But I'd rather you didn't mention this incident to anyone else. I'm sure I can rely on you."

"Oh yes, of course you can."

She'd had enough for now. She looked exhausted.

"I won't bother you any further this evening," Kate said. "Tomorrow, if you wish, you can go to your brother's cottage. Our forensic people have finished now and you should find everything more or less back to normal. However, while you're sorting things out, if anything in the least strange strikes you, then please let me know."

"What sort of thing?"

"Well, you might notice that something is missing, for example. It could be relevant."

"Oh yes, I see."

"One final point before you go. I'd just like to check whether or not your brother could swim."

"No, he couldn't. As a child Gavin was really scared of the water. We could never persuade him to go in."

"That fits," said Kate. She stood up. "Let's go and see if Carol has managed to book you in at Willow Bank."

Three minutes later, back in her office, Kate immersed herself in the ever-growing pile of paperwork. Finally, at around nine o'clock, when her eyes felt gritty with fatigue, she decided to call it a day. Just at that moment her door opened and Don Trotton stuck his head round. As he wasn't on the murder squad, she was surprised to see him at Aston Pringle so late in the day.

"Spare a minute, Kate?"

"I was just packing up anyway, Don."

He came right in. "I was thinking about your disappointment over losing that house, and I've got a suggestion. Would you consider renting a flat?"

She was at once interested. "Have you heard of one that's going?"

"Maybe. D'you know where I live, that big house with the peculiar turrets at Aylingbury, on the Marlingford road?"

"I don't think so."

"It's not much to look at on the outside, but inside it's very nice. Eight flats in all. Mine is one of the two on the first floor, but there's one on the second floor directly above mine that's likely to be vacant soon."

The thought of becoming a close neighbour of Don Trotton's didn't thrill her, but since when had beggars been able to make choices?

"Sounds promising, Don. Can you tell me which agency will be handling the letting? I'll get along to see them on Monday."

He shook his head. "No can do, Kate. The thing is, the chap who's got the flat now has been transferred to the Swindon branch of his firm, and it's such a long journey each day that he's looking for somewhere nearer to live. He might be leaving any time, but so far he's saying nothing about going. You can't blame him."

"Would he let me look at the flat, do you think? Then if he tipped me off the moment he gave the landlord notice to quit, I'd be first in line."

Don looked doubtful. "I wouldn't want him to think I'd been shooting my mouth off. He mentioned it to me in confidence. Tell you what, though, my flat's almost identical except that it's one floor down. How about giving that the once-over, Kate? Then if you like the look of it, I'll tip you the wink the moment I hear the move is official."

"Well . . ."

"It'll only take a few minutes. If you're packing up now, Aylingbury's scarcely a mile off your direct route home. Drop by and have a drink with me. Or a cup of coffee or whatever."

Don Trotton wasn't the best person in the world to be indebted to, she told herself; but on the other hand she couldn't afford to risk losing a possible home. She'd really wanted a small house with a patch of garden she could cultivate, but a flat would do.

"Okay, Don. Are you off home now?"

"Yep."

"Then I'll just freshen up and follow on in a few minutes. Okay?"

"Great! See you."

There was still a faint rosy light in the sky as she drove to Aylingbury. She identified the house at once from Don's description. Set in about an acre of ground, the building itself was somewhat forbidding. Institutional Victorian, Kate decided. But one can't have everything. And the moment she entered the main front door and looked around the spacious entrance hall with a massive stone balustraded staircase, she knew she could enjoy living here.

Don was at the door of his flat to greet her. He'd changed into white cotton slacks, and his pale blue shirt was unbuttoned to reveal a medallion on a gold chain. The gorgeous hunk image, so he fondly imagined. Poor Don!

"Come along in, Kate." His hand just brushed her shoulders as he ushered her inside. "Let's start with a drink. Have I got it right that you're a lady who's not averse to a spot of the malt?"

"Well, just a very small one," she said, not to sound unfriendly. "I'll be driving again in a minute."

The flat was nice, no question. A large living room with a bay window overlooking the garden at the rear, plus a side window giving a glimpse through trees to the river. Don had furnished it macho-man style—black leather upholstery; the walls, carpet and curtains in tones of cream and brown. State-of-the-art stereo and TV. Leading off this room was an adequate kitchen. The bedroom and bathroom made a separate unit across a small hallway.

"You don't have a second bedroom?"

Don grinned at her. "I don't need a second bedroom, Kate. One serves *all* my needs."

She ignored the sexy innuendo. "What about the flat above yours? Does that have a second bedroom?"

"No, just the one, same as this."

Her spirits took a dive. "That's a real pity. I'd certainly want to be able to accommodate the occasional guest, so I'm afraid it knocks the whole idea on the head. Sorry, Don, I should have checked that point first and saved you the trouble of showing me round."

"No trouble, Kate, far from it. Hey, you're not leaving?" he protested as she moved towards the door. "You must at least stay and finish your drink first."

"Well . . . okay."

"Come and take the weight off. By the way," he went on, as Kate took a seat on the leather Chesterfield, "thanks for letting me be the one to tell Jolly about wrapping up the Tillington break-in. He was delighted, and it'll help towards me getting my extra pip that much sooner." Don gave a slow, appreciative smile. "But that's you all over, isn't it? You're such a generous, warm-hearted lady."

"It's the first time ever another cop has called me that," she said dryly.

"Shame! You deserve it, and more. You've got everything, Kate. Charm and personality, and terrific looks." He perched on the arm of the Chesterfield and laid his arm along its back behind her. "You really turn me on, you know that? I could go for you in a big way."

With a derisive laugh, she put her glass aside and stood up. "Your dialogue stinks, Don. You've been watching too many old movies."

He wasn't in the least affronted. Rather the reverse, as if he appreciated her style. Smilingly he reached for her glass.

"Refill, darling?"

Darling! Time to depart, Kate, or the guy will really get ideas. But as she reached for her handbag to make a move, he quickly jumped to his feet and laid his palms on her shoulders.

Kate sidestepped and shook herself free. "I don't want a refill, Don. I'm leaving."

"Sweetheart, you can't walk out on me like this. It would be too cruel. Don't you see how I feel about you?" He moved to stand between her and the door.

"Drop it, will you?"

"Come on, sweetheart, you can't mean that," he said coaxingly, and once again laid his hands on her shoulders. "I'm sorry if I came on a bit fast for you."

"Just take your hands off me, Inspector Trotton, and get out of my way."

It took a mini-second for her words to register. Then his expression froze and his hands dropped away.

"Pull rank, would you?"

"You made a big mistake, Don. Let's just leave it at that, shall we? Good night."

His face twisted with anger. "This is the way you get your kicks, is it?"

Maybe she should have left without another word. As it was, Kate swung back to face him. "Why can't you grow up, Don? Just accept the fact that here's one woman you couldn't persuade to jump into bed with you."

"You're frigid, I suppose," he sneered.

"My God, you're pathetic."

She exited in a seething rage, slamming the door behind her. The rage was mostly against herself, for being such an idiot as to walk into Don Trotton's unsubtle trap. But as she drove home, the target of her anger switched to include men in general and their bloody arrogance. How dare they regard a woman as just a lump of female flesh for the use of.

Within minutes Kate was pulling up on the grass verge outside her aunt's cottage. There was another car parked there, which she recognized with a fresh blaze of fury.

"What are you doing here, Richard?" she demanded as she marched into the living room and found Felix and Richard Gower companionably chatting over a drink.

"Hey, what's eating you?" Richard got to his feet in the awkward movement dictated by his stiff leg.

"I've had a hard day," she stormed at him, "and I've just about had my gutful of men. Which is why I could have done without finding you here."

With admirable mildness, he said, "For your information, Kate, I dropped by tonight just on the off-chance that you might feel like coming for a drink and forgetting work for a couple of hours."

"Huh! You mean you wanted to see what juicy little morsels you could pick up from me about the case. There'd still be time to get something in the late editions of the Sundays."

"That's crap and you know it."

Kate didn't observe her aunt's apologetic jerk of the head towards the door. Richard took the hint and departed, saying over his shoulder, "See you sometime when you're in a better mood. 'Night, Felix."

When the two women were alone, Felix poured a stiff peg of whisky for them both, then began to chatter undemandingly about a Natural History programme she'd watched on television earlier.

She understood how Kate was feeling, having had a large hand in her upbringing since her mother died when she was only thirteen. She'd watched with pride as her niece had determined on a career and applied to join the police, following in her father's footsteps. With even greater pride she'd watched as Kate had overcome the shattering blow of losing both husband and young daughter in a horrifying accident, when they were struck down by a bank robbers' getaway car. Detective Chief Inspector Kate Maddox was a well-balanced, dedicated and extremely capable police officer. But there were times when the build-up of pressures brought her to snapping point.

"Another couple of fingers, Kate? It'll help you get a good night's sleep."

Nine

Inspector Massey followed Kate into her office when she arrived at the Incident Room on Sunday morning.

"You'd better see this right away, Kate. It was dropped through the letterbox during the night."

The note was short, typed (very neatly) on an otherwise plain square of white paper.

Why don't you stop hounding honest, God-fearing people when there is a vicious killer right under your nose? A man with a record of unspeakable villainy and depravity. Ask Jessop what he and that woman were up to at midnight last Wednesday.

"I wonder who the hell it's from," mused Frank Massey, re-reading the note over Kate's shoulder.

She didn't need to ponder the question for more than thirty seconds. "My money's on McEvoy, the chief clerk at Croptech. Among the people we've questioned he's the only one I can think of who'd write this sort of crap. I've got him pegged as a narrow-minded type, all prissy virtue. You can almost *feel* the quivering outrage in this note, can't you? *Jessop and that woman.* But the clincher to me, Frank, is who else at Croptech is likely to know about Jessop's prison record? Duncan McEvoy would have access to all the confidential staff records."

Frank Massey dug into his index-file memory. "Didn't he claim to be at home that night? And this was corroborated by his wife when DC Andrews visited her yesterday. So what was McEvoy doing observing Jessop at midnight?"

"That's exactly what we're going to find out, Frank. Where the hell is Boulter? I told him to be here sharp at eight-thirty this morning."

"And it's still only eight twenty-nine and thirty seconds, guv," said Tim Boulter cheerfully as he walked in the door.

"Don't try to be clever, Sergeant. I want McEvoy brought in for further questioning, and I want it done now. Go and see to it. You can read this afterwards."

Kate was aware of Boulter's silent exchange with Frank Massey over her head, though she pretended not to be. Yes, she was in a foul mood this morning. A restless night had left her with a headache which coffee and aspirin had failed to shift. It was totally irrational to allow the episode with Don Trotton to nag at her. Once having landed herself in that absurd situation last night, she hadn't really handled things too badly. But the aftertaste was still acid in her mouth. Damn the man, damn him to hell!

Honest, God-fearing people like the McEvoys wouldn't be Sunday morning lie-abeds. Kate wasn't surprised, therefore, that when Duncan McEvoy was brought in to her some forty-five minutes later, he was soberly dressed in a dark suit, white shirt and tie, with well-polished shoes. He looked perplexed, all of a fluster. But then, dropping his eyes from her hard stare, he took in the note lying before her on her desk. He turned pale. So, she'd been right.

"Sit down, Mr. McEvoy. This interview will be tape-recorded. Two tapes will be used, one of which will immediately be resealed and retained as evidence in any court proceedings that may follow. Sergeant!"

Boulter loaded the machine, pressed the Record button, and performed the necessary preliminaries . . . time and place, those present. He then informed McEvoy of his legal rights, and cautioned him. "You do not have to say anything unless you wish to do so, but what you say may be given in evidence."

"Now, Mr. McEvoy," Kate began, "I want you to tell me why you sent this anonymous letter about George Jessop."

"L—l—letter?" he stammered. "I don't know what you're talking about."

"Oh, I think you do. Of course, if you want to waste police time by forcing us to go through the tedious process of a forensic examination of the letter, then that is what we'll have to do. It won't be difficult to prove authorship."

This was a bluff. The likelihood of a forensic examination incriminating McEvoy beyond any doubt was far from certain. But luckily the bluff worked.

"It's true," he insisted on a high-pitched note of defiance. "Every single word is true."

"So you admit that you wrote the letter?"

He shrugged and looked sullen. Boulter said, "Please answer the Chief Inspector's question."

"I don't seem to have much choice, do I? All right, then—yes, I wrote it. But I don't see why you're treating me like this. You ought to be *grateful* to me, for putting you onto the murderer."

Kate fixed him with a direct look, and said, "When I interviewed you before, on Thursday, you stated that you'd spent the previous evening at home, except for going out to fetch one of your daughters from guides at around seven forty-five. Yet in this letter you refer to the activities of Mr. Jessop at *midnight.* How do you explain the discrepancy?"

He thought about it, while his gaze was held trapped by Kate's. Then he decided to bluster. "I don't have to explain anything to you."

"That is your right, of course, but you'd be well advised to give me an explanation."

More time for thought. A hand came up involuntarily, the thin fingers hovering around his mouth as if to guard incautious words. Finally, he muttered, "I . . . I had to go to the office for something I'd forgotten. I didn't mention it before, it seemed unimportant."

"What was it you'd forgotten, Mr. McEvoy?"

"Really, how can that be relevant? Surely it is what I *saw* that matters."

"Answer the Chief Inspector's question," came from Boulter again. "Remember that this is a murder enquiry, sir."

McEvoy still looked stubborn. Kate said, quietly but persistently, "If you refuse to answer, I'll be forced to extend my enquiries. Do you really want my officers interrogating your wife again, and your daughters, your neighbours, and all kinds of people who might conceivably help us to get at the truth?"

McEvoy's frame shook with panic, and Kate felt a momentary compassion for him. She watched his inner struggle, saw his realization of defeat. Each word was brought forth slowly, kicking and screaming with reluctance.

"I'll have to tell you everything, I suppose. There's nothing else for it. I am deeply ashamed to have to admit it, Chief Inspector, but I went to Croptech that night for an illegal purpose. In point of fact, to steal."

Kate stifled down her surprise. "To steal what, exactly?"

He sighed; a deep, juddering sigh. "A few months ago an old barn standing within the Croptech grounds was demolished as being surplus to requirements and not worth the expense of repairing. The stone blocks were stacked for possible future use as walling material. My wife and I had often talked of building a decorative wall across our garden to divide off the vegetable plot, and these blocks of weathered Cotswold stone seemed ideal. As we should only require a relatively small amount and as the firm had no plan in mind for it, I . . . well, I regret to have to tell you that I helped myself to a few stones from time to time."

Kate heard a stifled gurgle from Boulter, and she had a job not to burst out laughing herself. She asked incredulously, "Are you saying that you made a number of trips to Croptech in the dead of night for the purpose of removing some blocks of building stone?"

"Yes." He said it in a whisper. "You see, it's very expensive to buy, Cotswold stone, and . . ."

She wanted to ask him why the hell he hadn't just requested permission from Sir Noah to help himself to the stuff. But that wasn't relevant to her enquiry.

"And you went there on Wednesday night this week, the night that Dr. Trent was killed?"

"Yes. I didn't know about that then, of course, or I—"

"Tell me exactly what happened. Tell me what you saw."

"Well, I left home about half-past eleven and drove to Croptech. There's a side gate along the lane near Jessop's bungalow. On Wednesday night his lights were still on and I didn't want to risk his hearing me. So I parked my car a little way off, and waited for him to go to bed. But then his front door opened and the dog ran out, followed by Jessop and a woman. They were laughing." He said that as if it were the final obscenity. A man and a woman *laughing* together.

"Could you hear what they were saying, Mr. McEvoy?"

"Oh no, I wasn't close enough for that." His voice had lost some of its deep sense of shame now that he was discussing the iniquities of others. "They walked over to a car that I hadn't noticed before because it was parked round at the side of the bungalow, and they drove off in it with the dog."

"Could you identify the woman?"

McEvoy shook his head. "A large car came by just then, with its headlights full on. I was dazzled for a while."

"Would the other driver have seen them?"

"No, he couldn't have, not the direction he was going."

"You got a glimpse before you were dazzled," said Boulter. "Was the woman tall or short?"

"About average, I'd say."

"What was she wearing? Is there anything you can tell us?"

"No, not really. Just that she looked a bit of a . . . well, a tart. You know, lots of hair and the way she was dressed."

"What did you think at the time about where they were going?" asked Kate. "What they were doing?"

"Just that they were up to no good. I mean, a man like that."

"A man like that?" She let the query hang.

"Well, he's a gaolbird. Maybe you didn't know that, but I looked the case up in the reference library. He was sentenced to three years imprisonment for killing a young chap, a pupil at the school where he was a teacher. It all came out at the trial that Jessop and this boy . . . filthy stuff!"

"We are perfectly aware of Keith George Jessop's background, Mr. McEvoy."

"Oh!" His face fell with disappointment. "Well then . . . you know what a depraved character he is. And now he's carrying on with women. What I say is, if a man's killed once, then why not a second time and a third time? It stands to reason."

"My advice to you," Kate said, "is to keep your opinion of Mr. Jessop very much to yourself. Otherwise, you could end up in serious trouble. I shall probably want to talk to you again, but you can go for now."

He remained in his seat, looking at her anxiously. "What am I to tell my wife?"

"That's up to you. Just remember my warning."

"But . . . aren't I going to be charged?"

"What with?"

Bewilderment. "Theft, I suppose."

"We have had no complaint made to us about building stone being stolen from Croptech. However, I don't like people who write vicious anonymous letters, though I'm not proposing to take any action on that issue. For the moment."

After he'd been escorted out, Boulter returned and said, "I'd call him a prize shit, guv."

"Agreed. On the other hand, Tim, the police would have a nice cushy job if there were no worse villains than he is."

"You believe his story, do you?"

"I think he laid his soul bare to us. So, a further chat with George Jessop is indicated."

"I'll have him brought in, then."

"No, we'll go to him. I want to see how he reacts when we confront him with this. If necessary, we can bring him back with us."

A hullabaloo of barking greeted Kate and Boulter when they approached Jessop's bungalow. From inside a sharp order silenced the dog. A minute later Jessop came to the door. No punctilious, God-fearing churchman he! Sunday morning found him slouching around in pyjama bottoms and a crumpled T-shirt. His yellowish-grey hair was still uncombed.

"What do you want now? Can't you leave a man alone?" His manner was belligerent, but Kate saw a trace of fear in his eyes.

"I've a few more questions for you, Mr. Jessop. May we come in?"

"Could I stop you?" he asked, and stood aside.

The front door opened directly into the living room, where the dog, a cross-bred collie, had retired grumbling to an old blanket on the floor. The furniture in the room was minimal, shabby, obviously bought secondhand. Kate was a little surprised by the number of books around, stacked untidily on every ledge and dumped in piles on the floor. But perhaps it wasn't to be wondered at, given Jessop's background; books would be a solace for a man denied the more intellectual career for which he'd been trained.

"Perhaps you'd like us to wait while you get dressed, Mr. Jessop," Kate began politely.

"Why? Are you taking me away?"

"Not for the moment."

"Then I'll stay just as I am, for the moment."

"As you wish." He hadn't invited them to sit down, and for this interview Kate preferred the formality of conducting it on her feet. "Mr. Jessop, I want to talk again about Wednesday evening, the night that Dr. Trent was killed. You told Sergeant Boulter that after doing your usual round of the Croptech premises at approximately eight o'clo' ', you returned here and watched television for the remainder of the evening, going to bed at about eleven-thirty."

"What about it?"

"We now have evidence that this was not a true account. That in fact you were still up at past midnight, that you had a woman with you, and that you and she left here by car together, with your dog."

"Who the hell . . ."

"Go on, Mr. Jessop."

"Whoever told you that was lying. I was alone that night. I . . . I might've gone to bed a bit later than I said. And I did take the dog out for a bit of a stroll last thing."

"Why didn't you mention that to Sergeant Boulter?"

"It didn't seem important. It's just routine. A dog must have exercise."

"And who was the woman?"

Jessop glared at her. "I told you, there wasn't any woman." He gave a hollow, unconvincing laugh. "I should be so lucky."

"It's women you go for nowadays then, Jessop, is it?" asked Boulter.

"You've no right to let him talk to me like that," he said furiously, to Kate.

"It's a fair enough question in the circumstances," she said. "What's your answer?"

Jessop looked as if he'd like to hit her. The dog sensed this too, and gave a low, threatening growl. Jessop gruffly ordered it to be quiet. The interruption had given him a moment's thinking time.

"If you imagine I had anything to do with those two murders, you're completely up the spout. Beyond being the one to find Trent's body, I was in no way involved and I have no idea who killed them. That's all I'm going to say."

"That sort of attitude isn't going to help you," said Kate in an appeal to reason. "If you're innocent of these crimes, as you insist you are, then you have nothing to fear from our investigation. But we are intent on discovering the truth about that night. Just the truth."

"You wouldn't have such touching faith in British justice if you were on my side of the fence."

Calmly, Kate reverted to her earlier question. "Who was the woman? You might just as well tell us, because we are going to track her down in the end. We'll be discreet . . . as discreet as we possibly can be. But we have to know who she is."

"I'm telling you nothing."

"You still deny there was anyone with you on Wednesday night?"

"I'm telling you nothing. Now will you please leave?"

Boulter was about to object, but Kate checked him with a raised finger. "I'm going to give you the rest of the day to think things over, Mr. Jessop. If you're not prepared to be straight with us tomorrow, the consequences won't be very pleasant. Good day to you."

Boulter asked, as they were driving away, "You want a surveillance put on him, guv?"

"No, Tim. Leave him alone for the time being."

"You let him off pretty lightly, I reckon."

"Do you? The mystery woman might take a different attitude, when he tells her about our visit."

"Think he will tell her?"

"I'm sure of it."

"And she'll make him talk, is that your idea?"

"Something like that."

"Well, I only hope you're proved right." His tone said that he knew she'd be proved wrong.

Midday Sunday, Kate managed to get home for lunch. A rare treat! Stonebank Cottage was the one place she could relax. Felix put on cold chicken and various salads, with a bowl of ripe peaches to follow.

"This is my sort of food," said Kate, helping herself generously.

"I'm glad you appreciate me, girl."

"Oh, I do . . ."

"But?"

It followed logically for Kate to say, "I lost a house over at Ingram's Green yesterday. Just because I was too tied up to keep an appointment to view. Damn shame, it sounded ideal for me."

Felix nodded her head, and a few more stray hairs broke free from her loose topknot. She tucked them back absentmindedly, jabbing home one of the pins. "So that's what put you in such a disgusting mood last night."

"Mmm!" Kate's grunt was ambiguous. She had no intention of telling the whole sorry story to her aunt. Don Trotton was best swept firmly under the carpet.

"Something else will come along soon, girl."

"I'm beginning to wonder."

Felix took another spoonful of diced beetroot in sour cream. "Pity you had to snap poor Richard's head off like that."

"Poor Richard? Huh!"

"Yes, poor Richard. Being a friend of yours, he loses out professionally."

Kate raised her eyebrows. "Your logic defeats me sometimes, Felix. Elucidate."

"I shouldn't need to. Can't you see that if it wasn't for your friendship, Richard, as editor of the local paper, would be badgering you to death. Trying to trap you into making an unguarded comment and so on. As it is, he has to keep pussyfooting around you, hoping and praying that he won't miss out on a big story."

"Is that what he told you?"

"He didn't have to tell me. It's as plain as a pikestaff."

"Listen," Kate said crossly, "Richard Gower is first, second and third a journalist. Being a friend of mine comes somewhere around number thirty-three."

"That's what you think, is it, girl?"

Fiona Chapman was waiting for Kate when she got back to the Incident Room after lunch. There was now a trace more colour in her thin face, as if she was beginning to come to terms with the shock of her brother's death.

"Come on through, will you?" Kate invited, heading for her office.

"You said I was to let you know if I noticed anything strange at Gavin's cottage," Mrs. Chapman began, when they were seated. "I do hope I'm not bothering you about nothing, but . . ." She hesitated, looking uncertain.

"You think there's something missing, do you?"

"Well, no, it's the other way round, something that doesn't belong. It's probably not important and I'm just being silly, but . . . as you *asked* me to . . ."

"You were quite right to come," Kate assured her. "What was it you found?"

"It's this," she said, opening her handbag and taking out an audio tape in its plastic case. "I was sorting things out this morning, trying to decide what to keep and what to throw out or have sold, and I found this Tom Jones tape among Gavin's collection."

Kate took it from her and looked at the label thoughtfully. "What's so special about this one?"

"Well, it just isn't Gavin's sort of thing at all."

"It could have been a present from someone, couldn't it? Someone who didn't quite understand his taste in music."

"That's hard to imagine. After all, what friends did he have?"

"Not many, it seems."

"Virtually none. My brother, as I expect you've already realized, was a snob. An intellectual snob. And his snobbery extended to music, I'm afraid. Popular music of any kind was something he just couldn't stomach. He'd never have desecrated his personal library with a Tom Jones tape. It's past belief."

Kate pondered on how significant the find might be. "Could it have been a secret vice of your brother's? People are sometimes addicted to the very thing they most vehemently deplore."

"Not Gavin, I'm sure of it. The very lightest sort of music he could ever tolerate would be a Tchaikovsky piano concerto—something like that."

"So what do you make of finding this tape?" Kate asked. "Have you any kind of explanation?"

"No, I'm totally mystified."

"Let's go back to the idea that it was a gift. A gift, perhaps, from someone he specially didn't want to offend by refusing to accept it."

"I can't imagine who."

"Someone," Kate suggested, "with whom your brother was on intimate terms?"

Fiona Chapman gave a quick, nervous laugh. "Gavin?"

"It's often difficult for people to imagine their close relatives in a romantic or sexual involvement."

"I don't think so. Not Gavin."

Kate regarded her thoughtfully. She had no wish to distress Trent's sister, who already had plenty to contend with, but she couldn't let the chance go by of extracting a useful clue.

"Suppose," she said slowly, in a level, non-judgmental voice, "it wasn't a woman, but another man?"

Fiona Chapman looked up sharply. Not shocked, but deeply surprised. "You mean . . . gay? Oh no, I don't think so. In fact, I'm certain of it."

"What makes you so sure?"

The worried eyes were shrewd and candid. "I don't know, but I just am. After all, we spent our childhood together, and I think I knew Gavin better than anyone else could have done. No, Chief Inspector, I'll never believe that. And not just because I don't want to. If—and it's a big if—there *was* any sexual relationship in Gavin's life, it would have been with a woman. He'd have had to be really besotted if he actually managed to bring himself to *listen* to Tom Jones with her." Again that unamused laugh at the very idea of such a thing.

Kate had a thought, and rang for Boulter to come in. She introduced the two of them, then held up the tape.

"Sergeant, Mrs. Chapman found this Tom Jones tape at her brother's cottage. It isn't at all in line with his musical taste, and we're wondering where it came from. Check the fingerprint records and find out what, if anything, was found on it."

He was soon back, with some interesting information. "All the tapes in Dr. Trent's collection carried his fingerprints. A couple of them carried prints of one of the cleaners—presumably he'd happened to leave them out and they'd been put away in the cabinet. Or maybe, they'd liked the idea of music while they worked. But that Tom Jones one, in addition to Dr. Trent's prints, also carried prints of an as yet unidentified person."

"Mmm! Mrs. Chapman, I'd like to hold on to this tape for the time being. Sergeant, put someone on checking every retail outlet in the district, and see if anything emerges about who might have bought it. We can be pretty confident that it wouldn't have been Dr. Trent himself."

A couple more aspirins did nothing to subdue Kate's headache. She stuck grimly at her desk, trying to cope with the swelling avalanche of reports pouring in from the squad . . . routine interviews with each and every one who'd had any contact with either of the two dead men. From Frank Massey she already knew that nothing of import had come to light, but she still read each report meticulously in the hope of finding some hidden nugget.

By around eight-thirty even black coffee failed to keep her going, and she suddenly gave in and slammed the files shut. Her stomach rebelled at the thought of food. Bed beckoned urgently.

At Stonebank Cottage she dealt with Felix's solicitations in short order, climbed the narrow stairs and shut her bedroom door. Half an hour later, lying down with the curtains drawn against a spectacular sunset, she knew to her infinite relief that the throbbing was at long last abating and sleep was in her grasp.

Downstairs, the telephone rang. Felix answered it after a couple of rings. Kate tensed, awaiting the summons to go down, but it didn't come. She tried to settle back into the pre-sleep state, but realized from her aunt's tone of voice that she was arguing with someone. So it probably *was* for her, after all, and Felix was being protective.

With a weary sigh Kate pushed aside the covers and stumped downstairs in her pyjamas.

"It's Dr. Cheryl Miller," said Felix, covering the mouthpiece. "I told her you'd gone to bed, but—"

"Hand it over," Kate said. She was up now, so what the hell? "Chief Inspector Maddox here."

"Oh, thank the lord. Listen, can I see you?"

"*Now*, you mean?"

"Well, yes. I have something to tell you, and the sooner the better. As you're at home, shall I come to see you there?"

"No, I'll come to you. I remember where it is you live. About half an hour, right?"

"People are so inconsiderate," her aunt grumbled as she hung up. "Surely it could have waited till the morning, whatever it is? This won't do your head any good at all."

Kate laughed wonderingly. "The strange thing is, my headache seems to have gone."

"Oh well, I suppose it's no use arguing with you."

Minutes later, driving through the deepening twilight, Kate's head was as clear as a bell. Things were moving and she scented a breakthrough. But her buoyant mood was deflated by envy when she clapped eyes on the Old Rectory at Lower Aston. Dating from the good old days when a congregation of some twenty souls was felt to justify a parsonage of as many bedrooms, it was now converted into perhaps eight flats. You'd imagine, Kate thought sourly, that with so many of these old country residences that were too large for modern life being divided up into smaller units, there'd be a nook somewhere for her.

Cheryl Miller's flat was on the ground floor. The spacious living room must have once been the dining room. Long sash windows on either side of a central glazed door overlooked a paved terrace with an elegant stone balustrade and Grecian urns. *Oh, Kate, how happy you'd be if only this were yours.*

"Lovely place you have here," she commented.

Cheryl Miller nodded vaguely. This evening there was an air of uncertainty about her, which diluted her high-voltage sexual aura.

"It must be important, for you to ask to see me at this time of night," Kate went on.

"Yes, er . . . sit down, won't you? Drink?"

Kate sat, choosing for this formal occasion one of the two chairs at a small round table. "Nothing to drink, thanks."

"I hear you questioned George Jessop again this morning," Cheryl Miller said, pulling out the other chair for herself.

Kate didn't reply, keeping her expression neutral.

"It's about that I want to speak to you. You claim to know that there was a woman at George's cottage on Wednesday night, so there isn't much point in his going on denying it. Obviously you'll never leave him alone until you dig out the truth."

Good God, Cheryl Miller and George Jessop! Kate could hardly believe it. She said carefully, "I wish *he* could appreciate that fact."

"I've tried to make him see sense, but he can be so damned stubborn. I can understand his point of view, of course. A man with a record like his is scared to death of tangling with the police."

Where were the surprises going to end? "You know about all that?"

"Yes, I know."

"Let us get this quite straight, Dr. Miller, so there's no possibility of misunderstanding. You're saying that the woman with Jessop at his cottage on Wednesday night was yourself?"

"Yes."

"You and he are lovers?"

"No, we are not lovers." Some of her old spark returned. She said, ironically, "You find it hard to believe, don't you, Mrs. Maddox, that I could have any sort of non-sexual relationship with a man?"

"Jessop doesn't strike me as a man with whom a highly intelligent woman like you would find an intellectual rapport."

"George—or rather, Keith—wasn't always a caretaker. But then you know that."

"I understand he was formerly a schoolteacher. Is that sufficient to account for your interest in him? Or is it just that you like helping lame dogs? Incidentally, I'd be interested to hear how you came to know about Jessop's past. Who told you?"

"I didn't need to be told."

"You remembered the case, you mean, and somehow connected Jessop with it when he came here?"

"You could say that."

"Please, Dr. Miller, don't fence with me. You wanted to see me this evening because you had something to impart. So I suggest you get on with it."

Cheryl Miller's hands lay on the polished table top. She made no effort to conceal the fact that her fingers were clutching convulsively. "I told you that I was the woman with Keith that night. Surely that's enough?"

"It isn't nearly enough. I have to know *why.*"

In the silence could be heard, faintly, the sound of television from another flat. Kate waited, looking at her very directly. Ten seconds, twenty . . . then Cheryl Miller stood up in such a hasty movement that her chair toppled and fell to the carpet with a thump. She took no notice, but went to the empty fireplace and stood with her back to Kate, leaning her hands on the high marble mantelpiece. Then she suddenly swung round, and her eyes were bright with bitterness.

"All right, then, you'll find out in the end, so why not now? Keith Jessop is my husband."

Ten

Kate concealed her astonishment at this revelation. She said evenly, "Come and sit down and tell me all about it."

Dr. Miller hesitated a moment, then grimaced. "It'll be a relief in a way to talk, after keeping it dark for so long. Er . . . are you sure you won't have a drink?"

"Not for me, thanks. But you go ahead if you feel you could use one."

Kate's brain, after the fuzz of the day, was now needle sharp; she didn't want to blunt it with alcohol. She watched while Cheryl Miller went to a small cabinet and brought out a bottle of gin and a twist-stem glass.

Pouring a stiff measure, she swallowed it neat, then came back to sit at the table.

"Keith and I split up ages ago," she said. "We never bothered to get a divorce, though. Neither of us relished the publicity, for one thing, after that awful court case."

"Was that what caused the separation, his arrest and imprisonment?"

"Oh no, it happened a couple of years before that."

"How did you come to marry him in the first place?"

"You find it odd?" The wry laugh held a thread of sadness. "Keith didn't always look the no-hoper he does now. When we were at university together he was rather dishy. But then so were plenty of other men I knew, and I'd already had several flings. None of them serious. No way was I planning to get married at the tender age of twenty-two . . . there was far too much I wanted to do first. But with Keith there was something more than just physical attraction between us. Not love, exactly . . . not really. The point about Keith was—and still is, come to that—that he wasn't too strong on self-confidence. Not like I was. He needed someone to prop him up, to build his self-esteem, and the prospect of being the person to do that appealed to me. You see, all my growing up years I'd been unwanted. My mother died when I was only three, and my father remarried and started a new family. I was just a leftover, an encumbrance. Nobody ever *needed* me, not until Keith came along. It gave me a really great feeling to be important in somebody's life. That's why I married him."

"But it didn't last, that feeling?"

"In a certain way it did—and it's still there, even now. The problem was, Keith's sexuality was always somewhat ambivalent. I knew that he'd had a couple of homosexual experiments at university, but so had a number of other chaps. It didn't shock me. But when we'd been married about three years I discovered that he was fooling around with adolescent boys—kids he was teaching. We had a blazing row and Keith begged me to forgive him and swore that it wouldn't ever happen again. But then it did. Apart from feeling bitterly hurt—betrayed—I tried to argue him out of it for his *own* sake. I pointed out that he was playing with fire and that he'd lose his job if it ever came to light. Not to mention the potential for blackmail. But it wasn't long before I found that I'd been wasting my breath. That's when I decided I wanted out. Keith begged me not to leave him. He actually cried when I refused to change my mind."

"You didn't divorce him, though."

"One way and another I just never got around to it. I was in no mood to get married again. And I very much doubt that I shall ever want to now." She made a face at Kate. "You must have gathered my opinion of men."

"You've made that fairly clear."

"Would I be right in thinking you feel much the same way?"

"You'd be wrong. I was very happily married, some years back now, but my husband was killed." Kate forebore to mention that her three-year-old daughter had been killed at the same time; she wasn't looking for sympathy.

"Oh, I see. Tough luck! But you're on your own now, aren't you? There's been a lot of talk around here about you—that strange beast, a *female* Detective Chief Inspector."

"Being talked about is the price one has to pay for getting anywhere as a professional woman. You must know that."

"Don't I just! But you don't seem to mind."

"I mind like hell," Kate said, with feeling. "But there's not a lot I can do about it."

"No? I've found a few effective ways of cutting men down to size. They have such sensitive egos."

"You're an odd mixture, Dr. Miller. Contemptuous of men in general, yet protective towards one particular man."

"Must be a stray mother-hen gene in me, eh?"

"You haven't explained how it came about that Keith . . . that George Jessop came to work at Croptech."

Cheryl Miller's face clouded. "He'd had a rough time, poor devil. That boy who got killed . . . it was a pure accident, as Keith insisted in his defence. Of that I'm convinced. I'm not making excuses for him, Keith was a bloody fool. But that's all he was. He just isn't capable of deliberately killing someone to save his own skin—even though that boy was holding him to ransom. Yet the public was baying for Keith's blood as if he were a murderer. When he came out of gaol, he found that he hadn't a hope in hell of getting a job. No job of any kind. His reputation followed him around. I'd kept vaguely in touch with him while he was inside. There was never any question of our getting back together again, but neither could I abandon Keith completely. Anyway, when the caretaker at Croptech left, I jumped in and recommended Keith for the vacancy. I was totally straight with old Kimberley, and to do him justice he took it in his stride. I was able to guarantee Keith's honesty, and I pointed out that he had a practical bent when it came to doing odd jobs and repairs. Kimberley and I agreed that the truth had to be kept strictly under wraps. If it were to emerge, Keith would have been hounded out of his job by local public opinion. And very likely so would I."

"And you've managed to keep your relationship secret all this time? You must have taken a lot of care."

"And then some! Whenever we meet up at work, we never do more than just acknowledge one another, but we get together quite often. You may think that strange, but we always did get along on an intellectual level. Keith's got a good brain, a keen mind, and we enjoy talking things over. Besides, it's a relief to us both to be able to drop the pretence and just be ourselves. I always go to Keith's place, rather than have him come here, as there aren't so many people around. And I always go late in the evening, to be on the safe side. But it seems our luck ran out. Who was it who bloody saw us?"

"You're not entitled to know that," Kate said briskly. "I'll have to ask you to give me a formal statement about all this, Dr. Miller. But you needn't worry, it will remain confidential. Unless, of course, we have to bring a charge against either one of you. Or both of you."

Cheryl Miller's cool deserted her. "But I've explained everything," she protested. "Keith and I had nothing whatever to do with those murders. So what's all this about bringing charges?"

"Calm down and listen to me. You're far too intelligent to really expect that what you've told me puts you in the clear as far as those murders go. It's a well-known fact that you harboured a professional grudge against both victims. Added to which, you and Jessop made false statements about where you were last Wednesday night, the night Trent was killed. At this stage of my enquiry that puts you both on the suspect list. You must see that."

"I guess so, but—"

"But nothing! You've just claimed to be the woman seen with Jessop that night, but it turns out that you two are married. All the more reason, it could be argued, for you to lie to protect Jessop. Or you could both be in this together."

"For God's sake, you can't honestly believe that we—"

"What I happen to believe is beside the point. I still have to conduct this investigation strictly according to the book. That means following up any inconsistencies that show up, and each and every new lead, however come by. If I didn't, I'd be putting my head on the block." Kate grinned wryly. "There's quite enough hassle in this job without asking for trouble."

Cheryl Miller let out a long sigh of resignation. "Okay, you've made your point, but you'll find out I'm telling the truth." She looked at Kate with her head tilted to one side. "Being a high-level cop must be a tough job when you're female."

"It isn't easy. But then maybe I wouldn't want it to be easy."

"You like the challenge? The chance to prove yourself against men?"

"Don't *you?*"

Cheryl's mouth twisted angrily. "It doesn't matter how bloody good you are, the male establishment has always got the whip hand. We'll never overcome that."

Maybe, Kate thought, her passionate feminism could be turned to good use. "You know, you might be in a position to help me quite a bit. That is, if you choose to."

"Oh? How's that?"

"You knew both the murdered men, and a lot better than most people did. Especially Gavin Trent. You can probably tell me something about them that might give a new slant to the investigation."

"I can't imagine what."

"Think carefully. Did you notice any change in their manner towards you latterly? Or towards anyone else? Did you get the slightest hint that something might have altered in their lives? Were you told anything about either of them that might give me a lead? Or overhear anything?"

Dr. Miller was already shaking her head. "As far as Kimberley was concerned, I had very little to do with him. Deliberately. I felt pretty fed up with him ever since he appointed Gavin Trent over my head. As for Gavin . . . well, we'd reached the stage of hardly being on speaking terms unless it was directly discussing work. And even then it took all my self-control to be civil to the man. If you really want to know, he was a total shit. Apart from work, I scarcely ever saw him. So sorry, glad as I'd be to help, I honestly can't think of a thing."

"I understand that last Monday Trent lost his temper with Roger Barlow when a glass retort got smashed. Was that worse than usual?"

"I suppose it was, really. Gavin nearly went berserk. Come to think of it, the atmosphere in the lab during the previous few weeks had been marginally less poisonous than we'd all grown accustomed to. I don't mean that Gavin was any nicer to work with, but he seemed a bit less . . . how can I put it? He seemed more wrapped up in himself, and less bothered about what other people were up to. Less interfering, less ready to find fault. Am I making any sense?"

"You might be making a lot of sense. Can you amplify a bit more?"

Dr. Miller's hands clutched at the air, as if trying to grasp something intangible. "There was a sort of inner triumph about him. Smug satisfaction. As if he knew something the rest of us didn't know. As if he'd got something over other people. No, this is crazy. I'm imagining things. I'm too prejudiced against Gavin Trent to judge his behaviour impartially. Why don't you ask Violet Sneddon? She's the level-headed sort, and she'd tell you better than I can. Oh, I've just thought, you could ask the woman who cleaned house for him. She might know something."

"Dr. Trent didn't have just one woman, he used a contract cleaning service. They sent different people, whoever happened to be available on the day, so no one was able to tell us much about him."

"I'm talking about *before* that, a while back. It was a Mrs. Parkes. Joan Parkes, I think. She quit because she had to go and look after her grandchildren while her daughter was in hospital. She's back home now, though. I bumped into her in a shop the other day—on Friday—and of course she wanted to have a good natter about Gavin being murdered, and how terrible it all was."

Kate was cursing inwardly. As Chief Investigating Officer, the responsibility for the slip-up was hers. Which wouldn't prevent her tearing a strip off the two detectives assigned to interviewing the various cleaners, who had failed to elicit the fact that the domestic cleaning service had been doing the job at Trent's cottage for such a short time.

"Do you happen to know where this Mrs. Parkes lives?"

"Sorry. It's somewhere around Aston Pringle, but I'm not sure just where."

"Not to worry. We'll find her. Thanks for this."

"Will it help?"

"Could well do."

"I'm glad. Will you have a drink with me now?"

"Why not?"

Kate suddenly recalled the Tom Jones tape that Trent's sister had brought to her. The fingerprints on it had to be identified, and Cheryl Miller was one of the people to be checked on. She put it humorously. "D'you mind if we take a set of your dabs?"

Cheryl paused in the act of opening the drinks cabinet. "Hey, what is this?"

"We have a whole mass of prints from here, there and God knows where that we haven't yet pinpointed. We'll be asking a number of people to co-operate, so they can be eliminated."

"And I'm at the top of the list?"

"You're *on* the list. There's no order of precedence."

"It would be a waste of time asking who the others are?"

"A complete waste of time. Whisky, please, if you have any. With soda. Don't drown it."

Cheryl filled the glasses for them both, handed one to Kate and raised hers.

"Sod men!"

"Cheers!" said Kate, and sipped her whisky appreciatively. She had to admit that she liked Cheryl Miller. Much of the woman's abrasive style was explained by what she'd just revealed about her life. But a liking for Cheryl wasn't sufficient reason to put her in the clear as a suspect.

It was exactly the sort of assignment that DC Bell (Ringer to his mates) delighted in. A pleasant half day's outing (to London on this occasion) and a chance to use the shrewdness he'd developed in sixteen years as a detective constable. The job appealed to the actor *manqué* in him.

"We're treading delicate ground here, Graham," DCI Maddox had warned when she'd briefed him that morning. "If we put a foot wrong, Lord Balmayne could make big trouble for us." She told Bell the general line his questioning should take. "But nothing heavy, mind. I just want to have your impressions. I'm leaving the approach to you."

Bell took a train to Paddington and a tube to Warwick Avenue. Emerging to daylight, he first paid a courtesy visit to the local copshop to explain his intrusion onto their territory, and gladly accepted the offer of a mug of coffee and a sticky Danish. Forty minutes later, armed with directions, he found the address he sought. Little Venice, they called the area. A proper Millionaires' Row, by the look of it.

His ring was answered by a man so excessively short that Bell had to adjust his gaze to a sharply downward angle. Grey-haired, wrinkle-faced, he was dressed in black trousers and a white shirt with the sleeves rolled up to the elbow. Bell introduced himself, flashing his warrant card.

"Would this be the residence of Lord Balmayne?"

"It's his lordship's London residence."

"And you'd be, sir?"

"I am Jefferies, his lordship's manservant. If you're hoping to talk to him, you've made a wasted journey. He's presently staying at his home in Gloucestershire."

Bell knew this, but hid the fact. "Oh, dear. Perhaps I could have a word with you, then, Mr. Jefferies."

"I suppose so, though I can't imagine why." He stood aside for the detective to enter.

"To tell you the truth," said Bell with an air of confidentiality, "I can't see a lot of point in it myself. Still, it's not for the likes of us to question what our bosses want, is it?" He followed Jefferies through the hallway to a small sitting room at the rear of the house that overlooked a pretty latticed patio. "It's in connection with the death of Sir Noah Kimberley. I expect you've heard about that?"

"Yes, but what's it got to do with—"

"Not a blind thing, probably. This is just a matter of police routine. Somebody claims to have been at a certain place at a certain time, and we poor footsloggers are expected to check it down to the last tiny detail. In Lady Kimberley's statement she mentioned that she was staying here overnight when her husband first disappeared, and I've been sent all this way to verify that fact. My report will get fed into the computer and probably never see the light of day again. Hot today, isn't it? If you were to suggest a cup of tea, I wouldn't say no."

Jefferies caught on. "Or a nice cool glass of beer?"

"You've twisted my arm," said Bell, and made himself comfortable in an easy chair. In a few moments Jefferies, too, was seated. They raised companionable glasses.

"Mud in your eye," said Bell, and took a long swallow. "That's laid the dust very nicely. You've got it comfortable here, I must say, Mr. Jefferies. This'd be your room?"

A nod. "And upstairs I've a nice-sized bedroom with my own bathroom. You couldn't want a more considerate master than Lord Balmayne."

"Worked for him for some time, have you?"

"Nigh on twenty years, now."

"You've seen a few interesting things, then?"

A slight show of reserve. "I'm not one to talk about my employer."

"No, of course not. Naturally. I just meant . . . well, working for a leading public figure like you do, you must've met all kinds of top people in your time."

"My word, haven't I just! Politicians, show biz people. And pretty well everyone who's anyone in the opera and music world."

"Lord Balmayne does a lot of good work, I believe. Holding concerts to raise money for charity and so on."

"Indeed he does. His lordship is still financially involved in a number of operatic productions, of course, but he says he's past all the hassle of being a major impresario any more. These days he devotes more of his time to charitable work. He's always flitting around, here, there and everywhere."

"You don't go with him on his travels?"

"Not usually. I stay here. He likes to keep his various homes ready for instant occupation. He has a house in Paris, too, you know, as well as the one in Gloucestershire."

"Very nice for them as can afford it."

A couple more cans of cool beer were produced, poured and reflectively imbibed.

"He and Lady Kimberley have known each other for a long time, I believe?" Bell resumed.

"Oh yes, years and years. Back before my time, even. Of course, in those days she was still Vanessa Logan. Then she was made a Dame. I still call her Dame Vanessa when she's staying here."

"Comes often, does she?"

"Most times when she's in London. And Sir Noah, too. Well, he *did*. I wonder if it'll be back to the old days, now."

"The old days?"

The wrinkled eyes became reminiscent. "She was a damn fine-looking woman. Still is, of course, but . . . well, you know . . ."

"They got together, did they?"

"Well, off and on. He's always been quite a one for the ladies, but she's very special to him." Jefferies looked like a man who was suddenly afraid he might have said more than he should have done. He added quickly, "Mind you, there was none of that went on after Dame Vanessa was married. Definitely not. Oh, my word no!"

"You'd think they would have got hitched to each other. Or does he already have a wife somewhere?"

Jefferies shook his head. "A lifelong bachelor, the master is. Just not the marrying kind, I suppose."

The two men sat ruminating in silence for a bit. Then Bell pulled himself upright. "Well, I'd better get moving. This bit of nonsense that brought me here, can we just get that tidied up? The Friday of the gala, that's last Friday week . . . Lady Kimberley arrived here sometime in the afternoon, intending to take part in the show, but then she found that her throat was bad, and she couldn't sing after all?"

"That's right." But there was a sudden wariness in the little man's eyes.

"So instead she stayed put right here, nursing her sore throat, all through the evening and night. Have we got it right?"

"Correct." The confirmation was fast and emphatic.

"Nasty business for a singer, I should say, a throat infection. And coming just at the wrong time, too. It must have been very distressing for her."

Jefferies wasn't meeting Bell's eyes. He gave close attention to a speck on his trousers, picking at it with his fingernail.

"Very distressing, poor lady. She would have sung if she possibly could, I know her well enough for that. She'd hate to disappoint her public. But her throat just seemed to get worse and worse till she was really croaky."

"Lucky for her it didn't last long, wasn't it?" Bell squared up to his notebook again. "So, I'll just put down here that she arrived at . . . what time, exactly?"

"Let's see, it would have been about three-fifteen. Then she and his lordship went straight off to the theatre for the rehearsal, and they were back here at about five forty-five for some tea. It was then that Dame Vanessa finally realized that she'd never be able to sing that evening."

"I see. And from then on she didn't leave the house until . . . when would it have been?"

"Not until the next morning—Saturday. About ten-thirty."

"She was well enough to drive by then?"

Again a sudden wariness. "Well . . . I mean, a bad throat wouldn't stop her from *driving*, would it? She wrapped up well, of course. A scarf round her neck and so forth."

"What about his lordship's movements that evening? The Friday."

"His lordship? Oh, yes, well . . . he went off to the theatre for the performance. I mean, he had to put in an appearance, naturally. It was about seven or just after that he left the house. But at the interval he came home again, to be with her. Got here just after nine, I'd say." Jefferies pondered, then added, "They'd planned to go for a late supper at a restaurant after the gala, but in the circs I cooked them something light—just a soufflé."

"And he didn't go out again?"

"Oh no, he was at home all the time. They sat in the drawing room listening to music until Dame Vanessa went up to bed about eleven-thirty."

Bell wrote all this down in his notebook, then closed it with a snap. "That's that, then. Waste of time, really. Still, it's given me a trip to London and a pleasant chat over a beer, so I can't say it was all bad, can I?"

As he strolled towards Warwick Avenue tube station en route for Paddington, Bell composed in his mind the report he'd be putting in for the DCI. The gist of it, really, was going to be that twenty years' service with a generous and considerate employer could be counted on to buy a very special kind of loyalty.

Since Kate's promotion and transfer to the Cotswold division, she had grown accustomed to being discussed behind her back, to an awareness of mutterings and snide remarks which were cut off abruptly as she got within earshot. But all through Monday morning this seemed a great deal worse than ever before. It disturbed her, the feeling that something was going the rounds at her expense. In the end, she tackled Boulter about it.

"What the hell's going on, Tim?"

"Going on, ma'am?" That "ma'am" didn't pass unnoticed by Kate. She held out a temptation to Boulter's stomach, knowing that it never failed. "It's time for a bite to eat. Come on, let's go across to the Half Moon."

For once the sergeant didn't seem enthusiastic about the prospect of food. He was in a decidedly gloomy mood as he walked across the road to the pub with her. Kate ordered a pint of bitter for Boulter and a half of lager for herself, plus a plate of beef sandwiches. They retired to a table in a quiet corner of the bar.

"Right," she said. "Now spill it, Tim. Don't pretend you don't know what I'm talking about."

He looked thoroughly ill-at-ease. "It's nothing to do with me."

"Maybe not. But you know all about it. The lads are having a damn good laugh at my expense, aren't they? A lot more so than usual. And I expect you to tell me why."

Boulter gave an embarrassed laugh. "You ought to be able to figure it out, guv, the way you always seem to come up with answers to everything."

"Well, this time I can't." She added persuasively, "Come on, Tim, tell me as a friend."

The sergeant peeled back the corner of a sandwich and inspected the contents without interest, closing it again with a sigh.

"It's Don Trotton," he finally muttered. Then he burst out accusingly, "What the hell do you expect, getting involved with him like that?"

Kate felt a sick clawing in her stomach. "What are they saying, Tim? What am I supposed to have done?"

"You tell me." He sounded bitter. "You were there."

"All right, I will," she said on a note of cold dignity. "While you were in Cardiff, a chance of a house came up, but I lost it because Superintendent Joliffe held me up and I couldn't keep the appointment to view. Trotton happened to be around at the time and I let off steam to him. Later, he came back and told me there might be a flat becoming vacant where he lives. He said that his own flat was almost identical, and he suggested that I took a look at his to see if the one like it would suit me."

"And you went to Trotton's place?" asked Boulter incredulously. "Just like that?"

"Why the hell not? I realized immediately I got there that the flat wouldn't be any good for me, since it only has one bedroom. I told him so, and not to be too unfriendly I stayed to have a drink with him. Being Don Trotton, of course, he had to make a pass, and I had to slap him down—hard."

"That's not the way he's telling it," said Boulter grimly, and bit into a sandwich as if he didn't relish it in the least.

"Come on," Kate said, "I've got to know the worst. What's Don been saying?"

Boulter frowned into his beer. "Look, guv, it's not fair, putting the squeeze on me like this."

"You reckon it's fair for me to be slandered?" she retorted. "Not be in a position to hit back? I need to know exactly what story he's been telling."

"You won't get anything on Don Trotton, he's too bloody smart for that. It's all nudge-nudge, wink-wink stuff." And anyway, he was quite plainly thinking, most of what Trotton had hinted at was in all probability true. The thought that her sergeant felt disappointed in her made Kate feel twice as rotten.

"Okay, then, let me guess what Don Trotton is suggesting happened," she said sourly. "Kate Maddox jumped at the chance to drop by at his flat, and literally flung herself at him the minute she got there. Right so far?"

Boulter shuffled his feet under the table and stared down at his empty glass.

"All right, all right, don't answer," Kate said. "We can't hang about here anyway—we've got far too much to get through today. Drink up!"

But getting on with the job was easier said than done. It seemed impossible to make her brain function. Kate was tempted to have a real showdown with that bastard Trotton, but she knew it would be a useless exercise. As Boulter had pointed out, he was too bloody smart to have said anything she could nail him for. She'd end up even more humiliated than ever.

During the afternoon Richard Gower phoned to ask if there was any possibility of their getting together for dinner that evening. Kate was very ready to accept. When he added that he'd picked up a snippet of information she might find useful, it helped square her conscience about knocking off work earlier than she'd planned. It would be wonderful to get out of this hateful atmosphere for a while. To breathe some unpolluted air.

Kate went home just after six to bath and change. This evening she felt an urge to look specially feminine—for her own benefit as much as for Richard's. She put on a slim-cut dress in shrimp pink silk. Felix gave a whistle when she went downstairs.

"My word, that'll knock him sideways, girl. Special occasion, is it?"

"I just felt like dressing up a bit for a change. Ah, there's Richard's car. See you, Felix."

Richard drove her to the Old Tithe Barn, a classy restaurant near the Dodford polo ground. "My treat again this evening," he said as they left the car and walked towards the entrance.

"My God, you must be feeling flush."

"I just sold six full-page ads to the new supermarket that's opening in Marlingford. Twice what I'd expected to get from them. So you can indulge your expensive tastes to the limit."

"I never do come cheap," she threw back. They grinned at one another. *He's a really nice guy, Kate, a million miles from that turd Trotton.*

The overdone deference shown to patrons of the Old Tithe Barn would normally have stifled Kate. But this evening she felt in a mood to be fawned upon. Sitting over drinks in the intimate cocktail bar, the process of ordering their dinner became a summit conference at which headwaiter and wine-waiter engaged in grave debate.

When they were left alone, Richard said, "You look great tonight, Kate. And even more important, you look relaxed."

"About time, too. I've had a bitch of a day." She intended him to think she meant with the case.

"I almost hesitate to bring up my little item of news," he said. "You could do with a complete break from work."

"Spill it."

"I went up to London yesterday," he said. "It was a small get-together with some of the people at my old paper. The City editor is retiring, and he and his wife decided to throw an impromptu for intimates. As distinct from the official office function, that is. I was planning to ask you along, but after the treatment you gave me on Saturday night, it seemed best to skip the idea."

"Some other occasion," she said, with a grin of apology.

"Anyhow, the thing is I got talking to Hugh Bradley, the *Monitor*'s music critic. Knowing that I was now down in this neck of the woods, he soon brought the conversation around to our local murders. He's interested, of course, because one of the victims was Dame Vanessa Logan's husband."

"And?" Richard, being a journalist, liked to tell a story for maximum dramatic effect.

"Several fascinating things. Like, for instance, the reason Dame Vanessa suddenly decided to accept Sir Noah's proposal of marriage after ten years of beseeching on his part. Okay, okay, I'm getting there. At that time she was right at the top of the tree, as you know, but it seems that the word among the *cognoscenti* was that her voice was showing distinct signs of cracking up on her. Before much longer, everyone would realize it and she'd be past history as a prima donna. She decided that a romantic late-in-life marriage would make for a happier retirement."

"Like that, eh? Then it wasn't a love-match with Sir Noah?"

"More like an affection match, as far as she was concerned. Hugh reckons she was genuinely fond of the old boy. The chances are, though, that he'd never have won her hand but for the problem with her voice."

"But Lady Kimberley continued to sing in public. I gather she's done quite a number of charity galas since her marriage."

"Not quite the same thing, according to Hugh, as the strain on her voice of regular appearances on the professional stage. Besides, she can be selective about what she sings now, choosing arias that aren't too taxing vocally. Her technique, plus a benevolent audience, will obscure any weaknesses. Charity appearances offer Vanessa Logan a chance to stay in the public eye without risk to her reputation."

"So, she isn't quite the paragon she'd have people believe."

Richard shrugged. "Who is? Scratch the surface of anyone's life, and you get dirt under your fingernails."

"You don't need to tell me. Still, all this is food for thought."

"There's more."

"Out with it, then," she said impatiently.

"This is a bit more speculative, Kate. Good enough for a journalist to work on, maybe, but is it good enough for the police? It's being whispered around in musical circles that Logan's sore throat the other night was pure myth."

"That possibility occurred to me, too," Kate told him. "What's the theory based on?"

"Shrewd guesswork. She appeared at the theatre around four that afternoon, for a rehearsal. Which in this case merely meant a run-through of the programme with the orchestra. I gather that Logan didn't give her singing full voice, but this was a rehearsal, after all. There was no mention to anyone of her having throat trouble. Yet a couple of hours later it was announced that she was indisposed and unable to appear."

She'd been right, then, the sore throat was a fake. Should she believe anything else she'd been told about that Friday evening? Lady Kimberley and Lord Balmayne could have been anywhere during those vital hours, doing anything. The loyalty of the manservant, as reported by DC Bell, could probably be counted on to back up any kind of false alibi.

It was discreetly whispered in Richard's ear that their table now awaited their pleasure whenever sir and madam cared to make the effort of moving to the restaurant. Richard's limp was barely noticeable this evening, just adding a hint of mystery. Dressed now in a dark suit, groomed for an evening out, he looked damned attractive.

Seated at their table, he said, "So DCI Maddox has had one bitch of a day. Ditto on Saturday. Sounds as if something's badly wrong. Want to talk about it?"

Suddenly she felt ready to. "You want me to cry on your shoulder?"

"Why not, if it'll help?"

"The truth is, I'm in a flaming temper about men."

"Certain men in particular? Or the entire male sex?"

"Not far short." She related the events culminating in the sordid episode in Don Trotton's flat, leaving out the messier details.

"Tacky," Richard agreed, "and I'm really sorry about your losing the house. But come on, Kate, where's your sense of proportion? Any woman who's as attractive as you are must have hit this kind of situation before

. . . a cocky guy making a heavy pass, and turning spiteful when you smack him down. I'm not making excuses, but it happens. What's new?"

"What's new is what followed. All day today I've been aware of sniggering behind my back. At lunchtime I pinned down Tim Boulter. I couldn't make him tell me a lot, but enough to get the picture. Trotton's been spreading it around that sex-starved widow Kate Maddox leapt at the invitation to visit his flat. That she just couldn't wait to drop her knickers for him. And all conveyed with the sort of sly innuendo that I could never nail him for. If I dared try, I'd end up the loser second time around."

"I'd better sort that bastard out for you," said Richard, in an upsurge of anger.

"No, you keep out of it. That would only make the situation worse. This is my problem."

"So how are you going to handle it?"

"I don't know, not yet. But some way or other, you'd better believe it."

Richard regarded her with warm admiration. "You'll have me feeling sorry for Trotton in a minute. That guy's going to live to regret ever tangling with Kate Maddox."

When later they left the restaurant, it was a beautiful evening. Moonless, but bright with starlight. By mutual consent they strolled on beyond the car park and higher up the lane to a break in the trees. From there they could look over miles of open countryside, with clusters of lights that showed where the villages lay. A greater gathering of lights in the distance was Marlingford.

"Our territory," Richard mused, standing close beside her. "Yours and mine. Lucky, aren't we? Don't let that Trotton business get you down, Kate. None of this 'I will go sit and weep, till I can find occasion for revenge.' "

"Shakespeare?"

"Taming of the Shrew."

"Trying to impress me with your erudition, eh?"

"I find it works like magic to have a suitable quote ready for the right occasion."

Kate managed a flash recall. *"Brush up your Shakespeare, and the women you will wow."*

"Cole Porter?"

"Give the man a prize."

There was hardly a pause. "Kiss me, Kate."

"Brilliant. I don't know how you do it."

"I didn't say *Kiss Me, Kate.* I said, Kiss me, Kate."

She still didn't quite catch on until Richard turned her to face him. Then she went into his embrace with a soft sigh. It didn't seem a moment too soon.

Eleven

A Women's Institute coach outing to Windsor Castle had frustrated Kate's intention to interview Mrs. Parkes on the Monday. Only too often, regrettably, an important next step in an investigation had to be postponed for some such trivial reason. A police car despatched to her home first thing on Tuesday found the lady in. She arrived at the Incident Room visibly flustered but excited by the importance of the occasion.

Joan Parkes was shortish, plumpish, greyish. She was the sort, Kate noted with satisfaction, to have gimlet eyes at the back of her head.

"I'm sorry to have to ask you to come here," Kate began when they were both seated. "I want to talk to you about Dr. Trent. You used to work for him, I understand."

"That's right, I did. Poor man! You could've knocked me down with a feather when I heard about him being murdered. And that other gent too, Sir Noah Whatsit. What a world!"

"How long ago was it that you stopped working for Dr. Trent?"

Mrs. Parkes was immediately on the defensive. "It was only because I had to go and look after my grandchildren, no other reason. My Angie was expecting again and she had to go into hospital because of high blood pressure. So I had to tell all the people I did for that I wouldn't be able to come for a bit, not till after the babe was born."

Tactfully, Kate enquired of the grannie, "What was it, boy or girl?"

"Oh, a lovely little girl. Seven pounds three ounces. Ever so bonny, she is. Charlene Daphne, they're calling her."

"Congratulations, Mrs. Parkes. When exactly was it you went off to look after your grandchildren?"

"Well, let me think. It was just after the bank holiday."

"End of May, beginning of June?"

"That's about it. Since I came home a fortnight ago I've taken up all my other jobs again. Well, they were only too thankful to get me back after the rubbish they'd been filling in with. You'd never credit the stories they told me. But with Dr. Trent, I just kept mum about being back. My Angie said I was doing far too much at my age, and it was such a long way to that cottage of his on my bike. And so deathly quiet when I got there . . . I'd never clap eyes on a living soul the whole morning. So, like I say, I kept mum. I didn't want him begging me to go back to him, or I might have weakened." She sniffed. "I heard he'd fixed up with one of them contract cleaning firms. I can just imagine how the job gets done . . . a lick and a promise, that's all. The sort of people they employ, they've got no heart in their work, have they?"

Kate smiled. "I suppose you didn't see a lot of Dr. Trent while you were working for him? He'd have been away at the lab when you were at the cottage."

"That's another thing. Trust! Can you trust them other people, I wonder?"

Kate had to repeat the question.

"No, I never saw a lot of him. But you don't have to see a man to get to know him, not when you clean for him."

This one, Kate, is going to pay dividends.

"Dr. Trent seems to have lived a very quiet life," she said. "He wasn't the sort of man to make many friends, so it's been difficult for me to form a true picture of him in my mind. Which, I'm sure you will appreciate, is most important in helping to solve a difficult case of murder. That's why a chat with you could be so useful to me. I thought to myself, Mrs. Parkes probably knew Dr. Trent better than anyone . . . the private side of his life, that is. Anything she can tell me will be accurate, I can rely on it. That's what I thought." *God, will you listen to yourself, Kate Maddox!*

Joan Parkes resembled a plump pigeon, the way she preened herself. "Ah, well, you've certainly come to the right person. What is it you want to know?"

"I'm trying to make a complete list of the people he knew, apart from his work. He must have had one or two personal friends he saw occasionally."

But, disappointingly, Joan Parkes shook her head. "If he did, it's news to me. I've got loads of friends myself, but some folks . . . A funny old world, ain't it?"

"Did you take any phone calls for Dr. Trent while you were working at the cottage?"

"Only once in a blue moon. I mean, everyone would know that he'd be at work in the daytime. There were just one or two . . . queries about things he'd ordered from some shop, that kind of thing."

"How about letters? Personal letters?"

"His sister up north wrote to him sometimes. I'd see the letters from her. And a picture postcard now and then. I never read them, of course."

Perish the thought!

"Did anyone ever call at the cottage while you were there?"

"Well, there was a regular delivery of groceries every Tuesday from the shop in Aston Pringle." Mrs. Parkes screwed up her face in fierce concentration. "The telephone engineer came once to fix the phone. Dr. Trent told me to expect him."

Kate opened a drawer in her desk and took out the Tom Jones tape Trent's sister had brought to her.

"Do you recognize this, Mrs. Parkes?"

"It's one of them music tape things, isn't it?"

"That's right. It was found at Dr. Trent's cottage."

"Oh, he had heaps and heaps of them. Very musical gent, he was."

"But this one is quite different from all the others. It's a Tom Jones album. Not at all the sort of thing Dr. Trent enjoyed. I wonder if you know how he came by it?"

"I wouldn't mind betting his lady friend gave it to him." There was a crafty look on her round face as she said this. Kate realized that Mrs. Parkes had been deliberately saving up this morsel, savouring the effect it would have when she brought it out. The amazed expression Kate adopted gave her full value for money.

"He had a lady friend? I see. Do you happen to know who she was?"

"Had no way of knowing, did I? He never so much as breathed a word about her, and it wasn't my place to ask."

"So how did you know she existed?"

The scornful glance demanded, You ask me that, and you a woman! "I've got eyes, haven't I? And a nose. You can't miss perfume. Expensive perfume, too. It lingers. And *two* glasses on the table next morning. And that's not all, neither."

"What else, Mrs. Parkes?"

"Bed, that's what. When there's been a woman in a man's bed, her as comes to make it next morning can't help knowing. Oh, yes!"

Kate let an impressed moment go by. "Was this a regular occurrence? Was she there often?"

"Well, I couldn't really say that. I only went a couple of mornings a week."

"When was the first time you noticed anything?"

She scratched her head inelegantly. "Sometime beginning of May, it must've been. I remember it clear as anything. The minute I walked in that day, I thought to myself, Hallo, hallo, what's been going on here then? And when I was upstairs hoovering I found a lipstick under the bed."

"You haven't still got it, I suppose?"

"Course not! I'm not a thief. I don't take what's not mine."

You were too eager there, Kate. Backtrack.

"I didn't mean to suggest that for a minute, Mrs. Parkes. It's just that it would have been useful if you'd put that lipstick safely away somewhere. It's hoping too much, I suppose, that you might be able to remember which brand it was? Or even which colour?"

"It was one of them fancy ones. I tried a smear on myself but it never suited my complexion. Too vivid, a real bright scarlet. I always use English Rose."

"So what did you do with it?"

"I put it out where Dr. Trent would see it. I wondered what he'd think, knowing that I knew."

"Did he make any comment to you when you next saw him?"

"It was that very same day, as a matter of fact. Dr. Trent came home lunchtime, which was very unusual. He was ever so jolly for once, in a real happy sort of mood. Then when he spotted the lipstick—I'd put it on the table downstairs—he went bright pink and slipped it in his pocket quick. Not a word to me about it. Well, he needn't have been so embarrassed. I'm not narrowminded."

"Is there anything more you can tell me, Mrs. Parkes? Have a good ponder about it. You might be able to come up with some hint which will enable me to trace this woman."

Her eyes widened. "Do you think that she . . ."

"Whoever she is," said Kate, "I think she might be able to help us discover *why* Dr. Trent was killed."

Joan Parkes, she could see, would dearly have loved to produce the essential clue that led to the solution of the double murder. She would fancy herself as the vital witness for the prosecution who couldn't be shaken under intense cross-examination.

"I don't know as there's anything more I can tell you," she said regretfully. "I only wish I could. But there it is."

There it was. Tantalizing. Definitely a step forward, but how big a step?

By no stretch of imagination could Kate see Lady Kimberley as the woman involved with Trent. All the same, in view of Richard's revelation the previous evening, there were questions about her that had to be answered. A sideways approach seemed the best tactic in this instance.

She herself phoned Lord Balmayne's house, and fortunately he was at home.

"I wonder if I might come and see you this morning, sir?"

"I suppose so, if you must." He sounded cool. "I shall be setting out for Lady Kimberley's shortly, because I'm taking her out to lunch. Perhaps we could more conveniently talk there."

"I would prefer to talk to you alone," she said.

"Really? I can't imagine why. Oh, very well, Chief Inspector. When will you be here? I can't wait around for long."

"I'll come at once," she promised.

Kate easily found the house, an Edwardian mansion standing in several acres. Pitched red roofs and tile-hung gables; white-painted brickwork with louvred shutters at the windows. Nearby was a stable block (four or five horses were grazing in an adjoining paddock), garaging for several cars, and what Kate took to be an indoor swimming pool or gymnasium. Perhaps both. No doubt Lord Balmayne did a good deal of entertaining.

Grecian columns lent extra grandness to the portico. Kate anticipated a butler or manservant in livery, or at the very least a primly starched maid. But the door was opened by a homely woman in a blue nylon overall.

"His lordship will see you in the study," she informed Kate. "Will you come this way, please."

More columns in the hall, with gilded capitals; intricate cornices and a moulded ceiling. The stairway made an elegant double curve. Rich oriental carpets muffled footsteps. Kate followed the woman along a wide corridor until she stopped at one of the many panelled doors, tapped and entered.

"Detective Chief Inspector Maddox to see you, sir."

Lord Balmayne rose from behind a desk of Dutch marquetry, set before the high window. He was impeccably dressed—when would he not be?

"Come in, Chief Inspector." There was no welcome in his voice, but he was a man who believed in good manners. "Please sit down. May I offer you some refreshment? Coffee, perhaps?"

"I think not, sir, thank you."

With a small wave of his hand, the woman was dismissed.

"Am I to take it," he enquired, reseating himself at the desk, "that your presence here indicates a development in the case?"

"There have been several developments."

"Really?" A pause. "Does this mean that you are near a solution?"

"How near remains to be seen. I want to speak to you further about the events of the evening when Sir Noah Kimberley disappeared."

His lips pressed together in disapproval. "My man in London has informed me that an officer of yours was sent to interview him on this subject yesterday. Was that really necessary?"

"I've already explained to you that in an investigation into a serious crime such as this, we are obliged to check and recheck every statement made to us, no matter from whom."

He sighed and made a gesture of resignation. "If you say so. What is it this time?"

"I want to be quite certain in my mind of the reason for Lady Kimberley's non-appearance at your gala that evening."

"You *can* be quite certain. You have been given the reason."

"It has been suggested to me," Kate persisted in an even voice, "that the throat infection to which both you and Lady Kimberley referred was in fact no more than a diplomatic excuse to account for her non-appearance."

Lord Balmayne sprang from his chair and glared down at her, red in the face. Kate held his gaze steadily, anxious to avoid a confrontation if that were possible.

"This is monstrous," he protested. "Who dared to suggest such a thing?"

"I'm not at liberty to reveal my sources, sir."

He swung his back to her, staring out through the window as if fighting to control his anger. When he turned back, Kate saw that the battle had been lost. He was still furious. His eyes burned and his voice was harsh.

"You pick up a malicious rumour and immediately seize upon it as grounds for accusation. I will not tolerate this kind of treatment, Chief Inspector. I shall complain to the Home Secretary about it."

"You must do as you think fit, Lord Balmayne. But I cannot permit your unco-operative attitude to prevent me from performing what I see as my proper function."

For moments longer he remained standing, his mouth working. Then he reseated himself and challenged Kate with a penetrating gaze.

"What are you seeking to prove with these questions?"

"I am not seeking to prove anything," she said in a mild tone. "I am trying to establish the truth. A number of people are involved in this case, due to their connections with the two victims, and I am required to investigate all of them fully. Lady Kimberley, as the spouse of one of the deceased, is inevitably among that number. And you also, sir, as a close friend of the Kimberleys. If you are innocent, then I appeal to you to give me frank answers."

She allowed him a moment, noting the strain on his distinguished features. At length he said in a tired voice, "Lady Kimberley had nothing to do with the death of her husband. Neither did I. If you persist any further with this line of enquiry, you will be doing a great disservice to a fine artist and a remarkable woman. She is entirely innocent. Please leave it there."

"I cannot leave it there, Lord Balmayne. You must be able to see that."

He sighed heavily, looking beyond her from side to side as if seeking a solution there. When he spoke again, his voice was subdued. "It seems I have no option but to tell you something that I would much prefer not to speak about. I trust it can remain confidential?"

"That will depend, sir. I can't make any promises."

He nodded his head slowly. "As you probably know, Lady Kimberley and I have been close friends for many years, both professionally and personally. Some three or four years ago she confided in me that she feared she was losing her voice. The thought was terrifying to her, as it would be to any great singer. I, too, had suspected a lack of certainty in her approach to the higher notes, and I knew that her professional reputation was in jeopardy. If she continued to sing the demanding operatic roles for which she was famous, there was a danger that the vocal weakness would soon be spotted by the critics and *aficionados*. I arranged for her to see a throat specialist, but sadly he could suggest no remedy. A second leading specialist was of the same opinion. The voice is a very delicate instrument, Chief Inspector. It is subject not only to the afflictions of human tissue, but to all kinds of emotional stresses. My advice to Vanessa, in view of what she faced, was that she should retire from the professional stage while still at the peak of her success. A happy solution lay at hand. Noah Kimberley had been beseeching her to marry him for years. She finally accepted him, and—"

Kate interrupted. "I'd like to be clear on this point. Was Sir Noah aware of Dame Vanessa's anxieties about her failing voice? Or was he kept in the dark?"

"She . . . we both, felt it better that Noah should not be told." Lord Balmayne's expression was defensive. "It was a good marriage."

Good marriage or not, it was a strange situation when a lover of long standing urged his beloved into marriage with another man. The faintest hint of challenge was in Kate's voice as she asked, "There was no question, then, that you might marry her yourself?"

Lord Balmayne looked surprised. Affronted. Then he allowed his shoulders to relax as he made a shrugging gesture with his long-fingered hands.

"You are well informed, I see. The answer to that, I suppose, is that I am not a man for whom the state of matrimony holds any attractions. I would regard it as an intolerable intrusion into my freedom. Which is not to say I have anything but the highest affection and regard for the lady in question."

Kate considered a moment, then plunged in, "May I be totally frank, sir?"

He gave her a pale smile. "I doubt you'll be anything else, with or without my permission."

"After Dame Vanessa's marriage, did your former relationship with her continue?"

His lips tightened. "We remained close friends, certainly, but I am an honourable man, Chief Inspector, despite what you may be thinking. Once Vanessa became the wife of Noah Kimberley, for whom I have always had the warmest regard, there was never anything intimate between us."

"And now that Sir Noah is dead?"

He looked shocked. "I am sure the thought has not occurred to Vanessa, any more than it has to me."

But had, Kate wondered, he been shocked enough? She'd made a pretty outrageous suggestion, yet he remained in almost perfect control of himself.

"Perhaps, sir, we could go back to the matter of Lady Kimberley's throat infection on the evening of the gala."

He took a measure of time before he responded. Then he spoke slowly, calculating his words.

"Since Vanessa's retirement from the stage, she has performed on a number of occasions, mostly at charitable events which I myself organized. Each time she has been somewhat nervous, but her professionalism always conquered her fears. Whenever she performed she was invariably acclaimed with great enthusiasm, which naturally Vanessa found very heartwarming. She is an artist who has always been much loved by the public, you know. However, before this last gala her anxiety was worse than on any previous occasion."

"This was before she set out for London?"

"Indeed, yes. Several days beforehand. That was why she persuaded Noah not to accompany her. She couldn't bear the thought of making a spectacle of herself in his presence."

"What reason did she give her husband?"

"Something vague, I imagine. Obviously, Noah wasn't happy about it. She admitted that to me."

"I see. Please continue, Lord Balmayne."

"During the afternoon rehearsal at the theatre she was in an acute state of nerves. There was little real singing expected of her in the run-through and her near-panic passed unnoticed—at least, I trust so. But later, when we went back to my house for her to rest and have some tea, it became obvious to me that she could not possibly appear that evening without risk of a complete breakdown. It was I who suggested the pretence of a throat infection to explain her non-appearance. There, now you have it, the whole unhappy story."

A story that matched what Richard had told her about Vanessa Logan's failing voice. Kate found it a plausible explanation for the oddities and inconsistencies in the various statements made to the police, which had caused her to suspect that something was being concealed. But it still didn't put these two in the clear; by Lord Balmayne's own admission they had conspired to deceive her husband in the past. Might they not have conspired against him again? On that fateful evening they could have left Lord Balmayne's house in London and driven to the Cotswolds and killed Noah Kimberley. Their alibi for that night was dependent on the word of a manservant who had worked for Lord Balmayne for many years, and was perhaps ready and willing to lie for his master.

The time might come, she thought, when additional pressure would need to be applied to Jefferies to see if he would break.

Twelve

The Chief Inspector's briefing to Boulter had been succinct. She'd told him what she wanted him to do, but not how to go about it. This was a challenge which called for a pint of real ale and a lasagne and chips at the Half Moon to set his thought processes going. Well stoked, the sergeant made a call from the payphone by the door, then drove to the Croptech premises. At the laboratory building he told a white-coated porter who was wheeling a trolley loaded with plastic containers of some kind of fluid that he'd like to speak to Mr. Barlow.

When Roger Barlow appeared a minute later there was a surly expression on his good-looking face. "What do you want this time?"

"Just a few words, Mr. Barlow. Er . . . could we go somewhere private?"

"Sure thing, we'll go along to my personal private office."

Boulter let the sarcasm pass without comment. "How about taking a little stroll outside?" he suggested.

With a shrug, Barlow led the way back along the corridor. On the gravelled driveway the two men started pacing side by side.

"Chief Inspector Maddox," Boulter began, "is unhappy about the lack of corroboration of your movements on the two evenings when first Sir Noah Kimberley and then Dr. Trent were murdered."

"I've told you where I was those evenings. What more d'you expect?"

"You could rack your brains to think of something more positive to give us."

"I've already racked my brains," he muttered.

"Sometimes it's a help to reassemble events step by step. Suppose for starters we go through that Wednesday evening from the time you returned from Oxford and arrived at the Cricketers' Arms in Boscombe. Did you go up to the bar first?"

Barlow pondered a moment. "No, we didn't. They have waitress service there in the evenings. We found a place to sit, and ordered drinks."

"What was it you had to drink?"

"A pint of bitter. And Sandra had a glass of white wine."

"Where were you sitting?"

Again a pause for thought. "At one of the tables by those windows that overlook the village green."

"You had something to eat, too, didn't you?"

"Yes, that's right. Spaghetti bolognese."

"Did you tip the waitress?"

Barlow gave him a blank stare. "What's that got to do with anything?"

"She might remember you through that and be able to confirm your story. For instance, she'd have you down as a right mean bastard if you hadn't given her a tip."

"Well, I did. I remember now. Fifty pee, I gave her."

The sergeant smiled at him. "There you are, you're beginning to remember. The grub's not bad at the Cricketers', is it? In fact, it's a pretty decent pub all round. A good atmosphere to take a girl to. Mind you, though, it must've been pretty rowdy when that drunk climbed over the bar and started throwing bottles. At the busiest time of the evening, too . . . just before ten o'clock. It took three of our chaps to subdue him."

Barlow came to an abrupt halt in his walking. Then, recollecting himself, he started pacing on once more.

"To tell the truth, Sandra and I were . . . well, not really bothering about what was happening around us."

"Understandable! But you'd never have missed a fracas like that, not from where you were sitting."

"Oh yes, well, we did notice there was something going on. A bit of a fight. But we kept well out of it."

"A *fight?* At the Cricketers' on Wednesday evening? Nothing the police heard about. There was no trouble reported at all."

"But you just said—"

Now it was Boulter who halted, a grim expression on his face. "Oh no I didn't, Mr. Barlow. The fight I was talking about took place on Saturday. Wednesday at the Cricketers' was dead quiet, as per usual. To make quite sure of that, I phoned and checked with the landlord before I came to see you this afternoon."

Barlow went white. "You tricked me into saying that."

"I said nothing about a fight on *Wednesday*. And if you'd really been at the Cricketers' Arms that evening, you'd have told me that nothing of the kind occurred."

Barlow was looking terrified. "What happens now?"

"It's time for you to give us the straight truth, Barlow. And the police station is the right place for that." The surge of excitement he felt was nothing new to Boulter. A promising lead always had the same heady effect. But this was the biggest thing ever in his career. He'd unmasked a double murderer.

But his hopes were soon to be dashed. What Roger Barlow told him in one of the interview rooms, after being cautioned, had the ring of truth. What was more, the new alibi he gave was easily verifiable.

When Boulter reported back to his DCI, he was in a subdued mood. He felt almost apologetic that he wasn't able to present her with anything of positive value to the murder enquiry.

"It looks as if Barlow and his girlfriend are in the clear, guv. They spent last Wednesday evening, of all things, flying round the Bay of Biscay in Concorde."

"What?" Kate shrugged her shoulders impatiently. "Why the hell didn't they say so before?"

Boulter came over to her desk and sat down. "The thing is, those two have been acting like a couple of naughty kids and were terrified they'd be found out. It's all to do with Roger getting cheated by Croptech, as he maintains. A spot of sweet revenge. They've been having a high old time, eating out at fancy restaurants, booking the best seats at pop concerts and so on, and charging it all up to the firm. Sandra fiddled Kimberley's weekly expense account, which the old boy always signed without so much as a glance, then she drew it from McEvoy and deducted the extras before passing the proper amount over to her boss. They could only do it, of course, because of Kimberley's insistence on always dealing in cash. It was Sandra mentioning that which gave Barlow the idea in the first place."

"I'm surprised that Sandra thought it was worth risking her job for."

"She's totally besotted with the guy, I reckon, and she was probably scared stiff that he'd ditch her if she didn't go along with whatever he suggested."

Kate nodded thoughtfully. "That fits. How about the Concorde trip, though? Last Wednesday they knew that Kimberley was missing, so how did they expect to get their money back?"

"The Concorde flight was already paid for, booked in advance. Apparently Sandra spread the cost over several weeks so it wouldn't bump up any one expense account too much."

Kate pondered. On the one hand she ought to be feeling glad that the field of suspicion was narrowed. She could concentrate that much more on those people who remained on her list. But—and she'd experienced this irrational feeling before—the elimination of a suspect (in this case a pair of suspects) seemed to reduce her chance of ever solving the case.

"Get someone to verify the Concorde story, Tim. I haven't much doubt that it's true, but we must have confirmation."

The sergeant looked hurt. "That's already been put in hand, guv."

"Sorry, Tim, I must learn to trust you more." She grinned at him. "Not that I shall ever initial your expense chits without a second glance. I'm not gullible, like Noah Kimberley."

"I've never met a DCI who was, guv. In that respect you're no better than all the rest."

In that respect! *Nice one, Sergeant. You pack a subtle line of flattery.*

The post-mortem on Sir Noah Kimberley had produced an item of information that pinpointed the time of death with an exactness that succeeded Kate's best hopes.

"The examination of the stomach contents," she told her troops during another general briefing on Wednesday morning, "revealed that he'd eaten a fairly substantial meal not more than two hours before he was killed. Furthermore, the actual constituents of the meal have been identified, and they match precisely with the food he ate at his home on the Friday evening he disappeared . . . steak and kidney pie followed by black currants. We've rechecked that with his housekeeper. We know what time he had dinner that evening. He finished the meal at about nine and went out shortly afterward. So we can be sure that he died within, say, one and a half hours after leaving home." She glanced at a DC who showed signs of wanting to speak. "Yes, Doug?"

"I understood from the reports, ma'am, that the housekeeper said it was the deceased's favourite meal. Isn't it possible that he was still alive on a subsequent day, and repeated the same meal at some restaurant?"

"Good point. But the post-mortem finding was too exact for that to be a real possibility. Mrs. Byworth, the housekeeper, gave us a very detailed account of what she served, and the ingredients matched exactly. So we know when Sir Noah Kimberley died, but not where, because the body was obviously moved to the Tillingtons' residence. As to *when* it was moved, the evidence indicates that it was placed in the freezer not long after the actual killing. There was no onset of *rigor mortis* before freezing, and no sign of decomposition. So now let's consider what we have on the killer, and the person or persons who moved the body. Likely to be one and the same, but not necessarily so. A woman is involved, because a woman was seen driving the dead man's car in this area soon after midnight . . . and she seems to have driven it to Cardiff via the Severn Bridge and left it at the airport there. After that, we have no trace of her. Sir Noah is known to have received a phone call just before he left the house that evening, which may have been why he went out. It's a top priority to discover who that caller was. If anyone has any suggestions, they'll be welcome. You all know, to your cost, that we're in the process of checking through a long list we've built up of all Sir Noah's contacts we can track down, both business and personal."

At that point a WPC entered the room. Coming up to Kate, she murmured that a Professor Steinle was on the phone, wanting to speak to her.

"He's calling from Vienna, ma'am, and he says it's important."

"Professor Steinle? Did he ask for me by name?"

"No, ma'am. He asked to be put on to the most senior officer engaged on the Kimberley case."

"Right." Kate signed to Boulter to take over the briefing, and departed to her own office.

"Detective Chief Inspector Maddox here. What can I do for you, Herr Professor Steinle?"

"You are in charge of the enquiry concerning Sir Noah Kimberley's death, Frau Chief Inspector?" His excellent English was spoken with a marked accent. He showed no surprise to find that this senior police officer was female.

"I am. Do you have some information for me?"

"It is a possibility, I believe, that what I will now relate may be of much importance to your enquiries. Especially I think this, since it concerns the precise day of Sir Noah's decease. You must understand, Frau Chief Inspector, that I have only just today learned of this sad event, in a letter I received from a correspondent of mine who lives in London. I am much grieved, as Sir Noah was an old friend of mine. Let me explain. I am the Herr Direktor of a firm here in Austria which conducts business of a similar nature to Croptech in England. Landwirtschaftlichindustrie Steinle. The late Sir Noah Kimberley and I first met when we were both post-graduate students at the university of Cambridge, many years ago, of course. I speak to you now, Frau Chief Inspector, to inform you that on the Friday of last week, early in the afternoon, I had the unhappy duty of telephoning my good friend Sir Noah with some news of an unpleasant nature."

Kate's interest quickened. This must have been the call Sir Noah received just before Lady Kimberley left for London, which had seemed to upset him. She scribbled down an approximation of the Austrian firm's long name.

"What unpleasant news was this, Herr Professor?"

"I had received a communication from one of Sir Noah's most senior employees, offering to my company his services. There is nothing reprehensible, you may think, in such an offer. However, in this instance the man was most plainly suggesting that he would be able to bring with him to Landwirtschaftlichindustrie Steinle details of chemical processes developed at Croptech. In return for this information, he would expect to be paid a very large salary. Such confidential information, as this man well knew, would be of infinite value to my own firm. As a businessman, Frau Chief Inspector, I must of course consider what is profitable for my own organization, but I do not indulge in dishonourable practices. My initial reaction on receiving this proposal was to reject it outright with all the contempt it deserved. However, upon reflection it seemed more fitting that I should warn my old friend of this serious disloyalty in one of his employees. So I telephoned Sir Noah. To ensure that I was speaking to him privately, I waited until the early afternoon, knowing that his normal custom was to take luncheon at home with his wife. Sir Noah sounded deeply shocked on the telephone, as one would expect."

"What was the name of the employee concerned?" Kate enquired.

"It was Trent. Dr. Gavin Trent. To judge from his qualifications, he is a biochemist of considerable talent. But he is not, I fear, a person of whom his professional colleagues can be proud."

Kate broke in, "You are clearly unaware, Herr Professor, that Dr. Trent has also been murdered."

"*Wirtig?*" A shocked silence followed. "But this is terrible. How is it possible that both these two men—"

"Unfortunately, we still have no answer to that question, but your information has thrown new light upon my enquiry. Tell me, please, the communication you received from Dr. Trent . . . was it in the form of a letter?"

"Yes. Addressed to me personally, and marked *Confidential.*"

"I would like to see that letter, if I may."

"*Naturlich*, if that is your wish."

"Thank you. I will arrange to have it collected. Either one of my own officers will fly to Vienna to talk to you, or possibly the Austrian police can handle the matter for me. Whichever way, I ask for your co-operation in answering as fully as possible all questions put to you."

"Of course, of course, Frau Chief Inspector."

"One other point, Herr Professor Steinle. Did you telephone Sir Noah a second time that day, in the early evening?"

"A second time? I had no occasion to telephone him again. Why do you ask?"

"It's of no consequence. Did Sir Noah give you any indication of what action he proposed taking in the light of the information you'd given him?"

"No. He merely said that he was very distressed, as of course I knew he would be. Sir Noah's intention, I would imagine, was to take up the matter with Dr. Trent in the sternest possible way."

"Yes," said Kate. "I expect it was."

Thirteen

"Christ!" said Boulter, when Kate had imparted the gist of the phone call from Austria. "This alters the outlook more than somewhat."

Kate had had the advantage of a little time to consider. "How about this scenario, Tim? Noah Kimberley drives to Trent's cottage that Friday evening intent on having a showdown over the man's appalling disloyalty. The row ends in violence and Kimberley gets killed—either deliberately or accidentally."

"Do you reckon that either of those two was the type to get into a fight?"

"By all accounts Trent had the very devil of a temper. And don't forget, Kimberley must have been as mad as hell with him."

"So, if Trent killed Kimberley, who killed Trent?"

"One step at a time, Tim. Having a dead man on his hands, Trent panics. He's got to dispose of the body somehow. Inspiration dawns. The Tillingtons are away for several months, their house locked up. Hiding it there would be a way of buying time till he can think of something more permanent." She paused, and Boulter promptly nailed flaws in her line of reasoning.

"How is Trent supposed to know the way through the security system at Milford Grange? How does he know there'll be an empty freezer waiting for him there, big enough to take the body?"

"The freezer might have been a bonus he only noticed when he got to the house."

"And beating the security system?"

"We reasoned that Roger Barlow, with his scientific mind, might have figured out how to do it. Why not Gavin Trent?"

Boulter looked sceptical. Kate persisted doggedly. "Those unidentified fingerprints at Milford Grange. Were they checked against Trent's?"

"Can't say offhand, guv. I doubt it, considering that Trent was a goner himself."

"Well, have it done right away."

Only minutes later, Boulter burst back into her office alight with excitement, his scepticism about the DCI's theory forgotten.

"Bang on, guv. Those prints at Milford Grange are definitely Trent's. We're on our way."

Kate applied a dampener to his enthusiasm. "There are still several unanswered questions. First off, who was the woman in the case, the woman who drove Kimberley's car to Cardiff Airport that evening? And if and when we get a lead on her, we come back to who the hell killed Trent? And why?"

"Did *she* kill him?" Boulter floated. "Was there a row between them afterwards? Could Trent have threatened to expose her?"

"But he'd be exposing himself, too, if we're on the right track. We've got to find that woman, Tim. Whether or not she killed Trent, she's obviously a vital element in the case."

"Agreed."

"Okay then, let's consider what we know about her. Just a few stray bits and pieces, that's all, and even those may not all relate to the same woman. But let's assume for now that they do. We have two sightings of her on record—one by Giles Lambert, the car dealer. A lot of hair, was all he could say. The other sighting was by the man at the Severn Bridge toll gate, but he couldn't give any description apart from a guess that she was either drunk or crazy, judging by the way she drove. Or, we can suggest, possibly an inexperienced driver, or someone who was in a panic. We have strong circumstantial evidence from both Trent's sister and his former cleaning lady that there had been a woman in his life. What can we put together about *her?* That she used expensive perfume and wore a somewhat vivid red lipstick."

"And," Boulter put in shrewdly, "for some reason it was important to keep their affair secret. It couldn't have mattered a monkey's to Trent, so the need for secrecy must have been on her side."

"As in married woman, for instance."

"A whisky-drinking woman, too. Remember the half-empty bottle on Trent's table, almost certainly brought by his visitor the night he was killed."

"A lot of women drink whisky," Kate pointed out. "I do, for one."

Boulter chuckled. "Had I better caution you, guv?"

Kate screwed up her mouth pensively. "We also know that her taste in music was very different from Trent's. But again, a taste for Tom Jones is shared by a very large number of people."

"According to what Trent's sister told you, he must have been really besotted with this woman to have bothered to listen to the sort of music he despised. If he was so crazy about her, why the heck did he try to wangle himself a fancy new job in Vienna?"

"Good point, Tim. He might have seen that she was losing interest, and he just wanted to get away. Or maybe the plan was for her to leave her husband and go off with him."

"Could she have killed him—because he was coming on too heavy, maybe? He might have threatened to spill the beans to her husband if she didn't agree to do what he wanted."

Kate ruminated. "But if Trent killed Kimberley and she was in on it with him, they could hardly blackmail each other. It's possible she got scared that Trent might panic and let the cat out of the bag, incriminating her too. He was an unstable sort of character, don't forget, unable to control his temper."

"Assuming she did do it, she'd need to be one tough lady to drown him like that in the pond."

Kate tried to push away the nagging thought in her head, but it wouldn't leave her.

"Dr. Cheryl Miller," she said. "She's a tough lady, all right."

"She's married, too, in a way. Though I wouldn't have thought she'd care a damn if the whole world knew who she was doing a number with."

Kate shook her head slowly. "But with Gavin Trent . . . I just can't see it. I'd say he was the very last man she'd want to have an affair with."

"How about if all that guff she gave us about having such a contempt for Trent was just a smokescreen?"

"Why should she worry about putting up a smokescreen? You've just pointed out that she wouldn't care a damn who knew who she was sleeping with. On the other hand . . ."

"On the other hand, what?"

Kate talked herself through this new idea. "The way I read Cheryl Miller, she has a contempt for men—*all* men. Even Jessop, though she sticks by him because it gives her a good feeling to be needed. But Jessop apart, I think it's her aim in life to put men down. In her sexual involvements she doesn't fall for the man, she just uses him for her own amusement."

"Some men," said Boulter, rolling his eyes, "wouldn't mind being used by that one."

"Huh! They live to regret it."

"Or maybe die."

"You might be on to something, Tim. It's just conceivable that she deliberately set out to seduce Trent for the sheer hell of it. A chap who was short on experience of women the way he was might easily go completely overboard if a sexy woman like Cheryl Miller seemed to have the hots for him. Then comes the moment of truth, when she bitchily tells him to get lost. He threatens to blow the gaff about her gaolbird husband, and . . ."

"But how would Trent have known about Jessop? She'd have been too astute to confide that sort of secret in pillow talk."

"You're right, it's unlikely. I suppose Trent could have found out some other way."

"Anyhow," Boulter said, "Dr. Miller's prints don't match the ones found on that Tom Jones tape."

Kate was taken by surprise by the feeling of thankfulness that flooded through her. She and Cheryl Miller had little in common beyond the fact that they were both succeeding in a man's world. *We of the elite sisterhood, Kate.* Otherwise, they could hardly have been more different.

"I was overlooking that, Tim," she said, smiling. "We can't write her off as a suspect on that account, of course. But weighing up all the odds, it does seem to me highly improbable that she was the woman involved with Trent."

"You like Cheryl Miller, guv, don't you?"

"There's liking and liking, but yes I do. I respect what she's achieved, and I think I can understand what motivates her. She's a sad woman."

"Sad . . . her? She doesn't strike me as sad."

"Take my word for it. Life's treated Cheryl Miller pretty badly."

"She's not the only one," Boulter said, with a depth of feeling in his voice.

You bloody fool, Tim! Why can't you see that you've got it all on a plate? Men could have both an interesting career and a fulfilling family life. For women, it was usually a matter of choosing which.

"Back to business, Sergeant," she said irritably. "One way or another we've got to track down this woman. She's the key to the whole case. So let's sift through what we've got all over again."

Gavin Trent's funeral was scheduled for Wednesday afternoon. Kate wanted to attend, even though she couldn't afford the time, if only to give moral support to his sister and her husband, who was coming down specially. At the last minute she discovered a disastrous ladder in her tights, and she'd already used the spare pair she carried in the car. She popped out to the newsagent's just across Aston Pringle's wide main street from the police station.

Emerging with her purchase she saw a red Porsche pull up and reverse into a vacant parking space at the kerb. The first thing that caught her attention was its driver, Paula Kimberley. Then she became aware that the music issuing from the car was the unmistakable voice of Tom Jones. Deep, grainily smooth, it carried a throb that was incredibly sexy.

So Paula Kimberley liked Tom Jones. But ten million other women did, too.

The music ended abruptly as Paula switched off the ignition. Kate paused on the pavement, watching. Then as Paula got out of the car she went forward to speak to her, registering in that instant that Paula wore lipstick of a brightish red. But ten million other women did, too. A waft of expensive perfume reached her. But ditto, ditto.

"Hallo, Mrs. Kimberley. I was just thinking that I owe you a thank-you for your help over the robbery at Milford Grange. The information you gave us about what was missing was of considerable assistance."

In the first moment of seeing Kate, Paula had looked startled. Scared. Now her expression changed to relief and she gave a bright smile.

"That's all right. I was only too glad to help."

Not true, Kate. She had seemed very reluctant, and had been cajoled into it by her husband.

"We arrested the thieves and recovered the stolen items," Kate said. "But I expect you heard that."

"Yes, er . . . somebody mentioned it."

Smiling, Kate held up the package in her hand. "I just laddered my last pair of tights, so I had to dash over to restock. I seem to get through a hell of a lot."

"Oh, er . . . yes. They never last long, do they?" Paula Kimberley was clearly distrait, her mind elsewhere.

On a sudden snap judgment, Kate did her best impression of being taken short on a sneeze, then hastily opened her shoulderbag and fished for a handkerchief. At the same time, stealthily, she unclipped her wallet and loosened its contents. When she withdrew her hand with the handkerchief, the wallet came out with it, falling to the pavement and spilling driver's licence, banknotes, and other bits and pieces. For a frozen instant Kate gazed at the mess helplessly. Paula, as she'd hoped, immediately crouched down to gather the things together. Kate crouched to join her.

"Oh, thanks a lot. How stupidly clumsy of me!"

Acting a bit bewildered, she left most of the picking up to Paula, taking each item from her with babbled expressions of gratitude and slipping it back in her bag. To her great satisfaction she watched Paula pick up her rarely handled Kidney Donor card, gripping the smooth plastic firmly between her thumb and two fingers.

Back at the police station a couple of minutes later, Kate handed the card over to the office manager of the Incident Room.

"Have this dusted right away, will you, Frank. There'll be some prints on it that aren't mine. Will you get them checked against the prints on that tape found at Trent's cottage. The Tom Jones one his sister handed in. I'm off to Trent's funeral now."

The result of the fingerprint check was on her desk when she returned. Reading it, Kate felt a buzz of excitement. At long last, she knew, she was really getting somewhere.

After the encounter with Chief Inspector Maddox in Aston Pringle, Paula Kimberley felt slightly less fraught than she'd felt for days. It had been a good omen, something positive to tell Aidan about when he came home. He was in London this afternoon, having shot off there after spending the morning at Croptech again keeping things ticking over; to do otherwise would have suggested a lack of feeling towards his dead uncle's wife. But apparently his own business affairs had demanded his presence in Leadenhall Street.

Paula both longed for and dreaded her husband's return. Aidan was so bitterly hostile to her these days, so ready to snarl recriminations. It was so different from before when they'd had a relaxed, easygoing relationship at home, enjoying each other's company, and by tacit consent never asking awkward questions about what went on when they were apart. Now, she was almost afraid to open her mouth to Aidan. She was half terrified of him, yet she needed him. Without Aidan's support she would go insane.

It was almost seven when she heard the familiar note of his car turning into the lane. She closed the portfolio of designs for a new boutique in Cheltenham that she seemed unable to make any progress on, went through to the bedroom and swallowed down a couple of tranquilizers, then quickly checked her appearance in the mirror. God, she looked awful! Hastily she chewed at her lips and slapped her cheeks to bring some colour to her face.

She was halfway down the stairs as Aidan let himself in. Paula did her best to put on a welcoming smile.

"Hi!" she greeted him. "You must need a drink."

He nodded, tossed his briefcase onto a chair and headed for the living room. "Whisky. A large one. Anything happened?"

"As a matter of fact, yes. I popped into Aston Pringle for a few things I needed, and I bumped into that woman Chief Inspector."

He took the glass she handed him but didn't drink. "How did that come about?" he asked tersely.

"Sheer chance. I spotted a parking space outside the newsagent's and grabbed it. As I got out of the car, she came over to speak to me. She wanted to thank me for the help I gave the police when you and I went to the Tillingtons' place to tell them what was missing. I'm glad now that you made me do that, Aidan. It got us into her good books. She couldn't have been friendlier this afternoon."

Aidan tipped a long swallow of whisky, then frowned. "What's her game, I wonder?"

"No game. She just took the opportunity to say thank you."

He very decidedly shook his head. "I don't like it, Paula. You were officially thanked by Inspector Trotton at the time, and in the police's eyes that would be quite sufficient. The Maddox woman had an ulterior motive, I'm certain. You and I are still high on the suspect list, don't forget. That's inevitable in view of my close connection with Uncle Noah and Croptech. Thank God that whatever checks the police might have done into the firm's financial position are bound to convince them that Croptech was worth a damn sight more with Uncle Noah alive than it is now that he's dead."

"From the way she spoke to me today, Aidan, I feel sure we've got nothing to worry about."

"If you really think that," he said, with savage contempt in his eyes, "you're an even bigger fool than I took you for. You'd better tell me exactly what happened this afternoon, step by step, right from the moment she came over to you. What precisely did she say?"

"Just that she owed me a thank-you, because it was such a big help that I'd been able to identify things that were missing from Milford Grange. She mentioned that they'd caught the thieves. That was all."

He looked at her suspiciously. "And then you parted?"

"Well, we chatted for a couple of minutes."

"What about?"

"Nothing important. She explained that she'd just been to buy some tights, and we agreed that they never seem to last long. And then she spilled some stuff from her handbag."

His glance sharpened. "What the hell do you mean, she spilled some stuff from her handbag?"

"Well, she suddenly sneezed, and when she fished for a hankie she accidentally pulled her wallet out of her bag, too, and everything was strewn all over the pavement. I helped her pick things up."

"Go on," he said grimly. "What exactly did you pick up?"

"Does it matter?"

"Just tell me."

"Well, there were several banknotes . . . fivers and tenners. There was her driver's licence, a library ticket, and . . . and a National Trust membership card, I think."

"What about her police warrant card?"

"I don't remember seeing that."

"Credit cards?"

"No, they were attached to the wallet. She picked that up. Oh, and I remember, there was a Kidney Donor card."

"Which you handled?"

"Well, yes, I did."

Aidan took out his own wallet from the inside pocket of his jacket, and extracted one of the plastic credit cards from the concertina. This he tossed to the carpet.

"Show me exactly what you did. Exactly, mind!"

Paula stared at him, bewildered. "I don't understand. I don't know what you mean."

"For Christ's sake, it's simple enough. Pretend that I'm Chief Inspector Maddox and that on the floor is her Kidney Donor card. You said you picked it up for her. Give me a reconstruction."

About to demur again, Paula was stopped by the look on his face. She crouched down, considered for a second or two, then slowly picked up the card. Straightening, she held it out to Aidan. But he didn't take it at once.

"Is that how you held it, between two fingers and your thumb?"

"Yes, I think so. Yes, that's right."

"Then she took it from you?" He reached out and accepted the credit card, staring at it thoughtfully. "What then? Did she stuff it back into her wallet?"

Again Paula tried to recall the scene in her mind's eye. "Not actually. She'd already put the other things away, but she just stood holding the card as she thanked me again and apologized for being such a clumsy idiot. Then we said goodbye, and I went towards the newsagent's and she crossed the road on her way back to the police station." She added nervously, "For heaven's sake, Aidan, what's this all about?"

"I'll tell you what it's all about. That Maddox woman found a neat way of extracting your fingerprints from you without your being aware of it."

"Oh, but surely—"

"A clumsy idiot she definitely is not. You can't seriously imagine that she'd spill all that stuff *accidentally*. You bloody fool, Paula, you should have realized what she was up to. The problem now is, why was she so keen to get your prints? You must have left some at Milford Grange that night. Or in Uncle Noah's car."

Paula blanched at the thought. "But I couldn't have done. I was wearing my driving gloves all the time."

"You must have taken them off for some reason. It has to be that. And now that Maddox woman is able to make a comparison, she won't waste any time. So neither must we."

Paula looked at her husband in fear. "What are we going to do, Aidan?"

He didn't answer her at once, and she couldn't read the expression in his eyes. At length he turned away from her and went to pour himself another drink.

"You'll have to give me time to think. Meanwhile, what about getting me something to eat?"

Fourteen

Aidan Kimberley was dead right in saying that the Chief Inspector would waste no time following up the fingerprint lead. Even before he'd made that remark, just as soon as Kate had received a positive match on the prints on the Tom Jones tape, she had summoned Sergeant Boulter and discussed with him the implications of this new development.

"Let's see how Paula Kimberley fits with what we already know about the woman we're looking for," she said. "To start with, she has no alibi we can check on for the night Sir Noah died. Another thing, it looks as if she was more friendly with the Tillingtons—or at least with Mrs. Tillington— than she made out, so it's not beyond belief that she knew of a way to get into Milford Grange without setting off the alarm system. In which case, that was probably what gave birth to the idea of using their empty house to conceal the body. As for driving Noah Kimberley's car to Cardiff Airport—which was presumably done to explain his absence by suggesting that he must have left the country—there'd have been no problem about that. Trent could have driven to Cardiff too, in his own car, and brought her back."

Boulter granted all that, but he still had reservations.

"I can't understand how she ever came to be involved with Trent. If she was in the market for something on the side, you'd think she'd go for one of the rich beautiful people like herself—not a miserable loner like him."

"Maybe that was his appeal. Maybe it amused her to use her technique on a man like Trent and get him crazy about her. A bit like our reasoning when we cast Cheryl Miller in the role of his lady friend. I'm not suggesting that Paula Kimberley would have had anything more than a short fling in mind, of course."

"Possible, I suppose. But why go so far as to get mixed up in Kimberley's death? Or at least in covering up after his death."

"Maybe she had no choice," said Kate.

"And what about Trent's murder? Are you suggesting that *she* killed him? Could she have been ruthless enough?"

"If she felt sufficiently threatened, I think she could. Or perhaps it was her husband, if he found out about the affair when he came back from Hong Kong. But let's not go too fast, Tim. The more I think about it, the more convinced I am that Paula Kimberley is involved up to the neck in this business. But we can't build a case against her purely on the strength of her fingerprints on that Tom Jones tape. Aside from that, we've got damn all that would stand up in court."

"No solid facts," Boulter agreed lugubriously, in a fair take-off of Superintendent Joliffe.

Kate only half stifled a grin. "I think our best bet is to talk to Lady Kimberley and see if she can come up with any new thoughts. She knows Paula Kimberley better than anyone else around here."

"Right, guv, I'll fetch the car."

"No, I'd rather go alone. She'll talk more freely woman to woman. Though I shan't mind if Lord Balmayne is there. It might even be helpful to have him around. He's a very shrewd man. But Tim, make sure you stay at the end of a phone in case I need you for some fast action."

With the coming of evening the sky had clouded over and the air was sultry, a rainstorm threatening. At the Kimberley residence the housekeeper showed Kate out to the terrace, where Lady Kimberley and Lord Balmayne were catching what coolness they could.

"Mrs. Maddox, do sit down. I was intending to telephone you about a letter I received by the second delivery. Dotty, fetch it for me, will you, there's a dear."

The tiny woman trotted indoors and was back in an instant with a white envelope. She handed it to Kate, who glanced at Lady Kimberley.

"Am I to read it?"

"Please do. It answers a question that has been of some concern to you."

It was a letter of condolence to Lady Kimberley. The writer explained that his tardiness in writing was due to the fact that he had only just learned the sad news on his return from a business trip abroad.

I made your husband's acquaintance only very recently, when I played as a visitor at the Radlett golf course, but I found him most congenial. Accord-

*ingly, I invited him for a game at my own course near Cheltenham, and we
tentatively agreed on a date three weeks later. My business trip coming up
unexpectedly made this impossible, and I telephoned Sir Noah to postpone
our plans. From what I understand of the circumstances of your husband's
death, I believe that I must have been one of the last people he spoke to
before he met that terrible fate, as it was around seven forty-five that we
talked together. The thought fills me with sadness.*

Such a simple, innocent answer to a problem that had nagged at Kate
all through the investigation. Now, it was of no importance. Kate replaced
the letter in its envelope and laid it on the garden table.

"Thank you for showing it to me, Lady Kimberley. Actually, the reason
I've come this evening is because I think you may perhaps be able to help
me in another direction."

"Most certainly, if I can."

"The point is this: Certain facts have come to light which oblige me to
enquire into the precise nature of the relationship between Mrs. Paula
Kimberley and Dr. Trent."

"Their *relationship?*" Lady Kimberley looked bewildered. Lord
Balmayne remained silent, watchful.

"Mrs. Kimberley told me herself in your presence, if you remember,
that they'd known one another, having met on several occasions here at
your house. Beyond that, she said, she'd encountered Trent around the
neighbourhood from time to time. 'Just to say hallo to' was how she put it.
What I need to know is whether there was anything closer than that
between them."

"But surely . . . Paula is the one to question about this."

Lord Balmayne intervened, reaching over to lay a gentle hand on her
arm. "My dear, I am sure that the Chief Inspector must have a sound
reason for coming to you. What is it you are suggesting, Mrs. Maddox?"

"At this stage, nothing. However, I have cause to believe that Trent was
somehow concerned in Sir Noah's death."

They both reacted with incredulity. Lord Balmayne said, "Can this
really be true?"

"I have strong evidence to support that theory. I also have evidence
that Trent was secretly involved with a woman, that indeed it was this
woman who helped him remove Sir Noah's car from the locality in order
to mislead the police. It's vital that we establish her identity, and any help
you could give me would be of great value."

"But . . . but . . . Paula. I just cannot believe it."

"I do realize how distressing this must be for you, Lady Kimberley. But it's important that you should try to dismiss your personal feelings and be quite objective. Think back. Can you remember anything . . . anything, however trivial, that might point to a relationship between Trent and Mrs. Kimberley which was more than that of casual acquaintances?"

She shook her head, dazed and unhappy.

"Can you recall any specific occasions when the two of them were here together? Perhaps, for instance, when Mrs. Kimberley was present but not her husband."

"It's difficult to remember. Noah and I had so many people here. We *loved* giving parties. Aidan and Paula are usually down from London at weekends, as Aidan is so keen on polo, but sometimes his business takes him abroad and then Paula comes alone. In fact, this summer she has quite often stayed on at their cottage during the week." Lady Kimberley frowned in concentration. "Noah usually invited Gavin Trent to our parties, out of courtesy, but he didn't often come. However, I do recall one particular time when he and Paula were both here. It was during that last hot spell a few weeks ago and on the Saturday, after polo had finished, we had a swim party here and a poolside barbeque."

"A swim party? I understood from Trent's sister that he couldn't swim. That, in fact, he hated the water."

"You are quite right. Gavin didn't get into swimwear like the rest of us, which made him look somewhat out of place."

"And do you remember anything special about that occasion? Between Trent and Paula."

"As a matter of fact, I do." Her eyes were wide with dismay at where this seemed to be leading. "It was beginning to get cool and people were leaving the pool to get changed. The men used the summerhouse, and the women came indoors. Dotty was helping Noah set up the barbeque and I went to the kitchen for the steaks. I was surprised to see Paula there with Gavin Trent. They looked startled to see me, which I assumed was due to my rather sudden appearance. Paula was still in her bikini, and she explained she had been taking the shortcut upstairs and had run into Gavin, who was just returning from a visit to the toilet. The incident went out of my mind. I've not thought about it since, until this moment."

"Looking back," said Kate, "what do you think they were doing? Just talking? Arguing? Kissing?"

"Kissing? No, I don't think so." Lady Kimberley closed her eyes, casting back to the scene. "They were standing close, but not touching. It's possible they were arguing. He was certainly pink-faced, but I took that for embarrassment."

"Why should they have felt embarrassed, if they'd just bumped into one another as she said?"

Another pause while this was considered. "You know, I think it's possible that you are right, Mrs. Maddox, and there was something going on between them. Looking back now, with that in mind, their behaviour was certainly very odd. *Extremely* odd. And it was odd, too, that Gavin should have accepted the invitation to that party in the first place. Noah was surprised, I remember, because Gavin knew very well that most people would be swimming." Her glance sharpened. "If what you suppose is true, then . . . what does it mean?"

Lord Balmayne emerged from a long silence. "This may sound an outrageous suggestion, Chief Inspector, but is it possible that Aidan killed Trent? After discovering about Paula's affair with him, I mean."

Kate was astonished by his quick perspicacity. "It's a possibility I am considering, sir."

Against a protesting gasp from Lady Kimberley, he continued, "There is something I should reveal at this stage." He glanced at Vanessa almost apologetically. "You will be surprised by what I am about to say, my dear. But what I did, I did for your sake." He turned back to Kate. "On Sunday morning, Aidan Kimberley telephoned me at my home to ask if he could come to see me on a matter he described as very private and confidential. When he arrived he explained that he was in a difficult financial position because some speculative dealings of his had gone badly wrong, as a result of which he was unable to meet his commitments. He urgently needed four hundred thousand pounds, he told me, otherwise his reputation in the City would be ruined."

"Four hundred thousand pounds," echoed Lady Kimberley in horror. "Gerald, my dear, you surely didn't lend him such a large sum as that?"

He shook his head. "Aidan wasn't asking me for a loan. He offered to sell me his fifty per cent holding in Croptech for that amount, which, of course, I realized was a bargain price for the firm, even without Noah at the helm. He needed the money immediately, he explained, which meant that he couldn't offer the shares to you. With Noah's estate yet to be settled, he knew that you would never be able to raise a sum of that size at short notice. But he believed, rightly, that I could be induced to buy the shares, out of friendship for you. You see, my dear, I envisaged that you could buy them from me at a later date, if you so wished. Or, if not, that we could together offer the entire firm to someone who was looking for outright control. Aidan's suggestion seemed mutually advantageous; he needed secrecy, and I wished to avoid half of Croptech's shares falling into the hands of a stranger."

Kate's brain was dovetailing this piece of news with previously known facts. She said, "I get the impression, Lord Balmayne, that you now don't believe Mr. Kimberley was telling you the truth."

"I should have been suspicious at the time, Mrs. Maddox. My excuse must be that I was only too glad to be able to do something for Vanessa. But Aidan is an astute businessman, well accustomed to juggling the stock market. It is stretching credibility that he was in such dire need of four hundred thousand pounds as to be willing to offer the Croptech shares so cheaply. So I am wondering now if he saw this offer to me as a means of quickly laying his hands on a large sum of liquid cash."

"Which he could take with him out of the country if the need to flee should arise at short notice?"

"Precisely."

"And this Croptech deal has already been completed?"

"Oh, indeed it has. Aidan could already be in possession of the cash by this time."

Kate had no shred of doubt left that Aidan and Paula Kimberley were implicated in the two murders. Exactly how and to what extent each was involved were details that would have to wait. The imperative thing was to stop them from leaving the country, if that was what they were planning.

"I must get back to the office without delay," Kate said, rising to her feet. "Needless to say, it is most important that for the time being neither of you should speak of this matter to anyone else."

"Of course," they both agreed, and Lord Balmayne asked, "What action do you propose taking, Mrs. Maddox?"

"I'm afraid I can't tell you that, sir." Which was fair enough, considering that Kate was still undecided about that very question.

She took Boulter with her to the Kimberleys' cottage at Inchmere St. Mary. In a car behind them were a couple of uniformed men whom Kate had brought along as back-up, in case of need. Their instructions were to wait at a short distance, out of sight.

As a second home—a mere weekend retreat—the cottage was the sort of property to tempt an estate agent into hyperbole. Tawny Cotswold stone and gleaming white paintwork . . . that glorious combination. Climbing roses festooning trellises, clipped lawns and flowerbeds brilliant with colour. Immaculate. Expensive. Secluded. Paula Kimberley's red Porsche was parked on a paved area outside the double garage.

"Lucky sods," Boulter grunted as they got out of the car.

"Think so, Tim?" Reaching the front door, Kate pressed the bellpush and they heard silvery chimes within. They waited. Birds twittered in the trees. The air was very still.

No answer to the doorbell. No sign of life. Kate rang again. Still no response.

"Can you hear music?" she asked.

"Faintly." Boulter listened. "Radio?"

"Odd, if nobody's home. Take a look round the back, Tim."

He went off, and Kate rang a third time, then stepped back and surveyed the upper part of the cottage.

"Sounds to me as if the music's coming from upstairs," she said, when her sergeant returned. "There's a window open."

"There's also a window open at the back. The kitchen window." Boulter adopted a look of wide-eyed innocence. "I thought I could smell gas."

Can't give you marks for originality, Tim. Still, the old dodges often worked best.

"In that case, Sergeant, it's our duty to investigate. You'd better use that open kitchen window."

He vanished again, while Kate waited at the front door. Within sixty seconds Boulter opened it for her.

"No gas leak that I can find, ma'am," he said. "It looks as if I was mistaken."

"Would you believe it?"

The music was definitely coming from upstairs. They did a quick recce of the ground floor. Nothing of interest. Kate stood in the small hallway and called.

"Is anyone home? This is the police."

No response. The music played on. A solo piano. Debussy.

"We'd better have a look," said Kate.

The stairs did a quarter turn, ending at an oblong landing. Two doors stood half open . . . bathroom, and a room with a large table strewn with sketches and samples of fabric. Paula's workroom. The music was coming from one of the other rooms. Kate opened the door and peered inside. The master bedroom. Her eyes zeroed in on one of the twin beds, where Paula Kimberley lay under the covers. She was breathing heavily. Raspily.

"Mrs. Kimberley," Kate called in a good loud voice.

No response. She went over to the bed and touched the woman's shoulder. Boulter, behind her, said, "Look, guv!" and pointed to a small bottle on the bedside table with an empty tumbler beside it. Kate leaned forward and read the label. Mogadon. There was also a half full bottle of gin.

"It looks to me as if she's deliberately OD'd," Kate said, switching off the transistor radio. "Better call a doctor. We mustn't take any chances."

"Will do." Boulter went out to the landing and Kate heard him using his personal radio.

She tried again to rouse Paula Kimberley, shaking her gently by the shoulders and speaking her name. No response. Kate went into the en-suite bathroom and damped a face flannel with cold water. Returning, she dabbed Paula's forehead while she spoke to her again. She was rewarded at length by a slight stirring, a bleary half opening of the eyes.

Boulter reappeared at that point. "She's beginning to come round, Tim. Did you get hold of a doctor?"

"We're in luck. They've tracked one down right here in the village, and he's coming at once."

"That's a relief! Mrs. Kimberley, come on, wake up. Tim, quite likely the doctor will want to give her black coffee. Get some on the go, will you? Good and strong."

"And a cup for us?"

"Why not?"

A minute later a car drew up outside. The doctor, young and brisk, came bounding up the stairs. He'd already been told what to expect.

"Any idea how many of those she took?" he asked, with a nod at the bottle of sleeping pills.

"Unfortunately, not."

"But as there are a few still left in the bottle, we can probably take it she wasn't trying to finish herself off."

He examined Paula, checking her pulse, pulling back her eyelids. "It's the alcohol making things worse. What bloody fools some people are. She'll be okay, though. What's this, Sergeant, black coffee? You must be a mindreader. Come along, Mrs. Kimberley, we'll sit you up and you can take a sip. How many of these pills did you swallow?"

Paula Kimberley responded now, but she was obviously scarcely aware of who they were.

"Just . . . just a couple, I think. Aidan told me I must . . . must get a few hours' sleep. To . . . to be ready . . ."

Ready for what?

"Mrs. Kimberley, where is your husband?" Kate asked.

"Isn't he here . . . downstairs?"

"No, he's nowhere around."

"Nor's his car, ma'am," put in Boulter. "I took a dekko in the garage, and it's empty."

"But . . . where can he have gone?" Paula suddenly tensed, her eyes frightened. Then she reached out and grabbed Kate by the lapels of her beige linen jacket. "Aidan will come back for me, won't he?" she pleaded. "He will come back?"

He's abandoned her, Kate thought. Somehow he managed to get her to take an overdose of sleeping pills, to keep her knocked out while he skipped. And Paula, in her befuddled state, was coming to realize that she'd been deserted.

Kate glanced an urgent appeal at the doctor, who nodded his consent.

"Where has your husband gone?" she demanded. "Tell me!"

The mists must have cleared from Paula's brain, and she was beginning to get herself together.

"Why are you here?" she asked Kate in a clogged voice. "What do you want?"

Kate decided to take a chance. She wasn't prepared to waste time going round in circles.

"Your husband has run out on you, Mrs. Kimberley. You have to accept that. So tell me where he's gone."

But she'd succeeded too well in getting her meaning across. Paula was shocked into silence. She looked terrified.

Kate drew Boulter to one side. "Kimberley wanted to keep his wife doped and quiet while he made his escape. As I told you, it's clear from what Lord Balmayne said that he'd already made plans for a quick get-away, if need be. Something must have happened to scare him, and he's scarpered. He could be on the point of leaving the country by now. But how? Where from? By the time we can set something up at all points of departure, he'll be gone."

The sergeant nodded gloomily.

"He's unlikely to have booked a ticket in advance, Tim, if we're right that he's bolted in a panic. He'd go by air almost certainly, but how the hell can we pin down which airport, which flight? There are hundreds of planes leaving the country all the time."

"Not so many this late in the evening," Boulter pointed out.

"That's right, his choice would be limited." A stray thought suddenly crystallized in Kate's brain. "I wonder if . . . It's a chance in a million, of course."

"What is, guv?"

"Maybe Kimberley used the phone here before he left, to make a reservation. Worth a try."

She ran downstairs, Boulter following. The phone was in the living room, standing on a writing table in a small alcove. Praying for a miracle, Kate picked up the handset and pushed the redial button to get automatic connection to the last number dialled. The silence seemed to stretch for an age before the purr of the ringing tone. Then a gabbled response she couldn't catch.

"Who am I speaking to?" she asked.

It was the British Airways desk at Heathrow. Kate held down her leaping excitement as she identified herself.

"Now, listen. I need your co-operation, and I want it fast. This is urgent. Have you received a call today from a Mr. Aidan Kimberley— probably in the past few hours—to make a reservation on a flight this evening?"

"Which destination, please?"

"Unfortunately I don't have that information. It would be somewhere non-domestic."

The delay seemed interminable to Kate, though to be fair the woman was reasonably quick.

"We have no record of a passenger by that name today," she reported.

Damn! What now?

"Maybe that wasn't the name he used. Listen, ask around among your colleagues, will you? See if anyone can remember a man who wanted to make a last-minute reservation. It's possible that he wasn't fussy about his destination. I think he'd be travelling alone, and it's likely to have been just a one-way ticket. Please be as quick as you can. This is extremely urgent."

Another agonizing delay. Then a different voice came on the line.

"I believe I may have dealt with the gentleman you're enquiring about. A Mr. Kay."

Gotcha, chummie! Kate flicked Boulter a thumbs-up. "That'll be the man. Tell me about him."

"He phoned at seven forty-five and said he had the chance of a few days' holiday, so could I find him a flight this evening to somewhere pleasant. I booked him on the twenty-two-thirty flight to Malta. Just a one-way ticket. He said he'd probably return by a different route."

"Thanks a lot," said Kate. "You've been a terrific help."

"Another thing. I've just been informed that Mr. Kay collected his ticket from the desk a few minutes ago. They'll be boarding that flight shortly. Shall I have a call put out for him?"

"No, don't do that. He mustn't be alerted, whatever happens. Thanks again."

Boulter had been using his personal radio again. He showed her the number of Special Branch at Heathrow scribbled in his notebook.

"Thanks, Tim. What would I do without you?" Kate said as she punched out the number.

Special Branch wasted no time. In less than ten minutes they called her back.

"Chief Inspector Maddox? We've nabbed your man Kimberley, alias Kay, and we're holding him for you. And I've never seen anyone so taken by surprise."

"That's great," she said, with a rush of relief. "That's a pint all round I owe you."

"You may be interested to know that his hand luggage is a canvas hold-all packed with an enormous sum in currency. What was it, a bank raid?"

"It's his own money, would you believe?" she said with a laugh. "Legitimately come by."

The doctor gave it as his opinion that Paula Kimberley was certainly not fit to be interviewed at present, and was best left where she was for another two or three hours. Kate accepted this resignedly, though she was impatient for answers. She told Boulter to have a couple of WPCs come to guard her until she could be taken to divisional headquarters at Marlingford. Meanwhile, an escort was despatched to Heathrow to bring Aidan Kimberley back.

This meant that Kate had a brief respite, and she might as well make the most of it. She decided to go back to Stonebank Cottage to have a meal and freshen up before setting out for Marlingford and the heavy night that would await her there.

She headed her car homewards, taking a short cut through the darkening country lanes. It had started to rain and was getting heavier by the minute. After the long dry spell the air smelt fresh and cool as it drifted in through the ventilators. Kate wasn't feeling the least bit tired; the flow of adrenalin saw to that. She didn't know all the answers yet, didn't know what charges would have to be brought. But she was confident that by morning she'd have the case all wrapped up.

The rain was teeming down by now. Her headlights picked out the blurred figure of a man, running. He half turned and jerked his thumb, asking for a lift.

What *me?* A woman alone on a deserted road after dark. Think again, chum. Then she was close enough to see the man's face. It was Don Trotton.

She braked hard, and he ran up to the car as Kate reached over and wound down the window.

"Oh!" he said, taken aback and clearly not pleased to see who it was. "It's you."

He looked thoroughly wet and bedraggled. His hair was plastered to his head, and his sodden sweater and trousers clung to his body. And, Kate noted, there was a cut on his forehead, from which blood was oozing.

"What on earth's happened to you, Don?" she asked.

"Forget it," he snarled. "I'm okay."

"You don't look okay to me. If you're heading for home, you've still got quite a way to go. Get in and I'll drive you."

"But—"

"That's an order, Inspector." Kate wasn't about to have a member of the public come across an officer of the South Midlands force in such unfavourable circumstances. *Absurd* circumstances, she thought with an inward giggle. Already, she was mentally writing scenarios about what could have brought the swaggering, conceited Don Trotton to this indignity. Knowing him, a woman had to be involved, and it looked as if he'd been in a fight. With her? Had she been throwing things at him? Or was it an angry husband who'd beaten him up? Whatever, he'd somehow been rendered car-less and forced to get home as best he could. Then, to cap it all, he'd been caught in a downpour.

Trotton obeyed her mutinously, getting in the car and slumping back into the seat in sullen silence.

"Are you going to give me an explanation?" Kate demanded, as she started off.

"It's personal," he muttered. "None of your business."

"It is my business if you've been assaulted," she reminded him, enjoying herself hugely.

"Oh, for God's sake, can't you leave it alone?"

"The way it looks to me, Don, this is the evening when you've met your Waterloo. And not before time!"

He didn't answer that. But when, a few minutes later, she turned into the driveway of the big Victorian house where he had a flat, he said suddenly, "Look, Kate, there's no need to make a meal of this, is there? Let's just forget it ever happened, eh?"

"Hush it up, you mean? I'm surprised at you, Inspector Trotton, asking such a thing of a senior officer. Out you get."

Fifteen

Aidan Kimberley and his wife arrived separately at divisional headquarters but at about the same time. It was Paula Kimberley that Kate interviewed first, with Sergeant Boulter in attendance. When she later had Aidan Kimberley brought to the interview room, he was a changed man from the one she had met at his uncle's home. The suave self-confidence was gone, and so was his knife-crease grooming. He looked weary, dishevelled—and very nervous. This latter he was trying hard to conceal by adopting an attitude of impatience and outrage.

"Why the devil have I been brought here, Chief Inspector? The whole thing is ridiculous. A ridiculous mistake. I explained to the people at Heathrow that the money I was carrying is all my own. I can prove it."

"I've no doubt you can, Mr. Kimberley. You were arrested, as you were informed at the time, on suspicion of murder. My concern is with the deaths of Sir Noah Kimberley and Dr. Gavin Trent."

"You can't seriously imagine that I had anything to do with any of that," he protested. "If you're determined to go ahead with this charade, then perhaps I'd better have my solicitor present."

"That is your right, of course, as was explained to you when you were cautioned. Do you wish to have him sent for now, before we proceed any further?"

Kimberley gestured irritably. "What's the point? I have nothing to answer to, nothing to hide. So just get on with this and let me go."

"You haven't enquired about your wife, Mr. Kimberley."

On Kate's instructions he'd been told nothing about the police visit to his cottage and the discovery of Paula Kimberley in a drugged state. Watching his face, she guessed that he didn't know how to react to her remark without giving something away.

"She's at home, I presume," he said, with an exaggerated shrug of the shoulders. "What about her?"

"No, Mrs. Kimberley is not at home. In fact, she is here in this building. The reason you were kept waiting for me to see you was because I was interviewing your wife."

Kimberley's eyes flickered, and seconds of silence ticked away. Finally he asked in a taut voice, "What has Paula been saying?"

"She has given us a great deal of information," Kate said. "All of which confirms what we already suspected."

"What . . . what information?"

"She has admitted that she was an accessory in the concealment of Sir Noah Kimberley's body, following his accidental death at Dr. Gavin Trent's cottage."

Paula, in her fury at the way her husband had left her to face the music alone, had held nothing back. The whole story had come gushing out of her in a half-hysterical stream, with only slight prompting from Kate. Fidelity had never been part of the Kimberleys' marriage, it seemed, and each was free to go their own way. The unspoken deal was that they should be discreet and keep up the appearance that theirs was a successful match between two talented, beautiful people.

A surly loner like Gavin Trent had seemed an amusing challenge to Paula, and for a few weeks they'd carried on a clandestine affair. This hadn't been difficult, because in the summer months she often remained at Inchmere St. Mary during the week, when her husband returned to London. Her interior design work was just as easily carried on in the country, with many of her clients living in the locality.

Trent, almost totally inexperienced with women, had at once lost his head over her when she set out to charm him. The scene of his first seduction had been at his cottage, when Paula had called on him late one night bearing a bottle of champagne. But after a couple more visits there, she'd preferred their sex-sessions to happen in the luxury of her own home. This fact explained to Kate the lack of her fingerprints at Trent's place, except on the Tom Jones cassette.

Totally infatuated with Paula, Trent was soon trying to persuade her to get a divorce and marry him. When he started spouting wildly about how he had the chance to earn a very high salary so she could leave her husband and go off with him to Vienna, Paula knew that the time had come to end the affair. Anyway, the novelty had worn off and she no longer found him diverting. That was how matters stood when she received a panic phone call from Trent one evening, begging her to go to his cottage at once as he desperately needed her help. Arriving there, she had been horrified to find her husband's uncle lying dead on the floor. Trent had gabbled that it had been a terrible accident—the result, he insisted, of what he'd been trying to do for *her* sake, to make a new life for the two of them. Sir Noah had called round accusing him of disloyalty in wanting to leave Croptech and take a far better paying job abroad, and in his justifiable anger he had lashed out at Sir Noah, who had fallen and hit his head on the hearthstone.

"Gavin was just like a jelly and hadn't a clue what to do," she'd told Kate. "I could see that if I didn't come up with an answer there was going to be the most awful sordid scandal, with my name splashed all over the headlines." Her voice had dropped to a whisper, and Boulter nudged the tape recorder closer.

Kate said, "Tell us exactly what you did, Mrs. Kimberley."

"Well, first, I made Gavin help me wrap Uncle Noah's body in some polythene sheeting he had, and between us we carried it out to my car. I remembered about Milford Grange being empty while the Tillingtons were away in New Zealand and I thought that would make a good hiding place for the moment until we could work out a proper plan that was really safe."

"How did you intend to get into the house?" Kate asked. "You must have known there was a burglar alarm."

"Yes, I knew that, but several times when I'd been going back with Marjorie after we'd been shopping together, I'd seen how she shut it off. It gives you about half a minute after you open the front door before the alarm begins to ring. And once, Marjorie had forgotten her latchkey so I knew where they kept a spare one under a loose paving stone. Luckily, Gavin and I didn't pass a soul on the drive there and getting into the house was quite easy. Marjorie had talked about emptying her big chest freezer before she left, so it seemed a good idea to use that, to . . . to give us a bit more time to make our plans." Her beautiful face took on a hard-done-by expression. "If it hadn't been for those wretched thieves breaking in, we'd have got away with it."

"And afterwards," said Kate, "you drove Sir Noah's body to Cardiff Airport, and left it there? And Gavin Trent followed in his car to bring you back. Is that right?"

Paula gave a shudder of remembrance. "It was a simply terrible night. I knew we had to hide the car somewhere, get it well away from the neighbourhood. Gavin was just shot to pieces, so it was all up to me. I decided that leaving it at the airport would be a clever idea, to make it look as if Uncle Noah had gone abroad somewhere. With luck it wouldn't be found at once, so no one would be quite sure *when*. It was an awful journey, though, because I couldn't manage the gears properly, and I had a narrow escape on the Severn Bridge when I knocked into something."

"And Trent's death?" Kate asked. "Were you involved in that?"

"No!" Her eyes dropped and for several moments she didn't speak, while a perfectly manicured hand pushed back a streak of her blond hair that had fallen across her face. "Afterwards—after that night, I mean, I was terrified at what I'd helped Gavin do. When Aidan arrived back from Hong Kong, I told him what had happened. Everything. I didn't mean to, but I couldn't help myself. I was so scared, you see, and I felt desperate. Aidan was very shocked, of course, because he'd always been quite fond of his uncle, and he was absolutely furious with me. He called me all kinds of names for getting involved with a weak bastard like Trent and ending up in such a hellish mess. Then after a bit he cooled down, and said he'd decided to help us cover things up. It was an enormous relief, I can tell you, because I still hadn't been able to think what to do about Uncle Noah's body, and I knew that Aidan would be able to come up with some sort of plan. It was a bad mistake of mine, he said, to have returned to London. It would have looked much more natural if I'd stayed down here so as to be with Vanessa while she was so upset about Uncle Noah being missing. Right away, he phoned Vanessa and offered to help in any way we could. For the next couple of days I kept up the pretence of having flu, so I didn't have to go anywhere . . . I just couldn't face anyone. Gavin kept on phoning me to ask what on earth we were going to do and it was obvious that he was cracking up completely. Then on the Wednesday, Aidan told me he'd decided to drive down and see Gavin that evening, to make him understand that he'd got to pull himself together. And also to make plans with him about how to dispose of Uncle Noah's body. As a precaution, he said, it was best that nobody should know where he'd gone, so we agreed to say that we'd spent the evening alone together, if anyone should ever ask."

Kate cut in, "Your husband telephoned Lady Kimberley that evening, didn't he? Just after ten o'clock, I believe. Where was that call made from?"

"From the cottage. Aidan said he was going to drop in there first and phone Vanessa, pretending he was phoning from the Sloane Street flat, which would help support our story. And if anyone phoned while he was out asking for him, I was to say he'd gone to bed early with a headache and would return their call next day. Aidan thought of everything." Paula gave a deep sigh, then rushed on, "Anyway, when he got back home, which was very late, Aidan was evasive and I felt certain he wasn't telling me everything that had happened. I was sick with worry, but I didn't dare press him. Then the next day, after Gavin's body had been found and we heard from you that the police were treating it as murder, I guessed that *Aidan* had killed him. I knew it, really, but I was too scared to ask him outright. Aidan kept saying that everything would be all right now, as long as we stuck to the story we'd agreed on. He'd got everything under control, he insisted. Then yesterday evening when I told him about bumping into you in Aston Pringle and how you'd dropped your wallet, he said it was obvious that you'd used that as a trick to get my fingerprints." She broke off and looked at Kate. "Is that true?"

Kate nodded. "When I heard Tom Jones' voice on your car stereo it clicked in my mind that you must be the woman we were looking for—the woman with whom Gavin Trent had been having an affair. I needed to check your fingerprints against prints found on a Tom Jones tape we discovered at Trent's cottage."

Paula stared at her, baffled, seeming at a loss.

Kate explained. "Any other fingerprints you left at the cottage must have been wiped away during house cleaning, but the music tapes were all in a cabinet and the cleaners wouldn't have had reason to touch them."

"Oh God, if only I hadn't given Gavin that damn tape. It was a stupid idea. I knew he just hated any modern music like that, but I'm crazy about

Tom Jones and I couldn't resist making him pretend to like it to please me."

"Let's get back to yesterday evening. Did your husband finally admit to you that he'd killed Trent?"

Paula nodded, avoiding her eyes. "He said that he'd had to, for our safety, because Gavin was in such a state he couldn't be trusted not to break under questioning and tell the police all about Uncle Noah's death and how I'd helped him. Aidan swore that he hadn't *intended* to kill Gavin when he set out to talk to him, but when he saw what a state he was in he knew it was the only way." She blinked rapidly. "I . . . I'm not sure if that's true. I think that Aidan meant to kill him all along."

"I think so, too," Kate told her. "We have definite evidence that Trent's death was premeditated. A tree branch which we found beside the pond had been prepared in readiness to hold the victim under water, and I take it your husband knew that Trent couldn't swim?"

"He must have known. I mean, most people did because Gavin never used the pool at Uncle Noah's."

"And your husband was brought up in this area, wasn't he? So I presume he would have known that the pond in the woods was a particularly deep one."

"He must have done. He told me once that as a boy he spent a lot of time playing in those woods. Oh, God, I never realized before how ruthless Aidan could be."

"To return to yesterday evening, Mrs. Kimberley. When your husband worked out that I'd got your fingerprints, what did he say to you then?"

"He said that we'd have to get right away, out of the country, before the police came for us. He told me he'd made plans, just in case, and that he'd got plenty of money to take with us. But he said we needn't leave quite at once, and it would be a good idea for me to get a few hours' sleep first."

"He gave you some sleeping pills?"

"That's right. And some gin. Aidan said it would make the pills work faster. And then . . . oh, I can't remember properly. I think he gave me two more pills, saying I hadn't taken the others, though I was sure I had. I . . . I was confused. . . ."

It was armed with all this information that Kate had begun her interview with Aidan Kimberley. But she wasn't prepared to reveal everything his wife had told her, not yet.

"What was it you were escaping from, Mr. Kimberley?"

"I wasn't escaping from anything. I had some business to attend to. Urgent business."

"Where was that?"

"In Malta, of course."

"And what was the large sum in currency required for?"

"I don't have to account to you for what I do with my own money."

"It was the proceeds of the sale of your half share of Croptech, was it not? You told Lord Balmayne you needed it to meet commitments in the City, resulting from some unwise financial transactions. Will an investigation of your business affairs bear out that statement?"

Kimberley was clearly startled that she knew so much. "There is nothing you can prove against me."

"Why did you administer an overdose of sleeping pills to your wife?"

"Is that what Paula said? She took the pills herself. Anyway, it was only four Mogadons altogether."

"Enough to keep her from realizing you were deserting her. You plied her with gin first, so she was confused about the number of pills she swallowed."

"If Paula overdosed, that was entirely her own doing. She must have taken some more pills after I left."

"You plied Trent with drink, too, didn't you? It was no doubt he who drank most of the whisky you took with you to his cottage on the evening of his death, while you kept a clear head. You got him thoroughly befuddled, then you persuaded him to walk with you to the pond in the nearby woods, saying you thought that would be a good permanent hiding place for Sir Noah's body, provided it was well weighted down. Once there, you pushed him into the water and held him under with a tree branch until he drowned. Afterwards, you went back to his cottage, letting yourself in by the back door—which you had earlier surreptitiously unlocked for that purpose—and cleared away the signs of your presence there, before returning to London."

"That's ridiculous. I was in London the whole time this was supposed to be happening. You can't prove I wasn't."

Kate abruptly took another direction. "What precisely was the business you had in Malta, Mr. Kimberley?"

"That's my affair. It has nothing to do with all this."

"Why did you book your ticket under a false name?"

"There's no crime in that. My passport was in order."

"You had *no* business in Malta, did you? In fact, it was sheer chance that Malta was your destination. Merely that you were able to get a reservation at short notice on a flight that was leaving for Malta last evening. Almost anywhere would have done you as well, so long as it was beyond our jurisdiction. Hasn't it occurred to you to wonder how we managed to track you down so quickly?"

"Paula must have—"

"How could she possibly have known? You made sure she was lying in a drugged sleep before you put through that call to Heathrow. No, Mr. Kimberley, it was you who left a trail behind you. In your haste you overlooked a small facet of modern technology that could give you away. The last number you dialled from your home remained locked in the phone's memory. I merely had to touch the redial button to discover who it was you'd spoken to. I got straight through to the British Airways desk at Heathrow. They were able to recall their conversation with a Mr. Kay earlier that evening. A minor slip-up, but in your case a vital one." She paused, then added, "You shouldn't have made an enemy of your wife, you know. It will be on her evidence that you'll be convicted of murder."

"She's lying, the bitch."

The interviews with Kimberley and his wife had brought Kate a long way to an understanding of what had happened. But not far enough to make a charge of murder stick. She still hadn't one jot of firm evidence that Kimberley had been anywhere near Trent's cottage that night. If only someone could be found who'd actually seen him or his car in the locality.

Images flashed through her mind of the events of that fateful evening. It was possible that close questioning of the Inchmere St. Mary residents might turn up someone who'd seen Kimberley's car when he called at his cottage to make the phone call to Lady Kimberley. It was possible, too, that some late-night walker might have spotted a man who could be identified as Kimberley in the vicinity of the pond or of Trent's cottage. But how to find such a witness? Someone with a dog, perhaps? Which brought her to think of George Jessop. Could he and Cheryl Miller have seen anything, when they'd set out with Jessop's dog around midnight? Then suddenly her mind targeted on Duncan McEvoy, who'd been sitting in his car waiting for Jessop to go to bed before purloining some blocks of Cotswold stone.

That lane running past Croptech would be the route Kimberley must have taken as he headed back to London after drowning Trent in the pond and returning to the dead man's cottage to remove all signs of his presence there. She recalled McEvoy's statement. He'd been unable to identify the woman, he told her, because he'd been temporarily dazzled by a passing car's headlights. A big car. How many cars travelled along that minor lane around midnight—on any night? How many *big* cars?

It was the moment, Kate decided, to go out on a limb. She flashed a glance at Boulter to warn him something unexpected was coming.

"It's no use, Mr. Kimberley," she said, displaying impatience. "I have a witness who saw you in this area on that Wednesday evening."

"That . . . that's impossible."

"After you killed Trent, you headed back to London. Do you remember, as you went past the Croptech premises, a car was parked on the verge without lights? The driver of that car saw you, Mr. Kimberley. He saw you!"

The man shot her an evil look. Boulter was frowning tensely. Kate held her breath.

"All right, all right," Kimberley muttered at last. "But before I say another word I want my solicitor present."

Sixteen

"In future, Kate, when you solve a case," Richard grumbled, "kindly remember that the *Gazette*'s press day is Wednesday. By next week this will all be stale news."

She laughed at him. "Don't whinge, Gower."

It was Saturday lunchtime, and they were enjoying a drink and a chicken salad at one of the garden tables at the Wagon and Horses in Chipping Bassett. Felix would have joined them, but she was taking pictures at a Pony Club gymkhana at Dodford.

"Your press conference on Thursday," he went on, "was about as informative as a parliamentary answer. How about giving me the nitty-gritty, Kate?"

She tore off a scrap of bread and tossed it to a sparrow. "Strictly off the record?"

"Cross my honest old heart."

She owed Richard something, after all, for several instances of help he'd given her in this case. She treated him to a mildly edited version of the sequence of events leading to the arrest of Aidan and Paula Kimberley.

When she'd come to the end, he said, "That was a neat dodge, using the redial button of their phone to get onto Kimberley's trail. Clever stuff!"

"Tell Jolly Joliffe that. He took it in his stride as routine procedure."

Richard smiled sympathetically. "*I* appreciate you, Kate, anyway. So, it's all over?"

"You think? You'd never believe the paperwork."

"How's Lady Kimberley taking it?"

"So-so. It's been a tough time for her."

"What will happen at Croptech, d'you reckon?"

"I've no doubt that Lord Balmayne will advise her well. He's a good friend to her. One thing, I hope that whatever happens to the firm, Cheryl Miller doesn't get overlooked. She'd be more than capable of running the whole show. That is, if she wants to any more."

"What about those two who were on the fiddle, young Roger Barlow and the secretary . . . what's her name?"

"Sandra English."

"Will you be bringing charges?"

"I can't be bothered. But they'll be sweating, no doubt. Wondering." That made Kate think of Don Trotton, and she laughed. "They aren't the only ones sweating just now."

"Uh?"

"Don Trotton—you remember? He fell right into my lap the other night." She enlarged.

"Oho! Your chance for revenge. What are you doing about it?"

"Nothing. But Trotton can't know that. He'll sweat for days until it finally dawns on him that I haven't spread the story around. And then, he'll start sweating all over again wondering why."

"Serve the bugger right. This is really turning out to be your week, Kate, because I've got some good news for you."

"Good news?"

"I've found you somewhere to live. Somewhere very nice."

"You've *what?* Tell me, quickly."

"There's a stable block in the grounds of a big old house near Ampney-on-the-Water which the owner intends to convert into four residential units, and he's got planning permission. It's in a marvellous setting, and according to the architect's drawings, each unit will be pretty damn good. They're not too pricey, either, considering. And you can have first pick."

"That's incredible, Richard. Wonderful. How do I come to be so lucky?"

"The guy owes me some favours. Besides, I pointed out to him the security advantages of having a top brass police person living right on his doorstep."

"Richard, you're an absolute darling. Though how you could calmly sit there all this time and not tell me, I do not know."

"I was waiting for the psychological moment."

"When can I see the place?"

"There isn't a lot to be seen, as yet. Still, if we drive over there you'll be able to get a rough idea. And I've got photocopies of the plans in my car."

"Wow!" She jumped up and buttoned the jacket of her white blazer. "Come on, Richard, let's move."

"As soon as we've finished our lunch."

"For heaven's sake, who cares about food now?"

"I do." In leisurely protest, Richard set about making himself a sandwich, breaking open a length of French bread and stuffing it with the choicest remaining slivers of chicken from both their plates. Then he got up and walked limpingly over to where an impatient Kate stood waiting beside his Volvo. She looked good, tall and poised and confident, her short black hair riffled by the summer breeze.

He felt happier than he'd felt in years.

Erica Quest is the pseudonym for a husband-and-wife team living in West Sussex, England, who have written many successful novels. Their work has been published in a total of fifteen foreign languages. *Cold Coffin* is their fifth novel for the Crime Club.